# YOUNG ENOUGH

## THE AGE BETWEEN US (BOOK 2)

### CHARMAINE PAULS

Published by Charmaine Pauls

Montpellier, 34090, France

www.charmainepauls.com

Published in France

Cover design by Angela Haddon (www.angelahaddon.com)

ISBN: 978-2-9561031-5-8 (eBook)

ISBN: 978-1-7208118-4-8 (Print)

❈ Created with Vellum

# 1

*Jane*

Life is never just good or just bad. Mostly, it's a mix. My life is many kinds of wrongs, but it also has rights. A short while ago, my husband left me for his pregnant mistress. I lost my home in the process. I lost my stability and direction. I thought I'd lost everything, until a stranger broke into my property and ended up in my bed. He's not like any man I've met. When it comes to passion, he demands nothing less than the most extreme and forbidden corners of my fantasies. He gives light and awakens darkness. He gives darkness, and my light can't exist without it. It's the most explosive sex of my life, the most depraved and serenely beautiful acts I've committed.

Brian is everything I've ever wanted, the closest to happy I've been since my first love, Evan, died, which is why I'm ignoring that Brian is half my age. What we share is taboo. Which is why we're each other's secret. You could say I'm unlucky in love, like a fortuneteller recently told me when she gave a hair-raisingly accurate account of my life, but Brian makes me feel alive. He makes me feel desired. I've mourned a lost love to death. I've been left for another woman. But right now, I'm being coveted by a beautiful, sexually skilled man. I'm too weak to walk away from an affair that has no future. I want him too much. I need to breathe him like air and drown in him like water. I trust him with the darker side of my lust like I trust him with my body, because he earned it. He proved to me he's worthy of both, so I continue with my perfect, imperfect life, playing our game of secret love affair.

While Abby is with Francois, Brian and I spend the weekend together. We have sex as often as we can, anywhere we can. We're both shameless, but there is no shame in honest lust. The days we work together make up for the nights we can't sleep next to each other. Sometimes, we sneak off during our lunch break to make love in his truck at the dead-end road in Midrand with our clothes on or naked, lying amongst the grass that grows taller as summer advances. We're careful. We don't slip away together too frequently or raise suspicion with our behavior.

Toby likes Brian's Bakers idea, and Bakers likes it even more. By the end of the month, we're running their collectable card campaign. It's a major hit. Sales fly. They have to increase production for Christmas, resulting in an unexpected bonus for Brian and myself.

Abby is caught up in her studies for the year-end exams. The move from the only house I've considered my home, soon to be home to my ex-husband's mistress, doesn't come at the best time, right before the grade eight finals, but if we want to secure the cottage Brian found for me, we don't have a choice. If I weren't so worn-out from the last sprint before the end of the year at the office, I would've said tough luck and looked for something else after Abby finished her exams, but places like those don't become available every day. I'm not happy that Abby doesn't like the cottage, but as my good friend, Dorothy, said, she'll come around.

We arranged for Abby to be with Francois on the weekend I

move. Brian assured me he'd take care of the furniture. I can count on him for something other than sex, and it warms my heart.

I'm offloading kitchen appliances at the cottage when his truck pulls up. A guy jumps from the passenger side and another from the back. Walking toward them with a greeting on my lips, I stop in my tracks. They're Brian's buddies from the pool.

"This is Jane Logan." Brian points at the slender one. "This is Eugene Prinsloo." He slaps the chubby one on the shoulder. "And this is Clive Claassen."

They both stare at me as if my clothes are on fire.

I'm the first to recover. "I think we got off on the wrong foot the first-time round. Shall we start over?"

Eugene gives me a lukewarm handshake. "Uh, nice to meet you?"

Clive keeps his arms at his sides. "Hi."

"I appreciate your help. I hope Brian didn't bully you into it."

Clive snorts.

"No worries, Ms. Logan," Eugene says.

"Jane, please."

It takes us the whole morning and three truckloads to move Abby's belongings and mine. Brian transfers the security equipment from the house to the cottage while I put the smaller pieces of furniture in place. With the big furniture arranged, Brian connects the dishwasher and washing machine, and test both to make sure they work. There's no space for a tumble dryer, but we have enough sun—even in winter—and a line outside to dry our clothes.

I'm knackered by the time we're done, but eager to tackle the boxes. I want to have everything unpacked before I fetch Abby on Sunday. A tidy environment will go a long way in easing the change.

Thanks to Brian's thoughtfulness, we have a cold six-pack to swallow my picnic food down with. I offer to pay Brian's friends, but he refuses profusely on their behalf. He returns after dropping them off to help me unpack.

"I really appreciate your help." I hug him from behind, placing a kiss on his broad back.

"You didn't think I'd let you go through this alone, did you?" He turns to face me, his arms coming around me.

The hug is soft, but it's not tender. It's possessive and demanding.

One touch is all it takes. I gasp, burying my face in his chest.

"I want you, Jane." His tone turns desperate. "What are you doing to me? I want you all the fucking time."

"Then take me."

"That's the plan. On my terms."

My insides flutter in anticipation and with that pinch of wild fear his promises always evoke. "I can handle you, Brian Michaels. Take what you want."

His eyes darken. His whole body hardens against mine, every muscle drawing tight.

Lifting me, he carries me to the unmade bed and throws me on the mattress. Before my squeal has escaped, he's already covering my lips with his, swallowing my sounds as his hand moves between our bodies.

*Brian*

IT'S BECOMING HARDER to leave Jane. I'm torn in two, wanting to spend the first night in her new place with her, but I can't ask Clive to sleep over at my place after he's sacrificed his day to help with Jane's move. Finally, my responsibility wins over my desire. The result is a lingering ache in the hollow of my chest as I walk away from my woman at sunset with a bittersweet goodbye kiss.

After a hot day of strenuous work and fucking Jane twice, I

need a shower. I head straight for the bathroom when I get home, but as I pass Sam's room, I stop. She's sitting on the edge of her bed, staring at her toes. With a soft knock, I enter.

"Hey, piglet. What's up?"

She wiggles her toes on the worn thread of the carpet–I need to replace it sooner than later–but doesn't look at me. "Don't call me that."

"What?" I ask, baffled. "Piglet?"

She crosses her arms. "I'm not a pig."

Whoa. I've been calling her piglet since I can remember. It's because she loved Whinny the Poo so much.

I cross the floor and sit down next to her. "It's my way of expressing affection."

"It implies I'm fat."

"Where's this coming from?"

She turns her head to the side.

"Look at me, Sam."

Only her eyes turn toward me.

"Is it because I put you on a diet?" The last thing I want is to damage her self-esteem.

"It's the other girls," she admits meekly. "They say I'm fat."

My blood starts to heat. "The girls in your class?"

"Yeah."

"Why do you listen to them? You know better than to let someone whose opinion shouldn't matter upset you."

"They're my *friends*."

"Then you deserve better friends."

She jumps up. "You don't understand."

"Tell me." I hate seeing my kid sister like this.

"You *won't* understand." She pushes out her bottom lip. "You don't know what it's like."

"Try me."

Regarding me from under her lashes, she weighs my words.

Finally, she concedes with a theatrical sigh. "Lynette is having a party for her birthday."

"So?"

"So." She rolls her eyes, as if I should get the connection.

"Are you not invited?"

"Of course, I am."

"Then what's the problem?"

She slams a hand against her forehead. "Duh."

"Sam," I say sternly, "you're going to have to help me out here."

"I've got nothing to wear," she exclaims, "and even if I did, I'd just look fat."

Ah ha. For a minute I was working myself up, thinking it was something they'd done to her, because, let's face it, those girls may be young, but they're bitches in the making. I've seen how jealous they are of each other, how they gossip and tease with the intent to hurt and belittle.

The controlling part of me wants to forbid her to mingle with them. The protective part of me wants to refuse her permission to go to the party, but it'll only be a medicine to disguise a pain. It won't be a cure that heals the ailment. She needs to know how to stand up for herself. This will be a good learning curve for the future, because bullies are not limited to classrooms. My thoughts drift unwillingly to Monkey.

"You're not saying anything," she complains. "That means you agree. I'm going to look like the fat little pig."

"First of all, you're not fat." She has an extra bit of flab, which is my fault. I cooked too much pasta, but that's a thing of the past. "You're healthy and beautiful. Secondly, I didn't raise you to have such a low self-image. You're a bright, talented, and strong girl. You should act it, rather than brood over an image some bitchy girl from class put into your head."

She opens her mouth, but I hold up a hand.

"Lastly, since when do you care what others think? Whose opinion is the only one that matters?"

"Mine," she admits begrudgingly.

"Now that all that's out of the way, let's start over. You have a party to go to, right?"

"Right."

"I don't remember you asking permission."

"Briaaaaan."

"Sam."

The next sigh she utters signifies the world rests on her little shoulders. "May I please go to Lynette's birthday party?"

"When? Where? What kind of party?"

"Saturday before school ends. It's from six to ten."

"Whoa. At night?"

"It's at her parents' house, so don't sweat it. There will be supervision. We're going to have pizzas and play board games."

"Who's all going to be there?"

"Just about the whole class."

"Boys and girls?"

"Yeah," she says again, as if I should've known.

"I want her mother's number."

She narrows her eyes in suspicion. "What for?"

"To check if they'll be around all the time."

"Brian! You'll embarrass me."

"Plus," I hold up a finger, "in case of an emergency, I'd like to know she can get hold of me. That's the condition."

Her mouth falls open, and her arms drop to her sides. "Seriously?"

"Yes, Sam."

She throws up her hands, but nods with another eye-roll. "Fine."

I cup my ear. "I don't hear you."

"Thank you," she mumbles.

"That's better. Now that permission for the party's out of the way, we can move to the next problem."

"What to wear?"

Sam doesn't have much. She doesn't own pretty shoes or make-up and all the stuff girls like. It didn't matter as much when was she was younger, but she's growing up.

"We'll sort it, okay?"

"Really?" Her face lifts. "You mean I can get a new dress?"

"I think you deserve a new dress. Shoes and all."

She squeals and starts bouncing. "Really? Really?"

"If you stop hopping like a kangaroo."

She stills immediately. "I'll set the table every night, I swear. I'll even take out the garbage."

I get to my feet. "You don't have to do any of that for a dress. It's not an exchange. But–"

"I knew there was a but."

"It doesn't mean you don't have to do your chores."

"Thank you, Brian." She throws her arms around me, almost knocking me off my feet.

"You're welcome. By the way, did Tron check in on you?"

"He's been in and out a couple of times. Mom made him a cup of tea."

It's time to start dinner. My shower will have to wait. "Go have your shower. Dinner will be ready in half an hour."

She skips to the door. "Anything you say."

Before going to the kitchen, I look in on my mom. She's passed out on her bed. I cover her with a light blanket before turning my attention to our dinner menu. As I'm going through the fridge, Clive walks in.

"Beer?" I ask.

"No thanks."

I pull my head out of the refrigerator to look at him. Clive refusing a beer is like a snowstorm on the Magaliesberg Mountains in the middle of summer. I study him. His shoulders are tense and his arms rigid at his sides. He reminds me of a tightly wound top ready to spin.

"What's going on?" I ask carefully.

"You tell me."

"What do you want to know?"

"What's Jane to you?"

Her name on his tongue doesn't sit right with me. It bothers me without any explicable reason. "I think you know."

"You're dipping your dick, aren't you?"

Tension pulls my shoulder blades tight, my posture mirroring his. "Watch your mouth."

"It's serious?" he asks with disbelief.

Clive knows me well enough. I wouldn't mind his foul mouth if it weren't serious.

He nods several times, his look condescending. "You went back there, behind our backs."

"I don't need permission or approval from you for where I go."

"Some friend you are." He sneers. "You made me sleep here, taking care of your sister and mother so you could bang some uptown sugar mommy."

My vision starts to get fuzzy around the edges. I back away from the fridge, the tension a coiled-up spring driving me forward. My feet are moving, but I'm not aware of executing the action. It's like being in a dream where you float.

"You will watch your fucking mouth, or you'll leave here with no teeth."

He blinks, retracing his steps to the door. "Why did you lie, Brian?"

"I didn't lie."

"Are we not good enough for your uppity-ass *girlfriend?*"

In a flash, I see an ugly shade of crimson. Before I know what I'm doing, I'm in Clive's face, my fist punching the wall next to his head. Bits of flaking plaster fall on the floor. Pain explodes in my knuckles. It travels up my arm, all the way to my shoulder, but I push the sensory impulses aside. I can handle pain. I'll deal. It also brings me back to earth, preventing me from taking his head clean off.

"What the fuck's your issue?" I hiss.

"You'll choose her over us?"

"What are you talking about?"

"Our neighborhoods, they don't mix. Tell me it's just a fuck and–"

My fist collides with his jaw before he can form the next word. It's not a hard punch, but enough to make him stumble two steps sideways. His eyes are cutting as he grabs his jaw, moving it from side to side.

"I warned you."

"Yeah," he says. "I guess you warned me from a while back. I just didn't want to listen."

"What's your problem with Jane?"

"My problem? You're asking what's *my* problem? Dude, I hate to break it to you, but the problem's all yours."

"What's that supposed to mean?"

"I saw you today, the way you look at her. You're into her, as in deep."

"I don't see how that's a problem, least of all why you feel you should stir."

He laughs. "If you don't see the problem, you're as blind as a mole. She's twice your age. It can never work. Not as in long-term. Look where she comes from, bro. Women like her don't do boys from Harryville, not for serious. They do us to scratch an itch. It's the pool or garden boy, because they're bored. When they grow tired of the game, they chuck them out like old dishwashing water, because they can. That's the first of your problems. Then there's Monkey. Now that's a problem I don't wish on my enemy."

My finger is in his face, my anger radiating from me like toxic vapor. "If you know what's good for you, you'll put a cork in it."

"Question is do you know what's good for you?"

Lacing my fingers over my head, I tilt my face to the ceiling and move away from him. I want to smash his face in, but I can't do it for the truth. He's right about one thing. Monkey is a problem that's not going away. The desperation of the situation only makes me feel fiercer about what I want.

Jane.

I'm sick without her, and I don't mean physically. I mean in my head. In my chest. In my mind. It's something that's been chewing on me for a while. I want her wholly and completely. These bits and scraps aren't enough any longer. My mind and heart don't care that Monkey stands between us. My feelings don't give a shit about what he's capable of, because she takes up everything I have, everything I feel. We can make this work. I told myself I wasn't going to become that needy guy who demands more, but I can't help myself. With her, I can't get enough. I want it all. Everything.

Clive's tone softens. "Forget about the chick. Do what Monkey wants. You can do a lot worse than Lindy. Most guys will kiss her old shoes for the business that comes with her. Do you know how much Monkey's worth?"

I breathe in calm and breathe out my pent-up frustration. "I'm not most guys, and Jane's not most women."

He laughs softly again, shaking his head. "You're such an idiot."

"Maybe, but Jane is *mine*. The rest of the world, that includes you, better stay away from her."

"Are you thinking about your mother? About Sam?"

On cue, my sister's voice speaks from the door. "What's that about me?"

"Hey, Sam," he says, but his eyes are on me.

"Want to have dinner with us?" Sam asks.

"I was just leaving." He backs up to the door. "I'll see you around, dude."

He disappears through the frame. The sound of his steps falls hard on the porch and down the stairs. A moment later, an engine starts up. The sputter tells me he's borrowed his old man's car.

"What was that all about?" Sam asks.

"Nothing." I rub the back of my neck. That's not true. I never lie to my sister if I can help it. "Just grown-up stuff."

Spaghetti is my specialty, but I'm learning to broaden my cooking skills. Pulling up the recipe for ratatouille on my phone, I slice the aubergines and salt them to sweat. Then I tackle the sweet peppers and baby marrows. It's not as easy as you'd think. The onions burn while I'm still halving the cherry tomatoes. The peppers are overcooked, and the aubergine slices tear into unrecognizable pieces that look suspiciously like slimy snail. I didn't manage to rinse off all the salt before frying them, and with the Kalamata olives the dish is too salty. There's also that lingering bitter of the burn. I top it with a bit of mozzarella to make it easier to go down.

Sam pulls up her nose, but she eats what I serve her, probably because she doesn't want to evoke my irk before the party. After serving my mother a bowl in bed, I clean the kitchen and watch a movie with Sam. When she's in bed, I call up the app on my phone to test the security system at Jane's cottage.

The cameras work fine. They're motion triggered, meaning when set they'll take a snapshot if the lasers detect movement in the room. Within a second, I'll receive not only an alarm signal, but also a photo of whoever breaches her security. Since I have full control, the technology allows me to get feeds when the alarm is not activated. All I have to do is tap a command. I can make sure she's fine to set myself at ease and still my longing.

I flick through the rooms until I find her. She's in her bedroom, getting undressed. The image is high resolution. It's like watching a television screen. I move to the edge of the sofa bed, my breathing speeding up and my cock hardening. First, she pulls off a T-shirt. Then she wiggles out of her shorts. Her toned body looks good in pink underwear. It makes her tan stand out. My mouth goes dry as she unhooks her bra. My hand goes to my zipper. God, I'm a prick. I can't help it. When she slips her panties over her hips, my cock is already in my hand.

## *Jane*

NOTHING IS SAID about the coffee shop or Abby's birthday party when I pick Abby up on Sunday. From the haughty smile on Debbie's face, she looks as if she's scored a point. Several points, actually.

At our new home, things are not any better between Abby and me. She stops in the middle of her room, looking around. I've put daisies, her favorite, in a vase on her dresser and left the window open for the room to cool. A breeze moves the curtains, carrying the scent of jasmine inside.

"I hope you like it."

She walks to the dresser and runs her fingers over the flower petals. "Thanks for the flowers."

"You're welcome."

"I miss my own bathroom."

"You'll still have it when your father and Debbie move into the house."

"Only every second weekend. For most of the time, I'll have to make do with this." She waves her arm around.

"We were fortunate in Groenkloof. This is what I can afford," I remind her.

She turns to me slowly. "I know. It's just..."

"Just what?"

"Country living is not my thing."

"This isn't exactly country living."

She moves to the French doors that open onto the deck and peers toward the dam. "Whatever."

"If we both make an effort–"

"Mom." She rests her chin on her shoulder, looking in my direction but not quite at me. "I'll try, okay?"

"Okay." When only silence follows, I ask, "Are you hungry? I made *melkkos* with cinnamon."

"I suppose I can eat." She offers me a watered-down smile.

At least she's making the effort I demanded. "You can freshen up if you like. I'll set the table. After dinner, I can help you with your revision for tomorrow's exam. We can do a test."

"Dad already did, but thanks."

She squeezes past me and goes down the hallway to the bathroom. When she comes back, I'm done setting the table. It's a beautiful evening. I open the French doors to enjoy the view and fresh air.

"Tell me about your weekend," I say in a bright tone as we take our places by the table.

"I'm tired. Can we talk later?"

"Of course."

Our dinner goes down in silence. I wish I knew what to say to her or how to draw a reaction from her, but I respect that she's not in the mood for conversation. That's what I taught her. That it's all right to be quiet. It's all right to sometimes be sad. In all the years since Abby was born, I've been more sad than not, but I haven't practiced what I preached. I never showed it. Not to her as she grew. Not to Francois. Only to Dorothy, once a year. Now that sadness I thought would never lift is slowly dissipating, leaving room for happiness and peace. Leaving room for Brian or maybe he's the reason the suffocating pain is fading into nostalgic memories.

It's as if my recollection of the moments I spent with Evan is going through a filter. The hurtful ones are caught in the sieve while only the beautiful ones are distilled in my mind. A bit of hurt always slips through, but it makes the beauty bitter-sweet instead of unbearable. Even greater than the pretty of remembering is the thankfulness. The relief. God knows, I breathe better for it.

Abby is pushing the food around in her bowl. I frown, more concern settling over me. Like the flowers, this is one of her favorite dishes.

I'm about to ask what's the matter when Hilda knocks on the open doors and enters.

"Oh, I'm sorry," she says. "I didn't want to interrupt your dinner. I just wanted to say welcome."

"No worries." I glance at Abby's half-eaten food, now cold. "We're just about done. Would you like to join us for dessert?"

"May I please be excused, Mom?"

"This is my daughter, Abigail," I say to Hilda. "Abby, this is our landlady, Ms. Hilda Feldsmann."

Hilda extends a hand. "Nice to meet you, Abigail. Please, call me Hilda."

Abby stands and shakes the other woman's hand. "Hi, Hilda." She turns to me. "If you don't mind, I'd rather turn in. Tomorrow's a big day with the exam and all."

"There's sago pudding." Also Abby's favorite.

"Keep some for me for tomorrow. Good night, Hilda. Night, Mom."

She climbs the three steps and disappears down the hallway.

Gathering the bowls, I ask, "Sago pudding?"

"No thanks. We've eaten." Hilda follows me to the kitchen. "I'm sorry we weren't here when you moved in, but we just got back from Namibia."

"I didn't expect a personal welcome," I smile, "but thanks."

"If you need anything, we're only a short distance away."

"That's kind. I'll keep it in mind."

"Will it be just you and Abby staying here?"

"Abby's father and I are divorced."

"I assumed your boyfriend was moving in, too."

"Brian's not..." For some reason, I can't say it. I can't say Brian is nothing to me except for good sex. "What gave you that idea?"

"I suppose it's because he visited the cottage first."

"It's just Abby and me. For now." I cross my arms. "Would a boyfriend be a problem?"

Her cheeks flush. "The cottage is big enough to handle three people. We don't want hordes, though. Oh and no pets. I assume you read that in the contract."

"Got it. No hordes. No pets."

"Neither...indecency."

"Indecency?"

She shrugs. "Loud parties, questionable individuals, a loose lifestyle."

"Why would you think any of that would apply to me?"

I know exactly, but I want her to say it. I want her to hear what her hypocrisy sounds like when she tells me out loud I'm a *loose* person because I sleep with a younger guy.

"I don't. Just giving you the same drill we give all our tenants."

*Right.*

"Anyway, good night." She waves and walks to the door. "As I said, you know where to find us if you need anything."

I'm fuming when she's gone. Pretoria is a big city, but in many ways it's a small town where everyone knows everybody's business and judgment is disguised as good moral values.

I spend an hour cleaning the kitchen, but my tension won't ease. It's this quiet discord between Abby and me, the move, the Monroe account, and everything Hilda has said. If Brian is not my boyfriend, he's my lover.

Plain and simple.

Only, things between us aren't that simple.

It hasn't been for a while.

---

*Brian*

EXAMS ARE COMING UP. I can't afford to fail. If I flunk, I'll be kicked out of the course and lose my job at Orion. This is my only shot. I'll never get another chance like this. I'm studying like a lunatic and making sure Sam knows her tables and grammar for her own exams while cooking and cleaning when Mom's too trashed to do it. Every free minute is spent at Orion. I'm not seeing much of Jane in a naked way, except for a few stolen moments every second weekend. It makes me feel like a caged lion. I've adopted the filthy habit of watching her more and more on the security feed, especially at night when I jack off, her name always a whisper on my lips as I climax.

We don't have time to fuck, never mind to talk, but when I walk into her office on a bright Monday morning, I know something's wrong from the tense set of her narrow shoulders and the way she rubs her forehead.

I close the door and round her desk. "What's wrong?"

She shakes her head. Her pained expression scares me. Gripping her shoulders gently, I start a firm massage.

"Brian, you shouldn't-" She moans. "Oh, God. That feels good."

"Here?" I work my thumb over a knot.

"Ouch. Damn. Yes, just there."

"Talk to me."

"It's been a difficult morning. That's all."

"What's difficult?"

"There's this tension between Abby and me."

"And?" I push her forward so I have access to the muscles flanking her spine.

She groans. "Ah. So good. Don't stop."

"And?" I won't give up until she tells me what's gotten her into such a spin.

"Toby rejected my Monroe proposal. For a second time."

My hands still.

She swivels her chair to face me. "I'm going to lose the account."

Shit. Her salary will take a knock-the agency pays on a performance basis-but it'll also kill her career. If she loses her biggest account, or God forbid she loses the client to a competitor, no one in the industry will hire her. Toby won't have a choice but to get rid of her.

I swallow away the dryness in my throat. "What did he say?" She worked damn hard on that proposal.

"He said a country-wide kindergarten campaign will take too long to roll out, and it'll take even longer to see the revenue. Two years. Maybe more."

I grip the armrests of her chair. "Freddy needs to go digital."

"No." She pushes me away and gets to her feet.

"Jane," I plead as she walks to the window.

We've had this discussion. I don't understand her resistance to keeping up with trends. "Why not?"

She flings around. "So mothers can shove a tablet or smartphone in their toddlers' hands? This is exactly what the brand is not about. It's about interaction, mother-child contact."

"Times have changed," I point out gently. "The brand needs to evolve. Mothers are busy. They work, cook, clean, do grocery shopping." I close the distance, stopping close to her. "I'm not disagreeing with what you say. Yes, human interaction is important. That's a good value, but some electronic intervention isn't all bad."

"It's not what the brand is about, Brian. I'm not tweaking the values, not even to save my own ass."

"It's not about tweaking anyone's values. It's about adapting. It's about redefining outdated values."

"I'm not discussing this with you anymore. You know my take on digital. Any other brand, yes, but not Freddy. Consumers buy Freddy for the *outdated* values it stands for."

Her voice has been rising consistently, her cheeks growing red with anger. Standing there with her sleek, short hair, expensive jewelry, and designer dress, she's a sight to behold. All lady. All fire. A combination of adrenalin from the argument and not having my dick inside her nearly enough makes arousal explode through my body. All the blood from my head must've gone straight to my cock, because I'm lightheaded with want.

"What?" she asks, taking a step backward as I advance.

Her blue eyes grow large when her back hits the window. She knows me. She can probably see the hunger in my eyes, because I can feel it humming in every cell of my body, begging for her taste, her smell, and her skin under my hands. Her wetness around my cock.

"Brian, this–"

One hand dips under her dress to move her panties aside and cup her sex. I'm not wasting time. The other fastens around her neck, not with pressure, but with dominance. Ownership. Jane is her own woman, but right now, she's mine.

I trace the soft curve of her neck with my thumb. "You were saying?"

"Not here," she croaks. Her eyes dart toward the door. "Someone may walk in."

Why do those words make me so angry? Why do they make me want to punish her? Pressing her harder against the window, I rub my thumb in circles over her clit. Her knees buckle a bit. The minute moisture leaks from her slit, I coat my middle finger and breach the tight barrier of her asshole. She jerks and gasps, her eyes growing bigger as she clamps both hands around my wrist in a futile attempt to move my fingers away from her hot cunt. The effort only earns her more pressure. On her clit, in her ass, around her neck.

Her hands shoot up to my other wrist, the one taking away her air. It's not something we've played with yet, and I'm a bastard for not easing her into it gently, but I'm an exploding volcano. My lust and every possessive need that comes with it is boiling over. I can give. I can give her any fucking thing she wants. All the freedom in the world. Whatever she asks from me. As long as I know she's mine where it matters, in body and mind.

As her ass clenches on my finger, she increases her struggles, but it's hopeless. I've got her exactly where I want her. Close to coming. Her hips rock forward, and her eyes roll back in her head. A few more manipulations of my thumb, and she comes undone. I ease up on her neck as her abdomen contracts. She gulps in air. Her pupils dilate. I stop rubbing her clit, but I keep my thumb there, making her ride the ecstasy until it cripples her, until she sags in my hold and her back slides down the window. I'm not gentle when I extract my fingers. The risk that I'll start fucking her all over again is too big. The sooner I get my hand off her pussy, the safer. Before she can hit the ground, I catch her around the waist, dragging her body hard against mine. I want to make her ride my cock just like that, but it's close to nine, and Candice will soon do the tea round.

Testing her balance, I let her go. She slumps against the window, her chest heaving and her pretty lips parted. Her hand goes to her neck, drawing my gaze to the marks my fingers have left. I shocked her, but she liked it. Her wetness and climaxes don't lie. It's as if she comes to life in the next second. She pulls down her dress, straightens her jacket, and smooths a hand over her hair.

Like nothing happened.

"Don't do that," I grit out.

"What the hell, Brian? Are you out of your mind?"

"Don't make like you didn't just come the hardest in your life."

"We're in my *office*," she says through gritted teeth, "and you need to leave it now. This is a limit for me. You know that."

That's it. That's exactly it. It's not about the thrill of getting off in the office or getting caught. It's about that itchy, niggly, fucking damn limit.

"I'm tired of this." I motion between us.

Her breath catches on a hitch. "This? Us?"

"I'm tired of hiding." I'm crowding her, not giving her space to move away. "I'm tired of being your dirty little secret. I want to be able to show my affection for you openly, no matter who the hell is watching."

She's quiet for a moment, her palms pressed flat on the window behind her. "Voyeurism isn't my thing. I know you said–"

"I don't mean it literally. I don't mean I want to fuck you with

20

my fingers no matter who walks through that door. I want to hold your hand in public. I want to sleep next to you and wake up with your face on my pillow."

The weight of my statement drags me away from her. I take several steps back, giving her the distance she craved earlier. She remains plastered against the window, her face ashen.

Threading my fingers through my hair, I let my chest deflate, allowing the air to turn cold with the space between us. My voice is as despondent as the rest of me. "No more hiding."

A tremble runs over her body. She speaks so softly I have to strain my ears to hear.

"Are you giving me an ultimatum?"

"No, Jane." Defeated. I sound like what I feel, because there's the truth for you. "I'll take whatever you're giving." Stripped naked to the bone. "That's how desperate I am for you."

The seconds stretch on as we stare at each other, me vulnerable and her holding all the power. I've fucked her weak against the backdrop of everything she stands to lose, but I'm the one on my knees.

It's not her words that pour into my questions and fill them up, it's her silence.

Goddamn, it hurts.

I break first.

I'm the coward who walks away from the pain.

# 2

***

## *Jane*

**M**y body shakes so badly I battle to walk back to my desk. Flopping down in the chair, I wrap my arms around myself. I'm breaking apart inside. Brian is a man of his word. He means what he says. He'll take what I give, even if it hurts, and I don't want to hurt him. I've been cruel. I saw it coming, and I did nothing to stop it. I selfishly took the physical release he gave me, knowing very well his actions went way beyond. Installing security equipment, finding me a place to rent, moving my furniture, these aren't acts of a man who's only in it for the sex.

I lean my head against the cool surface of the desk, inhaling the fragrance of wood polish. It's not that I'm hurting less than Brian. It's that my guilt is bigger. Yes, I knew every step of the way where this was going to lead. To a futile dream and a dead end. There are many problems facing me, the biggest being the Monroe account, but I can't think. I can't operate. I can't do anything but feel, feel, feel.

It's agonizing, but I'm grateful. For how long have I prayed for this during my long, emotionless existence after Evan's death? To feel *something*. Now I do. In abundance. So much so I can't function.

Picking up my phone, I dial the only person I can. Dorothy.

"Jane, this is a surprise."

"Are you free?"

"What, now?"

"Yes."

"I have aqua gym, but I can wiggle out of it."

"Are you sure?"

"I wouldn't have offered if I weren't. Where do you want to meet?"

We agree on a nearby tearoom. Thirty minutes later, we're sat across from each other. I stopped to buy a scarf from the clothing store next-door to hide Brian's marks on my neck and am only a couple of minutes late.

"What's going on?" Dorothy asks, getting straight to the point.

I don't have time to waste either. "I met someone."

"I knew it." She flicks her fingers. "There was something different about you the last time we met."

"He's half my age."

"Oh. Like twenty-one?"

"Nineteen, actually."

"Oh. So, it's the sex."

"Why does everyone assume that?"

"Sorry. You're right. That was a horrible cliché. Is it? The sex?"

"Yes and more."

"You like him."

"He likes me, too."

"Then what's the problem?"

"He wants to go public."

"I see." She leans back and studies me. "You don't."

"We work together. What do I tell Abby? How will his friends look at me when we go out on a date?"

"Those are obstacles, not reasons to shun a potential relationship."

"A relationship going where?"

"Not all relationships are meant to go somewhere. It doesn't mean you can't enjoy each other while it lasts. You're both single, consenting adults. Why do you care about your colleagues, his friends, or even Abby?"

"Abby's my daughter."

"Your daughter needs to understand that you're more than a mother. You're also a woman."

"She may be too young to grasp that."

"I think you underestimate her. She's almost thirteen, not three."

"Are you saying, I should give it a shot?"

"I'm saying you should do what you want. You bloody hell earned it, don't you think?"

"Did I?"

"Jane," her voice is stern, "you've been mourning a man for years, and you're still paying for a mistake that..." She swallows and blinks away a tear. "A mistake that's mine."

"Dorothy, please."

"Let me finish. You married a man you didn't love because he took advantage of you when you were weak."

"Dorothy!"

"I'm not bloody done. You've been living dead. I've seen you more alive the last time we met than in twelve years. If you're making up excuses because you're afraid of getting hurt, grow up. What you and this man of yours do has nothing to do with anyone but the two of you. If you want to announce it to the world, go for it. If you enjoy sex with him, I hope it's a blast. If it doesn't last, own it. No one can judge you for it."

"Wow."

"It's not what you wanted to hear?"

"I don't know what I expected."

"That's not true. You expected me to give you the truth, and that's what I've done."

"Damn." I reach for her hand. "You should've been my mother-in-law, you know that?"

"Instead, you have a friend." Pain flashes through her eyes, but she frowns it away.

"I've been trying to do the right thing all my life."

"I know. This is a good time to stop. If you want to sleep with the king of Andorra, it's nobody's business."

I can't help the smile that creeps onto my face. "Who's the king of Andorra?"

"I don't know. Hopefully, someone Spanish and handsome and filthy rich."

This makes me laugh. The heaviness lifts from my chest. "Thank you, Dorothy."

She gives my hand a squeeze. "Shall we order? And I need to go to the powder room. All that talking made my lipstick run into the wrinkles around my lips."

I watch her as she makes her way to the ladies' room. I know she's escaping to go wipe away her tears, and I grant her the space. I love her so darn much, I dare say more than I loved my own mother. I've loved her from the word go, which is why I'd do just about anything for her, why I'd done what I did.

I FEEL CONSIDERABLY BETTER when I get back to the office. Brian looks up from his desk in the open-plan space when I enter. His eyes darken when they fall on the scarf around my neck.

I run my fingertips over his desk as I pass. "We need to talk."

He catches my wrist. "When?"

Candice looks our way. Her attention hones in on where his fingers are locked around my arm. A few others are staring, too.

"After your exam."

"Before."

I know that obstinate look. He's not going to budge, and I don't want to argue in front of the whole floor of workers.

"I'll ask a friend to pick Abby up from school."

He releases me slowly. "Five o'clock, when we knock off. I'll wait."

All eyes are on me as I enter my office. I shut the curious stares behind my door and sit down to get some work done.

The minutes tick by like hours, every other priority dimming in the light of what lies ahead. When five o'clock finally comes, I'm a nervous wreck. This can be our beginning, but it can just as well be our end. I'm not sure how Brian is going to take it.

We take his truck and drive to our favorite dead-end road. He cuts the engine but doesn't look at me.

Gripping the wheel so hard his knuckles turn white, he says, "Talk, Jane."

"No more hiding."

He turns his head toward me quickly, releasing his death grip on the wheel. "Do you mean that, or are you saying so because I pushed you into a corner?"

"I mean it."

One by one, his muscles give until his posture is relaxed.

"Why?" he asks.

"Why what?"

"Why did you make the decision?"

"Isn't it enough that I made it?"

"No. I want to be sure you're doing it for the right reasons."

"I was–am–afraid of getting hurt."

He twists in his seat and cups my cheek. "So am I. You have no idea, but you're worth the risk. I'm not going to hurt you. You have my word."

"How can you be so sure?"

"Because I'm not letting you go. No matter what."

It's a serious statement, one that requires commitment, and not just the sexual I-won't-run-around-on-you kind of commitment, but the kind that comes with death doing couples apart. Something about it lodges in my mind, like a red flag waving from very far, in sight but out of grasp. I don't take time to analyze it, though, because he grips my face between his palms and kisses me hard. My knees turn weak as he spears my lips, eating my mouth exactly like he goes down on me–like it's never enough. I moan when I run out of breath, pushing on his shoulders for air.

He lets me go an inch. His gaze is intense as it settles on my face. "How long do we have?"

"Loretta said Abby could stay for dinner." Setting me aside almost brusquely, he starts the engine. "Where are we going?"

"To get your car."

It's hard to hide my disappointment. "Already?"

"Then we're going back to your place."

My stomach flutters. I'm a puddle of pathetically happy endorphins.

He throws the truck into gear.

"What about your studies?" I ask. "And Sam and your mom?"

"My studies are up to date. I have a friend watching out for my sister and mom. I'll be home in time to make dinner."

My heart swells for the man he is, because even if he's barely past the legal age, he's more of a man than most men I know.

*Brian*

PEAK HOUR IS past when we get back to the office. It doesn't take us long to drive to the cottage. The minute Jane closes the door behind us, I tell her how the evening is going to go down.

On my terms.

I need this.

To give her the freedom she deserves, the freedom in which she will blossom and thrive, I need her to surrender her control. Even freedom has borders. Rules. These are my rules. She'll stay with me, and she can do and have whatever she wants. I'll do whatever it takes.

"I want to take you," I say, watching her from the door.

She stands in the middle of the lounge. A lamp illuminates the space. The light makes her platinum hair glow.

"I want you, too," she whispers.

"I wasn't finished." I close the distance so that I can undo the knot of the silk scarf around her neck. I want to see the marks I left on her skin. It's depraved, but I like it. "I want to take you from behind."

She stares up at me, waiting for me to continue.

"I want to take you from behind with a butt plug stuck in your tight little ass."

Her breathing accelerates then stops as I brush my knuckles over the hard tips of her tits.

"I want to take you from behind with a butt plug in your asshole and film every dirty minute of it."

She inhales on a gasp.

"And you're going to let me," I finish.

"I–I don't know."

Reaching for the zipper on the side of her dress, I pull it down. "What don't you know?"

"I'm not sure about the filming."

"You're going to love it."

"Brian–"

"You trust me, remember?"

She catches her bottom lip between her teeth.

"Do you trust me, Jane?"

There's no hesitation. No reflection. "Yes."

Her trust is the most powerful aphrodisiac. It gives me the control I crave, the power I need to give her freedom within a prison she doesn't know she's in. It doesn't matter. I'll make her prison a castle. She'll be my princess. Forever.

"Say it again." It sounds like a command, but it's a plea.

"Yes," she whispers.

"Good." I let her go, having initiated the undressing. "Take it all off."

She slips the dress over her arms and down her hips. Her underwear is the same color as her skin. I can guess the darker patches of her areolas and pubic hair through the lace, and it turns me harder than what I already was.

Her shoes follow next, and then the thigh-high stockings she favors. Her breasts fall free when she unclasps the bra. Firm and perfectly shaped with that slight downward dip, they're the prettiest curves I've seen. Her pussy lips are hidden under golden hair, but I know she'll be wet and tight on my cock.

My voice is gruff. "Hands and knees, on the bed."

I get a full view of her tight ass when she turns for the bedroom. My cock leaks pre-cum already. It's going to be hard to hold myself back.

Following in her footsteps, I'm the voyeur who watches as she obeys my command. She crawls onto the mattress, ass in the air and legs spread. The sight sends my libido into overdrive. Her pussy is already blushing pink and swollen. Moisture covers the outer lips. I place my phone on the nightstand before undressing quickly. Naked, I round the bed, dragging a palm over her back and slipping a finger down her crack to her slit.

"Do you have a butt plug?"

She shakes her head.

"Your vibrator will do."

"I'm not sure–"

I slap her ass. Hard. She yelps.

"You trust me," I remind her, massaging the sting away. "Say it."

"I trust you."

I'll wring those words from her as many times as I have to, just because they're music to my ears and fuel to my lust. Opening her nightstand drawer, I withdraw the toy and lube before climbing between her legs.

She glances at me from over her shoulder when I squirt a generous amount of lube down the crack of her ass.

"You're going to love every minute." I want to reassure her, because she's tensing up. "Take a deep breath. That's good. Now blow out."

When she exhales, I penetrate her ass with one finger. She wiggles a bit, but she takes me easily. A few pumps relax the tight ring of muscle, enough to stretch her with two fingers. It's not a big vibrator. She'll take it without pain. She moans when I pull out. Lubricating the vibrator, I push the tip against her anus.

"Deep breath."

She obliges. The blunt head spears her little rosebud. It takes more work to fit the rest, but I take my time. I don't want to tear her. When we get to the thickest part, I pinch her clit, rolling the nub between my forefinger and thumb. She arches her back and clenches her ass, sucking the toy deeper and past the thickest part.

I love playing with her like this. I love looking at her like this. She'll get on all fours and dirty for me just because I want her to. Me, I'll do anything for her.

"How are you doing, princess?" I ask, smoothing my palms up her back.

"Good."

I flick the switch on the vibrator, going straight for the highest setting.

Her back dips and her muscles tighten under my hands. "Oh, my God."

"Better?"

"Y–yes."

I knead her shoulders and massage her back until her body relaxes again, telling me she's adapted to the sensations in her ass. Dripping more lube around the intrusion in her asshole, I pull it out an inch and slide it back in. Her moan is the sign that she's enjoying this, that she can take more. I start fucking her ass gently with the vibrator. The tight ring stretches to take the toy, and my own ass clenches at the erotic sight. I study her pretty pussy from every angle as I make her ass work for me. Slipping the toy in all the way, I twist left and right before giving two shallow pumps. I find her clit and flick a finger over the nub while repeating the rhythm in her ass. A few seconds like this, and her arms collapse. She goes down on her elbows, her face sideways on the mattress.

"Stay like that." For good measure, I slap her pretty globe.

She moans and rolls her hips, greedy for more.

I set the focus of the video function on my phone and check the screen. With my arms around her waist, I drag her diagonally across the mattress until I have the view I'm looking for. Perfect. From this angle, I've got her splayed pussy and face in the picture. I activate the recording.

Time to get down to business.

The foreplay has primed her pussy. I don't have to check to know she's ready, but I drag a finger through her slit, anyway. She whimpers when I rub the wetness I've gathered around her clit. Grabbing her hip in one hand and my cock in the other, I position the head at her entrance. I nudge to give her a warning, and then drive home. She cries out, raw ecstasy transforming her pretty face, but she takes me beautifully. My balls are pressed against her ass. I'm as deep as I can go. Her heat is sleek and tight, her cunt lips stretched wide to accommodate me. I'm glad I'm filming this. The sight is too pretty not to enjoy over and over again. Her pussy tightens on my cock. I can feel the vibrations from the toy in her ass. I'm not going to last long.

I pull out until only the head of my cock is lodged in her cunt and slam back in. My thrusts are deep and fast, rougher than I intended, but I'm chasing both of our releases. The power with which I'm ramming into her pushes her body forward. Her legs give in, and she collapses flat on her stomach. I lift and hold her with an arm under her waist while I'm punishing us both with hard pleasure. She grunts with the force of every thrust, her breasts and body swaying from the impact. The sound of me fucking the air from her lungs mixes with the low hum of the toy and our groins slapping together. The room smells like sex, feminine sweat, and her grapefruit perfume. The sensations are overwhelming. I'm lost in us, everything but my senses absent. I'm an addict to this. This is my obsession.

My climax starts building at the base of my spine, pulling my balls tight and high. She needs a little extra to get there with me. My palm comes down high on her ass cheek, jiggling the toy. She screams. Begs. Her words are incoherent, but the way she slams back as I shove deep is an affirmation that she wants this as hard as I do. I need to stay in control. I count each spank I deliver until I reach ten and her ass is red on both sides.

"Touch yourself," I command.

Obediently, her hand moves between her legs. It's a grueling pace. I'm fucking her pussy raw while she's rubbing herself and her dark hole is filled to the brink.

"You're with *me*," I say, thrusting the meaning into her. "You'll stay with me. I'll do whatever it takes."

It's her desperate gasp and the way her muscles lock that sends me over. My load shoots in her cunt, filling her up as she comes on my cock. My dick swells inside her. My back pulls crooked as her pussy milks the last jets of cum until I'm empty and she's shaking.

Reaching over her, I switch off the video function on the phone. I barely have enough strength to catch my weight on my arms and not crush her. We're breathing in tandem, our pants evidence of how hard we both came. I kiss her shoulder and the marks I left in her neck. I kiss my way down her spine until my cock slips out and cum runs down her thighs. I let her lie down on her stomach to wiggle the vibrator from her ass. She whimpers, but she's boneless. Hell, so am I.

My arms protest as I push up. My skin feels raw all over, even where our bodies didn't touch. There's heat in my pores and deep satisfaction in my gut. I plant a kiss at the top of her crack, and drag myself to my feet and to the bathroom, where I wash the toy and wet a hand towel with warm water to clean her.

She doesn't contest my administrations. When I've wiped away the lube and cum, I fall down beside her and pull her into my arms. Then I kiss her, long and slow. Our tongues tangle in a sweet cool-down of the extreme passion we've shared. I want to kiss her like this forever. Tonight might have been on my terms, but she holds all the power. Always has. From the first moment she stepped out onto her deck to confront me in her pool. This woman can be the end of me if I let her. It'll be the end of me if she leaves me, but I'll never let her. I allow the knowledge to still the fear and uncertainty that worm their way into my gut at the startling revelation of exactly how much she means.

More than anything.

Without her, my life suddenly seems colorless. Black and white.

She stirs in my arms. "I have to pick up Abby soon."

From the lethargic look on her face I know it's hard for her to move. Picking her up in my arms, I carry her to the shower and give us both a quick rinse-down. She pulls on a T-shirt and yoga pants when we're done, watching me as I get dressed.

When I reach for my phone, she asks, "What are you going to do with that?"

I know what she's referring to. "Keep it."

"For how long?"

As long as I'm planning on keeping her. "Don't worry. It's for our eyes only."

"I know."

I cup her nape and pull her closer. "Kiss me."

She presses not only her lips, but her whole body against me. "I'll see you tomorrow."

"You will."

"I'm sorry you can't stay."

"Me, too."

"Good luck for your studies. Will you send me a text before you go to sleep?"

I smile. "What would you like me to say?"

"Anything."

"Then it will be anything." Anything she wants.

She gathers her bag and keys and walks me out. I insist on following her at least to Groenkloof where her friend lives. You never know. When I wave goodbye at her exit, I feel oddly alone.

We're public, but we're not together. Not yet. I'm a greedy bastard, always wanting more when I get what I want, but it's hard not to want everything with Jane.

---

### Jane

"I HAVE A FAVOR TO ASK," Brian says, curling one of my short locks around his finger.

We're lying on a blanket under the shade of a willow tree at the edge of the water. The picnic by the dam next to the cottage was my idea to take a break between Brian's exams while Abby is with Francois for the weekend.

"Ah ha. I knew there was a price for helping me move," I joke.

He remains serious. "Sam has a party in a few weekends' time."

"Yes?" I wait for him to elaborate.

"It's important to her. You know better than me how girls are. She's worried she won't wear the right clothes or do her hair the right way."

"She's worried she won't fit in."

"She's worried she'll look fat. She needs an outfit, and I'm not the best candidate to give her fashion advice."

"Would you like me to take her shopping?"

"If you don't mind." He brushes the curl from my face. "I know you're tied up with work and Abby's exams."

34

"Of course, I don't mind. How about in two weeks, when I don't have Abby? It'll give us time to do it right."

"I didn't know there was a wrong way."

"Shopping for the right outfit means trying on many. It's hungry and thirsty work. We'll have to stop for carrot cake and hot chocolate."

"I'm sure you've noticed, but Sam needs to lose weight, not pick up more."

"A treat on a special occasion isn't going to hurt. It's all about the balance."

"I'll try to remember that." He rests his palm on my belly, tracing a thumb around my navel. "Eugene is having a party next Saturday. It's his birthday."

"You don't have to warn me if you're planning on getting trashed." I wink. "I'm not the jealous type who waits up."

"Actually," he raises his gaze from my stomach, watching me intently, "I'm inviting you to come."

It catches me by surprise. "To Eugene's party?"

"With me."

We haven't been out together since we've decided to go public. We've both been caught up in family responsibilities, work, and exams. Neither have we told anyone, yet. We've decided to keep it quiet at the office, regardless. A relationship with his boss will make Brian's appointment look biased, and he's doing a great job. I'd hate to see him get fired over *personal interests* when he's got his future cut out for him at Orion.

"It's at Playback in Hatfield," he continues.

His fingers play lightly over my stomach as he carries on, watching me with that look. Fear. Fear of rejection. He's worried I'll decline.

"I'd love to go with you."

His relief is palpable. "It'll be a bunch of pimple-faced asses."

"I know what a student party looks like."

"Technically, they're not all students."

"I know." I place a hand on his cheek. "I've been to every bar in Hatfield before you were born."

He grips my hand and kisses my palm. "God, when you say it like that…"

I grin. "It makes me sound old?"

"No." His expression darkens. "It makes me think about every other dick in every scaly bar that's been around you before me."

"Ah, someone is the jealous type who waits up."

He bites down on the tip of my finger.

"Ouch! What was that for?"

"I trust you. It's the other five million penises I don't trust."

I laugh, then shudder as he sucks my finger into his mouth and licks away the pain while holding my gaze with that brutal look in his eyes that drips of sex and dirty promises. Of shared secrets. Of going public.

Where are we heading? Is there even a future for us? I don't ponder the question, because he pushes me down and rolls over me, his strong body pinning me to the ground.

"Tell me how you want it, princess."

He's giving me control, but even then, I'm in his power. Even then, he's pulling the strings. I can't help but ask how wide when he tells me to spread my legs. Then again, he doesn't have to tell me anything. Instinctively, we dance in tune. We're two of a kind. Soulmates. Born at the wrong time.

"Just like this," I say.

He knows what I like. He knows how I need it. Gripping both my wrists in one, big hand, he unzips his pants with the other and releases his cock. He hardly takes the time to move my underwear aside before he spears into me under the protection of my dress, taking me fully with the first thrust without foreplay or warning. The intrusion stretches me, but I welcome the burn. I crave it. I bite my lip to catch a scream as he fucks me with all the wildness reflecting in his eyes.

WHEN I WALK into the office on Monday, Brian and my weekend escapades are burning between my thighs. We've been rough and tender. We've been brutal on Sunday when he had to say goodbye. I flush a little at the memory, adjusting the collar of my dress. There's a buzz in my stomach at the thought of seeing him, but when I enter our floor, his chair is empty. He's in, though, because his phone is lying on his desk.

The knowledge of what's on that phone makes my insides twist. He shouldn't let it lie around like this. I glance in Candice's direction, but she's facing the filing cabinets. Slipping his phone in my purse, I walk to my office.

"Where's Brian?"

"Good morning to you, too." Candice straightens. "In Toby's office."

"What's he doing there?'

She shrugs. "Probably discussing the continuation of his internship."

I close the door and walk around my desk. Retrieving Brian's phone from my purse, I stare at it for a moment. I know his code. I've seen him use it enough times. After a second's hesitation, I unlock the screen. I go straight to Videos. There are a few, mostly of Sam. My hand trembles. I keep on looking at the door. I scroll up and down, but the one I'm looking for isn't there. I switch to Movies. There's only one file, a big one. It's titled Jane, but there's no preview image. When I click on it, a popup screen asks for a code. Thank God. He's encrypted it. Sighing with relief, I drop the phone on my desk and slump in my chair. We haven't watched the film or spoken about it after that night. How many times has he watched it? What has he done while watching our dirty little movie? I'm growing wet just thinking about it.

The ringing of my own phone jerks me from my untimely, lustful thoughts. It's Debbie.

"What are you getting Abby for her birthday?" she asks. "We want to make sure we don't get her the same thing."

"I'm getting her a chain with a heart pendant." It's one of those lockets in which you can put two photos. That's what she's asked for.

"Thanks. We'll get something different."

She's quiet.

I feel the need to make small talk. "How's the pregnancy going?"

"Fine. We'll see you on Saturday."

I'm still pondering the abrupt goodbye when Brian's phone buzzes with an incoming message. A photo pops up on the screen. I wouldn't have paid it any attention if it weren't a striking girl blowing a kiss. Long, blonde hair. Blue eyes. Young. I want to say the standard cliché, but she's even prettier than that. My eyes slip to the text. I will myself not to read it, but I can't stop.

*You owe me a date. Playing hard to get doesn't suit you. You told my dad you were waiting to get a better job to prove yourself to me. You got the job. I won't be patient much longer. Looking forward to seeing you at the party. Kisses. XOXO*

My heart turns inside-out. I place a palm on my stomach where I feel sick.

Not for one minute have I considered that Brian may have a girlfriend. Why hasn't it crossed my mind? It should've. What are the chances of a man like Brian being single? The girls must be all over him like ostriches over bling.

We never laid down rules. We never clarified what the explosive sex between us means. Exclusivity? Or just an extra on the side? Brian is banging my brains out every second weekend and during some stolen lunch hours. It doesn't mean he's not seeing someone–this girl–during the longer periods he's not with me.

Speaking of the devil. The door opens, and Brian enters. Spotting his phone in my hand, he stops in his tracks.

He closes the door before he speaks. "What the hell, Jane?"

"You tell me."

He walks to me slowly, eyeing the phone as if it's dangerous. "Are you checking up on me?"

"Should I?"

"What are you doing with my phone?"

"You left it lying on your desk. I was worried about the film."

"So, you checked and found it locked with a code."

"Yes."

"Told you, I'm not going to let it fall into the wrong hands. I'm not stupid."

*Don't say it. Don't be petty.* Ah, darn it. I guess I am the jealous type, after all. "Is this thing between us exclusive?"

His eyes widen and then narrow. "This *thing*?"

"Whatever we've got going on."

"You mean our *relationship*."

Or affair. "Are other sex partners allowed?"

His mouth sets into a hard line. "Fuck, no. Unless you want him to die."

"What if it's a she?"

"You want to bang another woman?"

"Don't be an ass." I shove his phone at him. "Check your messages."

He takes it with a question in his eyes and unlocks it with a frown. The frown deepens as he reads the message. When he looks back at me, his face is expressionless.

His voice is equally flat. "It's nothing."

"Who is she?"

"Nobody."

"My ex-husband cheated on me."

"I know. He's a bastard."

"I know what it feels like."

"I don't, but I can imagine. It makes me want to strangle him."

"I'm not doing that to anyone."

"You're not. I thought you trusted me."

"Don't throw that card at me. You're the one who said I can always talk to you."

His shoulders lift as he inhales deeply and fixes his gaze on a spot to the side. After a few beats, he looks back at me. "She's from a next-door neighborhood. We went to the same school. Her father was hoping we'd get together, but I'm not interested."

"She is."

"Doesn't change how I feel."

"How's that?"

He looks me straight in the eye. "I'm in love with another woman."

# 3

---

*Jane*

In a second flat, my heart goes from crumbling to soaring. The silence between Brian and me grows like our awareness of each other's feelings.

It's sweet.

It's scary.

It's a drug.

The dark lust that draws us together over the obstacle of my desk is a language we both understand. It's more potent than a touch or a word. He feels my need. He knows the depth of my desire. I'll let him do despicable acts of passion to me–tying me up, fucking my ass with anything he fancies, and filming us–because he had it straight when I said I trusted him. I don't care what the world will think of me, because I own those moments.

Dorothy was right. It feels good.

"I–"

He holds up a hand. "You don't have to say anything. I don't expect you to say the same because you think that's what I want to hear."

My words are soft. "Unless I mean them."

Uncertainty creeps into his tone. "Do you?"

"I'm falling in love with you, too."

I haven't said those words to anyone but Evan, and now that they've left my mouth, it's as if the spell that kept me bound to Evan's ghost breaks, and I'm free. I'm free to fall in love again. I'm free to feel, and it hurts like hell.

"Jane…" He swallows.

Where the admission on the one hand sets me free, it opens up a cauldron of problems on the other. If you don't care, there's no future to worry about, but if you're in love to the point of being addicted, the future shifts to the focal point. That's where the problem lies.

"There's no future for us, Brian."

Falling in love was futile. This is why I didn't want to care. Now I'm slain open, and that dragon he unleashed is demanding her pound of flesh, except there's no one else like Brian to give it, and there will never be. He's everything I need, everything I love, but his life is just beginning when mine is over the halfway line.

His expression heats with anger. "Bullshit."

"You're nineteen, for God's sake. By the way, you lied to me about your age."

"Don't throw age at me. Age is not a valid reason for us not to have a future."

"Think." I tap my temple. "How old will I be when you're forty?"

"This is your insecurity speaking."

"I'll be an old woman, and you'll be in the prime of your life."

"One," he holds up a finger, "you'll never be an old woman in my eyes. Two, this is the last time I'm telling you, it's not about age. Three, I fucking love your body, but it's *you* I'm head over heels in love with."

Silently, I consider his words. How much more shall I risk? The further our relationship goes, the harder I'll fall. Will I survive it, this time?

"Jane," his voice is pleading, "you're over-complicating this."

"It's this simple–What happens when you're fifty and I'm seventy?"

For a moment, I pinch my eyes shut, waiting for him to deal the blow, because not even Brian can be this ignorant, but he doesn't falter or wither. He faces me squarely. Certain.

"I'll still love you, and if I'm lucky, you'll love me back. *It's that simple.*"

God, I want to believe him, and the miracle is I do.

I can't let him go. I cling to him with my gaze, even as the door opens and Candice steps inside.

"Oh." She stops short. "I didn't know you were busy."

Clearing my throat, I force myself to look away from Brian. "Yes?"

"Toby wants to see you."

"Thanks." I have to clear my throat again before I can speak past the emotions. "I'll be right there."

Brian doesn't turn to look at her. He just stares at me, his eyes dark with a kind of possession I've never seen before.

---

*Brian*

LUNCH IS at Jane's place on Saturday. As usual, she cooked up a storm, knocking my socks off. God, I love her cooking. This lunch is different, though. This time, there are three of us. Abby is there.

I understand why Jane waited to introduce me to her daughter. You don't invite your bed partners to meet your kids, unless it's moving in a solid direction. The solid has been there all along. We only agreed to take it forward.

Solid.

Exclusive.

Public.

She's falling in love with me.

I still can't get over the high of those words. I'm like a kid with his first kite. Jane is my first in every way. The first woman I want more than sex with. The first woman with who I can picture a future. My first love.

*Fuck, she's in love with me.* I'm a lucky bastard, because I sure as hell don't deserve her sweet pussy, never mind her heart. Only, I was never going to stop until I had both. We're out in the open and so are our feelings. There's no turning back, but Abby is going to be a hurdle. I can see it from the way she crosses her arms and glares at me from across the table, which is set outside with a pretty tablecloth and colorful crockery. Jane is serving an Italian menu with pasta dishes. She declined my offer to help carry everything outside, I'm suspecting to give me time alone with Abby.

"Aren't you the security guy?" Abby asks.

"I helped your mom out with the installation, but I'm not with a security company."

"I saw you at our house." Her words carry an accusation. "I came home from ballet and you were just leaving. I recognise your truck."

"Your mother and I have been friends for a while." If Jane hasn't told her the nature of our relationship, I respect that. If it was anyone else, I wouldn't have hesitated to put the facts straight. I want the world to know Jane's mine, but not Jane's kid. Jane should deal with breaking the news when she's ready. I prefer to change the subject. "How do you like your new home?"

"Not much."

My brow rises at that. "Why not?"

"I ran into our landlady in the garden. She told me you chose the place."

"For the record, I found it, but your mother chose it. Is that why you don't like it, because you think I chose it?"

She snorts. "Don't be silly. I don't like that my mother lied to me."

Jane has been confiding in me about her strained relationship with her daughter and the way Abby is with Debbie. I don't point out that her father lied to her and her mother about his mistress, and she seems to be getting on just fine with her dad and his soon-to-be-wife.

"Don't be too hard on your mother. Moving wasn't her choice, and it's not easy on her, either."

"She *had* a choice." Before I can ask what she means, she continues. "You're her boyfriend, aren't you?"

Ah, shit. I can't lie at a direct question, not if I'm hoping to one day win her trust. "You should ask your mom about that, but yes, I like to think of myself as her boyfriend."

"How old are you?"

"Abby, it's not about–"

"Mom said you're twenty."

"Yeah." Almost.

"You're only seven years older than me."

I scratch the back of my head. "It's not about age. It's about maturity and compatibility, but I don't expect you to understand that, yet. One day, you will. I know your mom loves you, and she wants you to be happy, but she also deserves her own happiness, don't you think?"

Abby opens her mouth but shuts it when Jane exits the house with a tray. I get to my feet to take it from her.

Our lunch continues in a tense atmosphere. I get an inkling of how it must be for Jane. I'll have a word with Abby again when the next opportunity presents itself, but I should let her get more used to the idea of Jane and I as an item. I almost don't get through lunch with the way Abby slurps her spaghetti, but I crunch my teeth and make an effort for Jane. It takes counting to a thousand several times during the meal.

After lunch, I help to tidy up and then go home to spend time with Sam while Jane drops Abby off at her friend's house for a sleepover before getting ready for Eugene's party. I also get some equipment from Tron I want to set up in the cellar.

The plan was to pick up Jane at eight, but she sends a text to let me know she's running late and will meet me at the bar. With time to spare, I arrive early. Clive, Mike, and a few other guys are already there. By the looks of it, Eugene is well on his way to getting pissed. They would've pumped him full of shooters by now.

I put my arm around his shoulders and lead him to the bar. "Happy birthday, bud." I signal for the bar lady. "Let's get some water into him."

He makes a face when she puts a beer mug full of milky tap water in front of him, but he drinks it all.

"Alternate with water after every drink," I say, "or you won't make the end of the night."

Clive comes up with shot of tequila. He offers me the tot glass. "You've got some catching up to do."

"No thanks."

"Suit yourself." He throws the liquor back with a grimace.

The door opens, and a group of girls enter. I can pretend I don't see her, but I can't overlook the blonde in the center.

Eugene elbows me. He's seen them too. "Your date's here."

"My date's still on her way."

"No fucking way," Clive chirps.

"What's that?" Mike, who joined our party at the bar, asks.

Clive shakes his head as if I'm the biggest loser in the bar. "He invited his uptown girlfriend."

Mike stands taller. "The one who brought you lunch at the site?"

"She brought you lunch?" Eugene whistles. "Man, this is serious."

"She's a looker, that one," Mike says. "I don't know how you winged it, but she's got class."

"Big mistake." Eugene looks amused. "We're just a bunch of poor idiots. I don't think she'll fit in."

"Don't forget Lindy's here," Clive adds.

"Let me worry about my girlfriend and how she fits," I bite out.

"Is it official, then?" Eugene asks. "Last time we spoke about it you didn't want to admit shit."

"As official as it gets." Which makes me sleep better at night. She's my woman, meaning I get to play the hands-off card.

Mike looks at me with something like admiration. "You don't fool around."

Not when it comes to her. No fooling there.

Eugene orders a round of beers while Clive secures a pool table. My eyes are trained on the door, watching, waiting.

At eight-thirty, she walks in. I almost choke on the swallow of beer I've just taken. Jane is wearing long, lace-up boots with black stockings. The black shorts are tight with a high waist, showing off her firm ass and flat stomach. A red patent leather jacket and a fitted tank top rounds off the outfit. Her make-up is heavier than usual with dark eyeliner and red lipstick, and her hair is slicked back. Her only jewelry is big hoop earrings. I've seen her in all kinds of formal and naked, but this is new. Steaming hot. She's looking casual but classy in an understated and over-sexy way. It's not the clothes or the make-up. It's the attitude and that body. It's just Jane.

The bar hasn't exactly gone quiet, but everyone is looking. Mike is practically drooling. I have to shoulder him to close his mouth. The girls are more discreet, but they're staring just like the men. Even Clive is pussy-whacked. I feel like breaking a few jaws, starting with Mike just because he's unlucky enough to be closest, but then Jane spots me and smiles.

The fucked-up world I live in falls away. My sins don't matter, and the darkness of my soul has no consequence, because that smile makes everything okay. The only thing that counts is the woman who walks to me with a sway and confidence in her gait. She's a woman, not a girl, old enough to know what she wants. What she wants is me.

She's almost on top of me before I get back the function of my tongue.

"Hey, princess."

*Thanks for not standing me up. You look gorgeous. The room just got happier now that you're here.* All the things I want to say sound as cheesy as hell, so I rather keep my mouth shut. There are better things I can do with my mouth.

Cupping her nape, I draw her nearer and kiss those red lips. She smiles when I wipe her lipstick from my lips with the back of my hand. Does she know what I'm thinking, where I want those red lips, right now?

I'm so smitten, I've almost forgotten we've got company, but Jane remembers her manners.

She holds out a hand to Mike. "How are you doing, Mike?"

He fucking blossoms. "You remember my name. Good. I mean I'm good."

"Happy birthday, Eugene." She kisses his cheek and hands him a small parcel.

My friend blushes. I swear he must be red from his cheeks right down to his toes.

"Clive." She offers her hand.

This time, he shakes it, mumbling a greeting.

She motions at the gift. "Aren't you going to open it?"

Eugene fumbles with the giftwrap. It takes him almost a minute to tear it off. "No way."

Jane smiles sweetly. "I hope you like it."

"No ways."

Mike tries to look over Eugene's shoulder. "What is it?"

I'm as curious as hell, even if I won't admit it.

"Is this what I think it is?" Eugene asks.

"Yep. It's from the original movie reel."

"Shit. This is a piece of cult." Eugene holds a piece of film to the light. "The Empire Strikes Back, 1980. My all-time favorite Star Wars movie. You remembered. Thanks, Jane. This is really cool."

"Wow." Mike stares at it in wonder. "Where did you get it?"

"I worked at Disney World for a couple of months during my backpacking years. Got it at the souvenir shop."

"How did you even know it's his favorite?" I ask Jane.

"Eugene told me when we were moving."

"Thank you," Eugene says again. "It's awesome. You're the best."

"I'm glad you like it."

That was a nice thing to do. I'm sure the souvenir meant a lot to her. I'm not the only one to think so. The whole bunch look at her like she's made of fairy dust. I pull her to my side and put a hand on her lower back. I like to have her close and touch her, but it's also a warning to the rest of the assholes who are staring.

Brushing my mouth over her ear, I ask, "What would you like to drink?" The music isn't so loud she won't hear me, but I want to feel her body shiver. She doesn't disappoint.

"Beer, please."

I place the order and turn to introduce her to the rest of the crowd, mostly people from our class, but Jane is already taking care of herself. She's chatting to a guy with freckles who sat next to me in science class. It takes all of ten minutes for her to put everyone at ease. At ease is an understatement. Win them over is more like it. Her social skills are good. I guess when you move in her circles you get practice, but Jane has a quality of being genuinely interested in people. I think back to our first breakfast and her platonic interest in me, how it made me feel like the most important person in the world, the *only* person on the planet.

When the karaoke starts–a special exception for Eugene–she's on stage with all the other clowns. They're laughing their asses off, looking like they're having the time of their lives. I grab a seat at the bar from where I can watch Jane. It's not only to make sure she's safe, but I like being her spectator. I like watching her in a social setup. It's different. We haven't spent time with other people. It shows me another side of Jane, the fun and playful side. I imagined shielding her all night from curious stares and questions, but she's out there on her own, one of them. One of us. I wouldn't have minded holding her hand throughout the party, figuratively speaking. I accepted and looked forward to it as my duty, but seeing a different nuance to her is more fun.

The song ends with loud clapping. I stretch my legs out in front of me, expecting Jane to come to me and making space on my lap, but she tosses me a private sultry look and mingles with the group at the pool tables. They talk animatedly. She throws her head back in laughter. It's too far to hear what they're talking about, but I don't give a damn about the conversation. Not really. What I care about is the way she presses the beer bottle to her cheek, as if she needs cooling down. I care about the way her hip cocks slightly as she shifts her weight and how sassy her legs look in those boots. I care about how it looks as if she's really enjoying herself.

From the other side of the room, Lindy makes her way over. Our eyes connect. It's too late to get up and walk away.

She takes the seat next to me, her knees brushing my thigh. "I'll have a tequila slammer."

"Isn't that a bit strong for you?"

"Making decisions on my behalf? We're not even together, yet. Or are you just watching out for me, protecting your future interests?"

"Lindy." It's both a plea and a warning.

She tips her head toward the pool area. "That's what you passed me over for? Marilyn Monroe?"

"Don't be nasty. It doesn't become you."

"Are you buying my drink, or do I have to get it myself?"

I call the bar lady over and order the drink. When she's poured the lemonade, Lindy pushes the glass toward me.

"Mix it."

Placing a palm over the glass, I slam it down hard. The lemonade fizzes up to the rim. She takes it back and tosses it in one go.

Licking her lips, she watches me. "You didn't reply to my messages."

"It's not going to happen."

"You lied to my dad." She swivels her chair and rests her elbows on the counter behind her. "About why you got that fancy job."

"Lindy–"

"Don't worry. I won't tell. I figured out a few things about my dad since we last talked. He'll kill you, and you're no good to me dead."

"What are you playing at?"

She puts a hand on my thigh. "I'll let you have your fun with Marilyn. When you're done playing the toy boy, you'll come crawling to me." Leaning over, she whispers in my ear, "That's a promise."

I catch her wrist and move her hand away. "I think you've had enough. Your daddy won't be happy if you get home drunk."

Her eyes flash as I get off the barstool. I don't wait for her to say more. I turn my back on her and walk away.

What I can't walk away from, is dealing with Monkey.

It's going to have to happen soon.

---

*Jane*

EVERYONE IS IN HIGH SPIRITS. I'm having a good time. I'm learning things about Brian he never talks about, like how he got into detention for freeing the frogs from the biology class before they could become autopsy experiments. Brian's classmates are eager to tell the stories, and I'm a greedy listener. When I glance over to Brian, I spot her, the girl who sent him a photo text. She's sitting next to him, her lips pouty. He says something. She puts her hand on his thigh, and when she leans over to whisper in his ear, her gaze catches mine. I look away quickly.

The ugly, jealous part of me rears its head. I'm simultaneously embarrassed and hurt. It's just flirting. Why is it affecting me? I'm not in high school, for God's sake. Yet, I can no longer focus on the conversation around me.

"Everything all right?" Brian asks, suddenly next to me.

I shake away the feelings. "Yes. You?"

"I'm ready to go, unless you want to hang out here a bit longer." He brushes a strand of hair behind my ear. "Looks like you're having fun."

"Ready." I hand him my empty beer bottle.

He leaves it on a nearby table and takes my hand, leading me to the door. Outside, we stop next to my car.

"I want to show you something," he says.

"What?"

"Follow me."

Without another word, he walks to his truck. I'm needy and hungry for him. I want him to take me to bed, but when we get to my place, he tells me to lock my car and get into the truck.

"Where are we going?"

"You'll see."

As we cross over the highway and take the exit, our destination becomes clear. He's taking me back to his place? He hasn't invited me back since the incident with his mother, and I didn't want to invite myself. Heading over to see his family wasn't what I expected tonight.

We park under the awning, but instead of leading me to the back door, he guides me to the cellar.

The heavy hatch falls onto the grass with a thud when he opens it. He unlocks the security grid and removes the chain. When he flicks on a switch and light spills down the stairs, I suck in a breath. The place is completely transformed. The wooden staircase is solid. The walls are plastered, and the floor cemented. A sofa is pushed against the wall, facing a flat-screen television. A small bar-fridge stands in one corner and a cabinet with glasses next to it.

"What do you think?" he asks.

"When did you do all this?"

"In the evenings. There's a lot of work to do, still. It needs painting and a carpet, but it'll make a cozy den. Come on."

He goes down the steep steps first and offers me a hand. Inside, I turn in a circle, admiring his work. It's neatly done. The building experience came in handy. There's a coffee table in front of the television stacked with electronic equipment, mostly cameras.

I wave at the table. "What's this?"

"Old stuff I got from Tron. He gave me the television, too."

I don't ask what work he had to do to earn the flat-screen. "This is where you *chill*?" I quote his slang from when he first showed me the cellar.

"It's quiet when I need to study."

Sleeping in the lounge isn't ideal. Maybe this is a good time to bring up the issue that's been bothering me since he invited me home. I don't want him to think I'm interfering or questioning how he spends his money.

"Do you sometimes think of getting a bigger place?"

"All the time, but my mom can't leave here."

I almost bite my tongue for the stupid comment. "How about extending the house? With your new salary it would be possible."

"Sam's education is priority. She's going to a private school next year."

Of course. That's just what Brian would do.

"The school she's in now has a bad reputation. She's getting bullied, but that's not the point. She can handle herself," he says proudly. "The point is that there are no computers, no science equipment, and it's infested with drug dealers."

My heart softens even more for the man facing me, a man so much older than his years. "She's lucky to have you as a big brother."

"Come here." He pulls his phone from his back pocket and leaves it on the table. Then he sits down on the sofa and pulls me down to straddle him.

I push on his chest, glancing at the open hatch. "What about Sam and your mother?"

"Sam will be in bed already, and my mom never comes outside. No one is going to walk in on us," he says with a mischievous grin. He cups my jaw and draws me closer. "I've been wanting to do this all night."

When his tongue traces the seam of my lips, my belly flutters. I open my mouth to give him access and gasp when he steals inside, seducing me into a puddle of desire with a gentle kiss. He takes his time, molding his lips over mine in an easy and unrushed pace. He kisses me with his eyes open, taking in my expression with the intensity I came to associate with his brooding, dark eyes. The caress is tender and sweet, but my need skyrockets. My clit and folds swell. Wetness gathers between my thighs. Moaning, I grind down on his erection. His hands slip from my face to my hips, supporting me as I rock rhythmically against him while he sucks my bottom lip into his mouth and gives a gentle nip.

The leather of his bracelet chaffs my skin as our pace picks up. His fingers dig deeper into my flesh until I feel them to my bones. The tenderness transforms into the fire that always consumes us, our hands roaming and groping while our moans fill the space.

In one movement, he lifts me to my feet. "Undress."

As always, he watches me while I do. When I'm left with only the thigh-high stockings and boots, he says, "Leave them on. I've been fantasizing about these legs in those boots all night, too."

The confession pleases me. At least his fantasies were about me, even if another woman had her hand on his leg and her lips against his ear.

He reaches around me for his phone and a remote. A second later the television comes on.

"We're watching movies?" I ask, surprised.

"Yes. Come sit on my lap."

I like the idea. I'm about to climb on sideways when he catches my hips and turns me around. Pulling me back, he makes me straddle him again, but facing forward. My legs are spread wide and my pussy open and needy. My breasts beg for attention. He flicks a thumb over the screen of his phone. When an image of us fills the television screen, I understand what kind of movie we're going to watch.

I suck in a breath as sounds and motion unfold. My ass is high in the air, stretched by the vibrator, and my pussy is on display. It's weird to see myself like this. It makes me blush, but it also turns me on, and when Brian enters me with a violent thrust on the screen, more moisture leaks between my legs.

He pulls my chest against his back and tweaks my nipples between his fingers. "Does it turn you on?" he whispers in my neck.

Goosebumps run over my skin. "It does." Not only the lustful sounds and images, but also his hands on me now.

His voice is wicked. "Mm, let's see how much."

His palm flattens between my breasts. Slowly, he drags it down my body until he cups my soaking sex.

"This much," he says, his tone pleased.

Pressing two fingers together, he rubs them over my clit. My hips lift of their own accord. My head falls back, and my eyes flutter close.

He nips my ear. "Watch."

I do as I'm told. He's fucking me so hard in our private movie he has to keep my body up with one arm. The memory of those sensations deep in my core make my pussy clench. I need to touch him. He doesn't object as I lift to my knees to undo his zipper and free his cock. The head is wet with pre-cum. I use my hand to smear it over his long shaft, lubricating him before closing my fingers and squeezing.

He hisses. His grip on my hips tightens before he pulls me almost violently back down in his lap. His cock is jutting out in front of my pussy between my spread legs. I can't help but rock my hips forward, dragging my clit over his hard length.

"Goddammit." He groans.

I get no warning as he circles my waist with both hands, lifts me higher, and positions his cock at my entrance. He impales me with a hard thrust, slamming up as he brings my body down. Our groins crush together. He's so deep inside it hurts. There's no time to find my balance. He lifts me an inch and pivots his hips, ramming his cock into my body, but I'm wet and ready, taking him easily. Then he reverses the action, keeping still but lifting me up and down by the waist. He keeps a hard rhythm that's in sync with what's happening on the screen. I'm close, but I won't come if he doesn't touch my clit.

As if reading my mind, he slows his pace, rolling his hips rather than thrusting. His cock hits a spot deep inside that has my thighs clenching. I dig my fingers into the fabric of his jeans, trying to find leverage as he folds one big hand around my neck, pulling my back to his chest. Finally, his free hand moves to my clit. My back is arched in this position, pushing my pussy forward and spreading me wider. I cry out, trying to bite back a scream when he pinches my clit and rolls it between his fingers the way I like.

He's close, because he's swelling inside me. My release starts to build in par with the woman's on the screen. He rubs my clit harder and fucks me faster, deeper. The pleasure coils. It heats my body. I cup his balls as he slams his groin against my ass. If it weren't for his grip on my neck, holding me still, my body would've lifted straight off his lap. His fingers close marginally, not choking me, but claiming dominance.

Everything inside contracts as pleasure rips through me. My scream is an echo of the one coming from the screen. He curses and keeps still, his cock jerking inside me. He rolls his hips up, settling deeper as warm jets fills my channel. I let him wring every aftershock from me with his fingers on my clit until we both sag back onto the couch, spent.

He keeps his hand on my sex and caresses my neck and jaw with the other, stroking my shoulder, arm, and breasts. We take our time to come down from our high, the screen now black. When I've found my breath, he lifts me off his cock and makes me lie down on my back. Bending my knees, he pulls off his T-shirt and uses it to clean me. How does he do that? How does he control my orgasm to the point of perfect timing? He rolls the T-shirt into a ball and throws it on the floor. Then he plants a kiss on my clit before crawling up my body to kiss my nipples. It's like foreplay in reverse, like we went for the wild stuff first to enjoy the sweetness after. He licks and sucks my nipples until my need starts building again, and then he kisses my lips while he makes the sweetest, gentlest love to me.

Afterward, he pulls a throw over us, holding me in his arms. I'm sleepy and satisfied, but the night gets fresh quickly now that the heatwave has broken, and the cellar is cold. Soon, I start shivering.

He kisses my shoulder. "Let's get you dressed before you catch a cold."

He helps me dress and goes ahead of me up the steps to help me out. His chest is naked, but the cold doesn't seem to affect him. He makes me get into the truck and starts the engine with the heater on full blast while he goes into the house to get a shirt and jacket.

When he comes back, I'm halfway asleep. He gets in but just sits and stares at me.

"What?" I ask.

"I'm not leaving you like this."

"Like what?"

"Tired and cold."

"I'm fine. Better, actually. I'm fantastic."

"Stay the night."

"Here?"

"I can't leave my sister and mom alone, not the whole night."

"I understand, but what about them if we wake up together in your bed?"

"Sam's a big girl. She knows about the birds and bees, and it's not like I have to ask my mother's permission."

It's a long drive to my place, and it's late. The roads are not safe at this time of night. We're both tired. I'm not comfortable letting him drive back and forth. "All right."

Back in the house, he makes me tea and toast before ordering me to the bathroom. After a warm shower, he gives me one of his T-shirts to wear. We snuggle up in his sofa bed in the dark lounge, and although I'm not at ease with sleeping here with his mother and sister next door, I fall into a deep sleep in his arms, not waking until the sun is high and bright in the room. The only thing brighter than the sun is Sam's smile as she stares down at us.

*Shit!*

I jackknife into a sitting position, clutching the sheet to my chest.

"You're wearing Brian's T-shirt," she says.

Brian stirs. He stretches, opens his eyes, and blinks. "Hey, piglet. Did you wake Jane?"

"It's ten o'clock."

Brian yawns. "We had a late night."

"Is that why she slept over?"

He sits up, pulling me closer with an arm around my shoulders. "No. She slept over because that's what girlfriends do."

My insides heat at the statement. I'm proud to be with him. I'm proud of everything Brian is.

"Mom's making breakfast." Sam turns and leaves.

YOUNG ENOUGH

I glance at Brian. This is going to be awkward. He cups my face and kisses me as if I'm made of spun glass.

"Morning. Sleep well?"

"Great, thanks."

He throws back the covers. "I'll get you some pants."

A moment later, he enters with a pair of his sweatpants. I have to roll them up at the waist and ankles. After finger brushing my hair and teeth, I go down the hallway to join Brian and his family in the kitchen. From the laughter that reaches me before I round the doorframe, it's a jovial affair.

Music is playing on the radio. Jasmine is frying bacon and eggs while Sam is making toast. Brian is in charge of the coffee.

"Good morning." Brian's mother greets me with a warm smile. "I'm Jasmine."

"Mom, this is Jane."

"Nice to meet you, Jasmine."

"The plates and mugs are over there." She points at a cupboard.

Locating the crockery and cutlery, I set the table while they finish preparing breakfast.

"How was last night?" Jasmine asks when we sit down.

"Fun," Brian says. He puts rashers of bacon and a slice of toast on my plate.

Sam leans her chin in her hands. "Who all was there?"

"Elbows off the table, young lady," Brian says. "Just about the whole class from school."

Sam sits up straight, resting her hands in her lap. "That must've been boring. Most of them are losers."

Brian gives her a warning look.

I laugh. "I got to hear all the interesting stories about your brother."

Jasmine chuckles. "I can see how that must've been fun."

The ringtone of my phone sounds from the lounge.

I get to my feet. "Excuse me, but it may be my daughter."

As I suspected, Abby's name shows on the screen. I close the door, because I can't explain Brian and his family's presence, yet. Abby wants to know if she can stay until early evening. She wants to go shopping with Jordan and Loretta for new clothes for Jordan. Since she doesn't have an exam on Monday, I agree. Time with her best friend will do her good.

"Everything all right?" Brian asks as I reenter the kitchen.

"Fine. It was Abby." For Jasmine and Sam's benefits, I add, "My daughter. She's spending the day with a friend." Maybe it's a good opportunity for Sam and I to also do some shopping.

After breakfast, I run the idea past Sam, who's jumping up and down at the suggestion. Brian is planning on closing himself up in the cellar to study and has no objections. It strikes me as odd that Sam asks permission from Brian and not her mother. Either way, I want to be sure Jasmine is fine with me taking her daughter to the mall, but after I've dressed in my clothes from the night before and go look for her, she's in her room, having what Sam calls her mid-morning nap.


BRIAN DROPS Sam and I off at my place to get my car and a change of clothes. Sam walks through the cottage, admiring the stone walls and panoramic views while Brian pulls me into a hug.

He kisses my forehead. "I'll miss you."

"We'll be back before teatime."

"I'll keep my phone on. Call if there's a problem."

His protectiveness makes me smile. "There won't be, but thanks."

He shoves a roll of bills in my hand. "I really appreciate this."

"I'm looking forward to it."

I'm not a big shopper, but Sam's excitement is contagious, plus I get why this is a big deal for her.

We drive to the Menlyn mall where there are a variety of stores. After visiting five clothing shops and letting Sam try on countless dresses, T-shirts, and jeans, we settle on an ensemble of a dress and denim jacket with sandals. The color compliments her eyes and skin tone, and the style is versatile enough to be worn to casual parties or fancier events like weddings. My gift is a pair of earrings to match. After hot chocolate and carrot cake at Mugg & Bean, we call it a day, tired but happy. We've accomplished our mission.

It's just after four when I drop off Sam. She scurries into the house with her loot, unpacking everything on the kitchen table for Jasmine to admire.

"That's pretty," Jasmine says, holding the dress up to Sam's body. "You're going to look beautiful." She hands Sam the dress. "Put it in the hamper. We'll rinse it before you wear it, and go put away your earrings so you don't lose them."

As Sam skips out of the kitchen with her parcels, Jasmine sits down at the table and lights a cigarette.

Since Brian's truck is in the driveway, I assume he's still in the cellar. "I'll go say hi to Brian, and then I must be off. I have to pick up Abby in an hour."

"Sit." Jasmine lifts her eyes to me. "If you have a minute."

"Of course." I sit down in the chair opposite her.

She tips her ash. "Thank you for what you did for my daughter, today."

The words are loaded, but even heavier are the words she didn't say. Thank you for doing what she can't.

God, what a sad thought. For her sake, for Sam and Brian's sakes, I hope she'll seek help. The psychological illness that is driving her to drink and self-imprisonment isn't going away by itself. I'm not a psychologist, but I know how crippling fear and depression can be. How do I broach the subject without being offensive? I'm a stranger. It doesn't seem right to meddle in her private affairs. Will she be angry with Brian for confiding in me? Do I dare risk his trust by telling her I know? Before I have time to decide if I should say something, she speaks again.

"I want to apologize for how we first met, or rather for what happened when you first came over. Sam told me."

"Don't worry about it." I decide to risk it. "Brian told me what happened."

She takes a deep drag and crosses her arms. Smoke escapes from her nose when she speaks. "He did, did he?" She blows the rest of the smoke from the side of her mouth. "It's not your business."

"I'm sorry. You're right."

"You seem like a nice person, Jane. I like you."

"Thanks. I like you, too."

"If you care about my son, you'll stay away from him."

I do a double take. I expect this speech from many people. Why did I think Jasmine's opinion would be any different?

"He deserves a girl his own age," she tips her ash again, "someone who can give him children. Someone he can marry and grow old with."

"What Brian seems to need right now is me," I say as honestly and respectfully as I can, but there's truth in her words, and that truth lodges like a splinter in my heart.

I get to my feet. "It's getting late. Thank you for the breakfast." I head to the back porch, but her words stop me in the door.

"I'm forty-one."

She doesn't need to say more. I'm one year older than her. I don't look back as I leave the house. I walk straight to the cellar. Brian sits on the sofa, his elbows resting on his knees and books open in front of him on the coffee table.

He gets up when I climb down.

"How did it go?"

"Great." I walk over to him. "Sam's really happy with her new dress. We got a denim jacket and shoes, too."

He cups my ass and drags my body against his, letting me feel the erection growing against my stomach.

"I appreciate it, and I know Sam and my mom do, too."

Flattening my palms on his chest, I push away. "I came to say a quick goodbye. I have to fetch Abby."

"Hey." He grabs my wrist, pulling me back to him. "What's wrong?"

"Nothing."

"I know you. You're upset."

"I have to go."

"Not until you've talked to me."

"Brian, please."

"We agreed to always talk to each other."

"It's just something I haven't considered." No, that's not true. It's something I didn't want to consider.

"What?"

He stares down at me, holding my wrist locked in his fingers. He's not going to let go until I give him something.

I wet my dry lips. "Do you want children?"

"Not particularly. Do you? I mean you have Abby, but do you want more?"

"What's the point of bringing more children into this crazy world? What kind of future can we guarantee them with global warming and terrorist attacks happening everywhere?"

He searches my face. "You brought Abby into this world."

I hesitate, but he deserves the truth. "Abby was an accident."

"Say it, Jane."

I frown. "Say what?"

"Tell me the real reason why you don't want to have kids, and don't give me some bullshit excuse about global warming or terrorist attacks."

"I don't know what you mean."

"You can be honest with me. Always. I'm not going to judge you."

I look away from his intense gaze that seems to see right through me. The answer isn't simple, and yet, it is. I just haven't admitted it to myself. Despite what he said, fear of judgment

63

makes me weak with the fear that he'll like me less, the fear of losing him. Taking a deep breath, I steel myself. "I'm not the motherly kind."

His face softens with a smile. "I didn't take you for motherly kind. You're more the executive type."

I try to pull away again, but he holds fast.

"All kinds of people are needed to make the world go round, Jane. It's okay to not go gaga over a baby. It's okay to want different things."

"It's just…" I chew my lip, searching for the right words. "It makes me feel like a failure as a woman."

"Don't. Being a woman doesn't come with pre-programmed DNA that makes you broody at a certain age. Each person is unique. Why should women have a common trade?"

"Sometimes, I'm not even sure I'm a good mother to Abby."

He cups my face and tilts my head up to meet his eyes. "Just because she wasn't planned and you're going through a rough patch because your family structure is being redefined doesn't mean you're a bad mother. You're being too hard on yourself. You love her. You do everything you can for her. You're doing your best."

It's as if a stone rolls off my chest, and I can breathe again. The uncertainties I've guarded for myself feel smaller now that I've shared them with him. True to his word, he's not judging me. He's not like the men I grew up with who divide roles with clear-cut lines. Women in the kitchen and men around the barbecue. He's not the norm in so many ways, and my heart beats clearer for it. I know with unmistakable clarity he's The One.

"Tell me about him," he says, his hands, eyes, and voice tender.

My body goes rigid. I can't talk about Evan in this moment. I'm about to say so when he says, "Tell me about your ex."

The breath goes out of me. Relief flows back into my muscles. I let them go soft, one by one. "Francois is not a bad person."

"Do you love him?" He wipes a thumb under my eye. "It's okay if you do."

I pinch my eyes shut for a moment before forcing out the horrible truth. "Not in the way a wife should love her husband."

"Why did you marry him?"

Should I tell him? It feels unfair to Francois, but Brian told me about his mother, and if we're going to be together, he needs to understand the dynamic of the relationship between Francois and me, between Abby and Francois and me, because it will always stand between us.

"What happened?" he asks. "What aren't you telling me?"

"I wasn't well when Evan died. My parents were still on their way from Cape Town after the news. I went back to the university dorm to wait for them. The doctor had pumped me full of drugs to calm me and help me sleep, and Francois came to my room that night."

His hands still. I didn't realize he was stroking my back until now.

His body tenses. "Did he rape you?"

"No. I didn't want to sleep with him, but I didn't say no. It was soothing in a kind of way."

"You were drugged." He sounds angry. "He took advantage of you."

"I allowed it."

"You weren't thinking straight."

"It doesn't matter. It happened, and neither of us can take it back."

"That's why you married him? Because you fell pregnant?"

"It seemed like the right thing to do. The only thing to do."

I was backed into a corner. Fragile. Scared. Weak. I could've said no when Francois gave me a ring. It's not his fault. The guilt for our failed relationship is all mine. Maybe that's why I'm not fighting him for the house or furniture. The only thing worth fighting for is Abby. I've always fought for her, especially when I said yes to a man I didn't love.

"I do love him," I confess, "in my way. Like a friend. I would've stayed. I would've honored my promise."

"You would've settled for second best," he says gently.

There are many things I wish I could take back, but regret doesn't allow for weakness. You need to be strong to survive regret. You need to be strong to move on.

"I wish things were different," I whisper. I wish I could go back to that night in Evan's house and not have another drink. I wish I'd been strong enough to fight for Abby alone. "I wish I could give you the younger version of me."

"I don't want the younger version of you. It won't be who you are *now*, because everything that happened to shape you into the person you are wouldn't have happened."

"As much as I selfishly want to keep you, you deserve a young woman, someone who can grow old *with* you, not before you."

"That won't be fair to her or any other woman, because I'll always go to bed with thoughts about you, and my wet dreams will all be about you. Every woman deserves the over-the-top, I'll-fucking-die-without-you feeling I have for you. I won't degrade a young girl to second best simply because you reject me, so don't even think about it. I'd prefer to be alone."

Leaning against him, I nestle deeper into his embrace. Just when I think there's nothing more he can give, he surprises me again. He's like a sky without a ceiling of clouds. The blue stretches into forever and deeper into my soul.

Most of all, now I know I not only can trust him with my body, but also with my heart.

# 4

*Jane*

A short while ago, I stood in a house that was mine, and Francois stood in the entrance, looking out of place. Now, the roles are reversed. My shoes are sinking into the Moroccan carpet I chose and paid for with hard-earned money not so long ago, but it feels as if I haven't been living here in years. It feels weird. I'm a stranger. Here. To myself.

Francois clears his throat. "Come through. The party is at the back."

"Thanks." I remove my jacket and hand it to him to hang on the coat stand.

We walk down the hallway and through the lounge. The furniture is the same. So are the paintings and ornaments. Through the open door, I see the kitchen. Everything is exactly where it used to be. Debbie hasn't changed a thing.

Voices and music filter through the sliding doors before the deck and backyard come into view.

"Wow." I stop dead.

There's a gazebo on the lawn with a stage and rows of chairs with white chair covers and pink ribbons. Cocktail tables and Chinese lanterns burning in the heat of the day take up the rest of the space. Waiters in tuxedos are carrying trays with what looks like Kir Royal, and staff in chef tunics are spinning candyfloss and flipping pancakes for a bunch of girls, Abby being in the center.

Debbie is standing at one of the cocktail tables, surrounded by a group of women, probably her friends. They all turn their heads toward me as she leans into their circle and says something. She's wearing a black cocktail dress–a brand with Loretta's stamp on it that shows off her pregnant belly–as are all her friends. I guess she forgot to put the dress code on the invitation.

I turn to Francois. "Isn't this over the top? She's thirteen, not twenty-one."

Francois and I have always agreed to material moderation where Abby is concerned. We want her to understand and appreciate the value of things.

He looks uncomfortable. "It's her first party."

Meaning, Debbie.

Abby comes running when she sees me. "Mom!"

"If you'll excuse me," Francois says. "I have to attend to our guests. Make yourself at home."

He almost bites off the last word, as if he realizes too late what a stupid statement he's made.

"Isn't this great?" Abby squeals when Francois walks off. "Wait until you see what's coming."

Loretta waves at me from across the lawn. She and Ralph are conversing with a couple of men wearing suits and ties.

I take Abby's hand. She's wearing a white, A-line dress with a black collar. "You look beautiful, honey. Are you enjoying yourself?"

"Are you kidding? This is the best party of the year in the whole school."

"Happy birthday." I hold out the gift box. A table near the stage is stacked with gifts. "Shall I leave it there?"

"Can I open it now?"

"Of course. It's your gift. You can open it whenever you like."

She tears away the wrapping and lifts the lid. "Oh, Mom, it's beautiful." She hugs me. "Thank you. It's exactly what I wanted."

"Would you like me to put it on for you?"

She turns so I can fit the locket around her neck.

"There." I adjust the chain. "It suits you. Delicate and pretty."

Jordan comes running up. "Hello, Ms. Blake."

"It's Logan now," I remind her. I took back my maiden name after our divorce.

She grabs Abby's hand. "Come on. They're making candy apples."

I watch the two girls skip off together. Still so young, yet not babies any longer.

A voice echoes my thought. "Aren't they growing up fast?"

I turn. Loretta stands next to me with two glasses of Kir Royal. She hands me one. "Cheers."

I take a sip and glance at the women in black. "I didn't know it was a bring-a-parent party."

"You're being mean."

"Sorry." I take a bigger sip. "I can't help it."

"Before you say anything about the dress, I couldn't say no. Debs wanted me to help her choose something for the party."

I absently watch the commotion of waiters and chefs on the lawn. "I wasn't going to say anything."

"You haven't spoken to me since the episode in Mugg & Bean."

"I've been busy."

"Look, what was I supposed to do? It was the day we went shopping for the dress. We stopped for a quick coffee."

I face her squarely. "You don't owe me an explanation. I already told you, I don't have exclusivity on your friendship."

"You're angry."

"I'm not."

"Then why haven't you called me?"

"I said I've been busy. Why haven't you called me?"

"I was waiting for you to call first."

"Christ, Loretta, we're not in first grade. What is our friendship worth if it can't survive a divorce?"

"You know what? You're right." Her gaze moves to Francois who has joined Debbie and her friends. "I guess this party breaks the ice. At least the wedding will be less complicated."

I frown at her.

"You know?" she says. "Abby's wedding. Divorced parents are always forced together at birthdays, graduations, and weddings. At least this way the ice is broken."

"You're repeating yourself."

Francois and Debbie walk to the stage. He picks up a microphone.

"Speech! Speech!" a few of the men call.

Some of them are his colleagues from the office. The others I don't know. Must be friends from Debbie's side.

"No, no, it's not the speech, yet," Francois says into the mike. "If you'd all please take a seat, we have a surprise for Abby."

Loretta takes my arm. "We're having a barbecue by the pool next Saturday. Ralph invited Francois and Debbie. Since Abby and Jordan will be at the year-end class party, you should join us. Especially now that the first party with the three of you in the same room–or garden–is out of the way. It'll be good for you. I promise." She winks. "You can bring your date."

People start taking the seats in front of the stage.

"The guy you disapprove of?"

"Look, you were right about that, too. Whatever kink you're up to is your private business. I just worry about you. I don't want to see you go down a destructive road because of what happened between you and Francois."

Debbie and Francois take the front seats while Abby and her friends fill up the rest of the row.

"Fine. I'll come. Happy?"

"Do I finally get to meet your mystery man?"

"I'll ask him."

"Good. Great."

"We should probably take a seat."

I'm about to drag Loretta to the gazebo when a raucous noise breaks out under the girls. They're screaming and clapping. It looks as if Jordan is going to faint. Their gazes are trained on us. Looking over my shoulder, I grasp the reason for their behavior. Tom de Lange, the biggest local pop star of the moment, has just walked through the sliding doors. A few of the women are fanning themselves as he strides down the aisle between the chairs and hops onto the stage.

"Good lord," Loretta mumbles. "How the hell are we supposed to live up to this standard? Can you imagine the kind of party Jordan will demand for her next birthday?"

I can see how a sleep-over with movies and popcorn waned compared to Tom de Lange. How much is Francois forking out for this party?

Tom is good. I have to give him that. He puts up one hell of a performance, calling Abby onto the stage for the last song, which he dedicates to her. After the show, he hangs around long enough to have a drink and sign a few autographs. When it's time for Abby to open her gifts, Debbie hands her a huge box with a red ribbon that Francois brings from the house. She kneels on the grass to tear away the paper. Opening the flaps, her mouth forms a big O before she slams a palm over it.

"Oh, Daddy. Debs." Abby lifts a Golden Retriever puppy from the box.

It's the cutest thing ever. Abby has always wanted a puppy, but we couldn't get one because of Francois' allergy.

I go over and crouch down to pet him. "He's gorgeous. What are you going to call him?"

"Dusty," Abby says, her eyes shining. She presses the bundle against her chest while her friends coo over the fluff ball.

Straightening, I say to Francois, "That was a very thoughtful thing to do. What about your allergy?"

"I'm taking medication."

"Actually," Debbie says, "it was my idea. Abby told me how much she wanted a dog."

In all the years I've nagged, Francois refused to take the medicine because he didn't want to risk the side-effects.

"Thank you," I say, meaning it. "I know how happy this makes Abby."

She looks at Francois with a smile. "I suppose I managed something your ex-wife hasn't."

Then she looks straight at me, and her smile vanishes.

---

*Brian*

SITTING IN THE CELLAR, I worry about my problems instead of studying. Avoiding Monkey isn't going to make the volatile situation go away. I was hoping Lindy would've backed off after seeing Jane and me together. I got the idea she believed I lied about having a girlfriend.

*Damn, a girlfriend.*

Jane is that and much more. It's like a wild, reckless dream come true. I've never gotten anything I wanted in life, especially not something I wanted this badly.

I rub the photo of Jane absently between a thumb and forefinger. I see that look on her face all the time, especially when she thinks I'm not watching. There's shit in her past. My job is helping her deal. Making her happy. Protecting her. I can't do that with Monkey breathing down my neck and Lindy harboring fairy tales that will never come true.

I slip the photo into the back of my Human Communications guidebook, lock up the cellar, and close the hatch. The hatch is watertight, which also makes it airtight. I'll have to do something about the canals leading from the street, roof gutters, and drain that are crisscrossing over the cellar. The rainy season is coming fast. Inundation will be a problem and I can't keep the hatch closed with no other means of ventilation. Committing the task to the back of my mind, I go to the house to tell my mom I'll be leaving.

She sits at the kitchen table, listening to a radio broadcast.

"I'll be out for a couple of hours."

"Where are you going?"

My mother has never asked before.

"To see Monkey."

Her right eye jumps, a sign she's stressed.

"Don't worry." I put a hand on her shoulder. "It'll be fine."

"You can't be with her, Brian."

"What?"

"Jane. You've got to forget about her."

I don't mean to sound harsh, but I can't help it. "You've never told me what to do. Don't start now."

"I'm sorry." She reaches for her drink. "You're right. It's going to backfire, though, unless you tell Monkey what he wants to hear."

"Let me worry about Monkey."

I grab a sweatshirt and am out of the door before she can say more.


MONKEY IS AT THE GYM. He's not working out, but he watches the guys who train in the boxing ring.

"'Bout time," he says when I walk up. "Come to ask for Lindy's hand?"

"I've got someone else."

He flicks a finger, and the pounding in the ring stops. The room goes quiet.

He turns slowly to face me. "What the fuck did you say?"

"I've got someone. Here's the deal. I marry Lindy but keep a mistress." No damn way I'll ever treat Jane as a mistress, but that's what I say, anyway. "Is that what you want for your daughter? A guy who'll never love her, never make her happy?"

He jumps up so fast the chair crashes to the floor. "Here's the *deal*, you little punk. In twelve months, I walk my daughter down the aisle and give her away to *you*, you skunk-assed, fucking loser, because Ingrid wants a year to organize the biggest wedding the fucking city has ever seen. You'll put a ring on my daughter's finger, and you won't as much as look at another pussy again, or I'll make good on my threat. You'll treat Lindy right, you'll give us grandchildren, and you'll grovel to make her happy, if that's what it takes. You'll prove what you have to with your new, fancy job and then you're in the business. *My* business. Are we clear?"

Rage rushes through my veins. I want to smash his head on the concrete floor and kick out his teeth, but I keep it in, let it fester and clump in my throat.

"Get out of here, you lousy piece of shit," Monkey yells. "I don't know what the fuck Lindy sees in you." He spits on the floor, right next to my tennis shoe. "Fucking punk."

Our stare drags out for a few furious heartbeats. Bit by bit, I squash the anger until I'm calm enough to jerk off my sweatshirt and tackle the weights. I came here not only to find Monkey, but also to train, and that's what I'm going to do. The guys watch warily, waiting for Monkey's next move, but he only kicks the chair and motions for them to continue the fight before his shoes pummel the floor to the exit.

Needing the burn, I pack on extra weights, maybe more than I can handle.

*Fuck it all to hell.* Can't say it wasn't worth a try.

*Jane*

THE DAY IS WARM, and the sky clear. It's a perfect day for a barbecue by the pool. Brian and I arrive at Loretta and Ralph's place at twelve. We had to stop on the way to pick up Loretta's meat order from the butchery.

I glance at Brian before ringing the doorbell. "Are you sure you're okay with this?"

I don't want him to feel uncomfortable because my ex is here, plus he'll be the youngest by far.

He puts an arm around my waist and kisses my neck. "Don't fuss." As if making a point, he rings the bell.

"Whenever you want to go–"

He shuts me up with a kiss. It's a soft, lingering one that makes my knees weak, and it's not finished when the door opens.

"Oh." Loretta coughs. "Hi."

I try to pull away, but Brian doesn't let go immediately. Loretta and the rest of the world don't matter to him, not when he kisses me. He ends the kiss with a soft peck and a smile in his eyes that holds a private message. It tells me he's fine. We'll be all right. Instead of embarrassing me, the tender caress sets me at ease. Only then does he turn his attention to Loretta.

"This is Brian," I say.

He shakes her hand. "You must be Loretta. Thanks for the invite." He holds up the cooler box of meat. "Shall I leave this in the fridge?"

"Um, sure." She pats the ends of her asymmetrical bob. "The kitchen is at the end of the hallway."

"I'll be right back," he says to me with a wink.

He's giving Loretta and me time alone for a girls' chat. He's hardly gone before she dives in.

"Oh, my God, Janie," she whispers.

"He's handsome. I know."

"I was referring to his age."

"He's young. So what?"

"You're into schoolboys, now?"

"Don't exaggerate."

"This isn't what I expected."

"Who did you expect?"

"I don't know. A divorcé. A widower. Someone with gray hair."

Brian saves me from defending my choice of a partner by returning with two beers.

He hands me one. "Is a beer all right, or do you prefer wine?"

"Perfect, thank you," I say, grateful for more than just the beer.

He turns to Loretta. "Can I get you a drink?"

She touches her hair again. "Um, mine is outside. Come on. I'll introduce you."

We follow her to the pool deck out back. Debbie and Francois plus another couple are already there, mingling around a table set with appetizers. The conversation dies down when we walk outside.

"Meet my friend, Jane," Loretta says to the couple in an overly-jovial voice. "And this is…" Her voice trails off as she looks at Brian. "I'm sorry. I'm so bad with names."

What's wrong with her? Is she so shocked she can't remember his name? I hug Brian tighter. "This is my boyfriend, Brian."

Debbie's gaze trails over him, her eyes a bit too wide to hide her shock. Francois' expression is unreadable, as always. Loretta introduces the other couple as Mona and Jack, the husband being a colleague of Ralph's. Mona must be about ten years older than me. Her reaction to Brian is similar to Debbie's. Ralph and Jack are polite, if a little distant, when they greet us. Brian seems unaffected as he shakes their hands and exchanges pleasantries about the traffic and weather.

"What do you do for a living, Brian?" Debbie asks.

Brian puts his arm around my waist, pulling me to his side. It makes me feel sheltered under the scrutiny of the six people watching us, and I relax against him.

"I'm still studying, but I'm doing an internship at the firm where Jane works."

Mona lifts a brow. "Is that how the two of you met?"

Brian gives me another one of those private smiles. Turning to Mona, he says firmly, "No," but he doesn't elaborate.

His look is assertive as he continues to hold her gaze. The only person who appears comfortable with the silence that follows is Brian. Mona looks away first.

"How did you manage an internship at Orion?" Ralph asks.

Ralph doesn't as much as glance at me, but he doesn't have to. The insinuation is clear.

"Jane got me an interview," Brian says without blinking, "for which I'm mighty grateful."

I feel like I have to defend him. "He earned the position. You know how high Toby's standards are."

"Where are you from?" Jack asks.

"Harryville," Brian replies, not an inch of shame in his tone even as another hush falls over the conversation.

God, I love that about him, that he's not ashamed of where he comes from, and he doesn't allow money or status to determine who he is or, in this case, who he isn't.

"How about you, Jack?" Brian asks. "Are you and Mona from around here?"

"We're all neighbors," Loretta says. "Ralph, you better start the fire, or it'll be dinner instead of lunch."

Peering up at Brian, I give him my own private smile, one that tells him how much I admire and appreciate him.

Ralph busies himself with stacking charcoal while we make mindless small talk. Was it really a good idea to come? I love Loretta, but this feels like a waste of time. I shouldn't have let her bully me into accepting the invite, or maybe I was tired of hiding. Maybe I just wanted Brian and me out in the open.

"Dammit," Ralph says, throwing a burning match into the coals. Nothing happens.

"You and your fires." Loretta huffs.

Francois fiddles with the firelighters, sticking more into the pile of coals, but he does so daintily, with the tips of his fingers, as if he's scared to get his hands dirty. It's probably because he's wearing white slacks. All he manages is making smoke.

"Let me." Brian takes the matches and sticks his hand right into the middle of the coals, restacking the firelighters.

He's not wearing fancy chino pants, and even if he were, I bet he wouldn't mind getting them dirty.

In no time, flames leap up in the air.

While we wait for the coals to be ready, the conversation flows like it usually does at these kinds of barbecues with the girls talking kids and the guys talking business.

Francois is droning on about his new hotel project and how they're missing deadlines due to a shortage of clay, which means a shortage of bricks.

"Not that I expect you to follow any of this," he says to Brian. "We're being rude, Ralph. We should talk about rugby."

"No worries," Brian says. "I get it. It'll be more cost-effective if you replace clay with sand lime since sand lime bricks don't need plastering. Personally, I'm not into rugby. I'm more of a cricket guy."

I hold back a laugh. That should teach Francois to be condescending. I'm not going to tell him Brian was a bricklayer.

When the meat is finally sizzling on the grill, I pull off my dress. I'm wearing my bikini under. It's the hottest part of the day, and I can do with a dip in the cool water.

"Join me?" I say as I walk past Brian to dive in.

The water is heaven. I let the coolness slide over my body and penetrate my skin. When I surface at the shallow end, Brian is standing at the edge. He's pulled off his shirt, exposing a set of muscles that has to draw attention, no matter where. The women's gazes are glued to his back, even Debbie's, who's pretending she's not staring from behind her wide-rimmed sunglasses. He walks into the water with a grin, splashing me, and then he's against me and I'm wrapped around him.

"I recall a time when I was in your pool," he says in a low voice against my ear.

Shivers run over my body under the water. "Do you, now?"

Nibbling on my earlobe, he swims me to the deep-end. "There was only one thing I wanted."

"What was that?" I ask, slightly breathless.

"You in the water with me."

"You ordered me back into the house."

"Only because you chased me away."

"You didn't expect an invitation, did you?"

"Didn't need one."

"No?"

His tone is playful but his eyes serious as he stares into mine. "You were meant to be mine. I would've made it happen, regardless."

"Regardless of what?"

"Everything."

The answer is simultaneously non-disclosing and all-compassing. There are no lengths he wouldn't have gone to. No one has ever been this committed to me, not even Evan who walked away when I needed him the most to stay.

A tremor runs down my spine at the memory. It's a place I don't want to go, not with Brian's arms around me and his groin cushioned against mine.

"You're cold," he says with a frown.

I let him believe the lie, allowing him to lift me out of the water onto the side. He grabs my towel from my bag and spreads it out on a deckchair.

"Come here," he orders.

I go to him as if I've always been going to him and spread my body out in the glorious sun as if he's always been the steadfast path to my destiny. He disappears, returning a moment later with my sunglasses and a bottle of water. I reach for both gratefully.

He uncaps the bottle before handing it to me. "It's hot," he says. "I don't want you to dehydrate." Going down on his haunches, he places a hand on my stomach. "Are you hungry? I can get you something to eat." He grins, glancing back at the grill. "It may be a while still before the kebabs are ready."

Ralph is no barbecue master. Neither is Francois. They probably let the coals burn out and now it's too cool to cook the meat.

"I'm good, thank you. I had a few appetizers. I appreciate the offer, though." It's nice to be taken care of.

"You didn't put on sunscreen this morning."

"I was running late after dropping off Abby."

"You'll burn." He takes the bottle of sunscreen from my bag and squirts a blob in his palm. "Turn over."

I turn obediently, letting him massage the cream into my shoulders, back, and legs. When he's done, he does my front. There's nothing inappropriate about the way he's touching me. He's not going near my breasts or unfastening the straps of my top to get to the parts under the spaghetti strings, but he may as well have from the way the others are staring. Flipping the sunglasses down over my eyes, I block out their faces and concentrate on soaking up the sun. Brian takes the chair next to me, interlacing our fingers.

Sweat is running in rivulets down my back when Ralph announces that the food is ready. The older men are still dressed in their golf shirts and chinos. Loretta is wearing a designer bathing suit with a sarong tied around her waist, and Debbie sits on the edge of the pool, her legs dangling in the water, but no one else swims. Loretta will be worried about her hair. It takes her an hour to blow-dry every morning. I don't know what the others' excuses are, but it's a pity not to enjoy the pool on such a splendid day.


WE'VE BARELY EATEN when thick, purple clouds start rolling in. The smell of rain is heavier in the air than the chlorine from the pool.

"Damn," Loretta says. "There wasn't anything about rain in the weather forecast."

That's the thing about these summer thunderstorms. They're highly unpredictable. They almost always arrive in the late afternoon or early evening when the worst heat dissipates.

"I made marshmallow tarts for the grill," she complains.

"Better get them quickly," Ralph says. "I don't know how long the weather is going to hold before it pisses down."

"You sit," I say to Loretta. "I'll get them. You've been running around all morning."

Dropping the towel I had wrapped around my body, I pull on my dress. Brian is engaged in a conversation with Jack. Their chat seems amiable enough. I gather it's safe to leave him to his own devices. The vultures won't rip off his head in the short time it'll take to fetch the dessert.

I locate the aluminum cupcake holders lined with cookie crusts and filled with chopped marshmallows and chocolate chips in the fridge. As I turn with the loaded tray, Francois enters the kitchen.

"What the hell are you doing, Jane?"

I'm so baffled, I almost drop the tray. He hasn't shown me a speck of emotion during all the conflicts we've had in the twelve years we've been together, and he's stalking toward me now, bristling with anger.

"Getting our dessert," I say, flabbergasted.

He takes the tray from me and plonks it down on the counter. "You know what I mean. You're old enough to be his mother."

Anger sparkles in the nerve endings on my skin. The hair on

my arms and neck rises. "That's rich coming from a man who dates a girl young enough to be his daughter. I guess that makes you a hypocrite."

"It's not the same," he hisses. "You're a woman, and he's a boy."

"Now, that makes you sexist."

"Call it what you like. *It's not the same.*"

I cross my arms. "How is it different?"

"For starters, you're mature. Secondly, a man is the breadwinner. He's a toy boy. That makes you a–" He bites his words off angrily.

"Say it."

"A sugar mommy."

As if Brian would only be with me for money. I let the insult settle. "Anything else?"

"I don't want him around when Abby's with you."

"Too late. She's already met him."

He slams a hand down on the counter, making the tarts bounce and me jump. "You're a bad example for her."

"For Abby?" My indignation escalates. "You're a fine one to talk. I was *single* when I met him."

"Don't." He points a finger at me. "Don't even try that one on me."

"You expect me to stand here and accept your double standards?"

"I expect you to act your age." He narrows his eyes. "For the sake of your daughter."

I can't believe my ears. I don't even know what to answer. "It's all right if you do it, committing adultery in the process, but it's not okay for me?"

"I don't give a damn about your feminist arguments. That's all good in theory, but it's not the way the world works. You're embarrassing yourself."

I lift my chin. "That's your opinion, and you don't get to have one of my life, any longer. My business is no longer yours."

As he opens his mouth, Debbie steps into the room. She stops just over the doorstep, her gaze moving between us. The air is sizzling with so much tension, if there was a voltage to it, we'd be charcoaled.

Debbie's huge, brown eyes brim with hurt. "You were taking so long I decided to come look for you."

Francois picks up the tray. It takes him three seconds to school his features into a mask of indifference. "I was just bringing these out."

When he turns to Debbie, it's as if I don't exist. It's as if he never lost his cool, had an outburst, or said unjustly things. It's like it's always been between us. He walks past her through the door, the tray like a shield of armor. She stares at me as if she's going to say something, carrying all that hurt on her sleeve, and just as I'm about to tell her it was nothing, she spins around and follows him.

Lightning ripples through sky when I get outside. The crash of thunder follows two seconds later. Always in sync with my mood, Brian looks up. His expression turns broody.

*It's okay,* I mouth.

Big, fat drops start falling. They plop on the table and make a hissing sound as they hit the coals. We scurry to gather what we can from the table and rush it inside.

I catch Debbie in the dining room. "Stay here," I say over the peppering of water on the roof. "You can't risk slipping and falling."

The rain is coming down so hard and fast, the deck is already a centimeter under water when I get outside again. My bare feet slide over the wet, varnished wood. Drops pelt my face and body. It feels as if the sharp stings penetrate bone-deep. It's freezing cold. Jack managed to save the tarts, and Ralph and Brian are working as fast as they can to close the two canvas umbrellas lest the fabric tears from the weight of the water. Those giant umbrellas cost a fortune. Since Mona and Loretta are clearing the last of the glasses from the table, I grab the designer cushions.

We're all soaking ducks, dripping water on Loretta's hardwood floor. Thunder and crisscrossing bolts of lightning rip the sky apart.

"Bloody hell." Ralph drags a hand over his bald head.

Francois wrings the water from his golf shirt. He's standing in a puddle of water stained brown from the mud on his shoes.

"I can do the tarts in the oven," Loretta offers, patting her ruined hair.

"I better get Debs home and into dry clothes before she catches pneumonia," Francois says.

"You're probably right." Mona takes Jack's arm. "I wasn't planning on swimming, but the rain took care of that."

"Can't control these things," Ralph mumbles.

"The weather forecast said clear blue skies," Loretta whines. "I'm so sorry about the dessert."

"It was a great lunch." I put my arm around Loretta. "Don't worry about the dessert."

It feels like a big anti-climax. Loretta's effort to break the ice between Debbie and Francois and Brian and me didn't work out as planned. I offer to help tidy the kitchen, but Loretta declines fiercely. I guess she's worried about what Brian and Ralph would talk about if they're the only ones left.

The sky is still rumbling violently when we say our goodbyes. Brian pulls his jacket around me and shelters me under his arm as we run to his truck. He lets me in first before rushing around to his side. He closes the door on the wetness, but the noise of the water punishing the metal roof continues. He first buckles me in and then himself. Droplets of water runs down his temples and into his soaked T-shirt.

"You okay?" he asks me as he starts the engine.

I'm scared of all this water and the force with which it's coming down on us, but the question has nothing to do with the storm. It's about what happened between Francois and me in the kitchen.

Brian doesn't ask straight-out. He gives me an opening to talk about it if I wish.

I put my hand on his thigh. His skin is warm under the wet fabric of his swimming trunks. "I'm glad the party rained out."

He covers my hand with his. "Let's go home and have a warm shower."

"Yes." It's the only answer I can ever give him. "Let's."


"I WANT TO TAKE YOU SOMEWHERE," Brian says later that afternoon.

We're cuddling on the sofa in front of the television. We still have until nightfall before I have to fetch Abby from her year-end school party.

He wipes a curl away from my forehead. "Somewhere you've never been."

My excitement perks up. "Where?"

"A club."

"As in dancing?"

His dimpled smile makes the dark look in his eyes slightly less dangerous. "Not exactly."

"Oh. What kind of club, then?"

"A strip club."

"What? As in Teasers?"

He trails his fingers up my arm. His voice is low and seductive. "Would you like that?"

"I don't know."

"There's one way to find out."

"Why do you want to take me?"

"To show you who I am. I want you to know all there is to know about me, just as I want to know everything about you."

It sounds sweet and scary at the same time, but he's already on his feet, offering me a hand.

"Now?" I ask with a tinge of panic as I accept his hand.

His smile turns mischievous. "There's no time like the present."

I look down at my skinny jeans and loose T-shirt. "I'll have to change."

"Not for where we're going."

"Are you sure?" My attire isn't exactly club style.

"Come on." He pulls me gently to the door.

We drive toward Waverley and park in front of an unassuming building with no sign.

"You come here often?" I ask, peering through the windscreen.

"That's why I wanted to show you."

He comes around to open my door and takes my hand, not letting go even once we're inside. I'm grateful for the silent support, because when he's showed our IDs and we step into a large room with pumping music, I need it more than ever. I understand why my clothes weren't of importance. Most of the people are naked. Men and women mingle around a stage where a couple is in the last throes of fucking. The woman comes with a loud moan just as we slide into a padded bench at the back. The man pulls out his cock and ejaculates on her stomach a second later. Thank goodness for the low lights. I'm not a prude, but my face is hot. The man kisses the woman passionately before draping a gown around her and leading her off the stage.

Brian rests his hand reassuringly on my thigh while he orders two beers from the waitress. I glance around. The people who aren't naked wear sexy outfits while others parade in daring lingerie. I must be standing out like a lighthouse in a storm. Most couples are openly fondling, and some are having sex. I swallow, grateful for the beer that arrives to relieve my dry throat.

Staff are cleaning the stage and wiping down the hardwood bench on which the couple fucked.

I motion at the raised platform. "What was that?"

Brian leans over. His lips brush my ear. "Couples come here to fornicate in public."

I stare at him open-mouthed. "They're not paid to put on the performance?"

"They're part of the audience like you and me."

The *you and me* part jars me. "You don't want to...?" I can't finish the sentence.

His chuckle is deep. "No."

I sigh in relief.

"I don't want to fuck you on the stage, because I can't bear the thought of other men looking at what's meant for my eyes only, but you can kneel between my legs."

"What?"

He leans back, spreading his legs. "Kneel between my legs."

Another naked couple walks on stage. The woman gets onto all fours on the bench and the man takes up a position behind her. The stage starts turning. Every person in the room will have a glimpse at every possible angle of their coupling.

"How can they be comfortable with this?" I ask more to myself than to Brian.

"They're voyeurs just like everyone else here. They also enjoy being looked at."

"Do you?"

"I like watching, but I don't like sharing." He regards me with his penetrating gaze, the one that cuts right into my soul. "Does watching turn you on?"

I glance at the stage again where the man is now kneeling on the floor, eating out the woman. I can't deny that my sex is swollen. How am I supposed to feel about that? Does that make me a pervert?

"Down, Jane," Brian says, a dare in his tone. "You don't have to undress."

Taking a fortifying breath, I slide my ass off the bench to the floor and sit on my heels between Brian's legs, facing him.

His instruction is calm and collected. "Take out my cock."

The command makes the swelling between my legs throb, but I shoot a worried glance around.

"No one will see," he says soothingly. "Your head blocks the view."

We're in the corner, but I don't understand how he can be so blasé about flaunting his penis. Despite my unease that someone will see him naked, something dark stirs inside of me, begging me to do as he's demanded. I reach for the button of his jeans tentatively. He doesn't rush or aid me. He simply waits patiently for me to pull down his zipper and free his cock. His flesh is velvet hard and warm in my hand. I cover as much of the length as I can with two hands. His gaze is approving, heating my belly.

Leaning over, he grabs my beer mug and brings it to my lips. "Take a sip." He smiles. "You look like you need it."

I comply. My throat is as scratchy as sandpaper. He kisses my lips before depositing the glass on the table and sitting back again with his arms draped over the back of the bench. Behind me, the couple on the stage is panting. The woman moans loudly and then cries out as a smack reverberates through the space.

Brian cups my head with one hand, his look tender. "Now suck me off."

I should resist. I should demand privacy, but nothing in me objects to his suggestion. If anything, I want to. Spurred on by the sounds of flesh slapping together and ecstatic grunts and mewls coming from the stage, I open my lips wide and take his length to the back of my throat. He groans. I feel the vibration rather than hear it. As I speed up my act, the show gets louder, but Brian isn't looking at the stage. He's focused on me. His eyes are riveted to my face. His thumb caresses my cheek, and his fingers play gently on the side of my head as I suck and lick. The only indication he gives of his arousal is the way his hips lift off the seat with every pull of my lips. His scent is musky, and he tastes of salt. I can't get enough. The cocktail of dirty sounds combined with the way he feels on my tongue and how much pleasure I'm giving him is a heady aphrodisiac. The silk of my underwear is soaked. I open my throat and breathe through my nose, swallowing him deep. His fingers tighten on my scalp, and his face contorts in an agonizing expression, but the concentration in his eyes doesn't diminish as he watches me.

"I'm going to blow," he grunts.

His seed shoots down my throat and coats my tongue. I lap up everything, making sure he's clean before I free his semi-hard cock with a pop. He's breathing hard, his eyes shining like tiger stones and his smile appraising. The praise is all for me.

He pushes his cock back into his jeans and adjusts it before zipping himself up. Then he offers me a hand to help me up. Instead of letting me take my seat next to him, he pulls me onto his lap facing forward. His arms come around my waist as the full onslaught of the show hits me. I've watched some porn, but never live. This is different. The man is pounding into the woman, making her whole body sway. Her face is a mask of undiluted pleasure. He bends over her to stroke her hair and kiss her shoulder. The look she gives him is not only lustful but affectionate. Their bonding is unashamed and exposed. While I'm enraptured by the scene, Brian opens the button of my jeans and slips his hand down the front of my panties. I'm close to coming from the blowjob and visual stimulation alone. His fingers on my clit are heaven. It feels so good when he pushes two digits inside that I don't object. I lean back against his chest, watching the play on the stage near its end while he brings me to my own crescendo. I come with a violent spasm, my inner walls sucking his fingers deeper.

"Don't stop," I whisper with my face turned into his neck.

He obliges, gently playing with my clit while pushing his other hand up under my T-shirt to massage my breast. He tweaks first one and then the other nipple until my need is climbing again. The stage is once again empty. From my exposed position, people can clearly see what Brian is doing, but it's hidden under my clothes, and I find I don't care, not when I'm so close to coming again.

"Oh, God." I moan softly, grinding my hips down on his groin.

Reading my signals perfectly, he starts fucking me again with his fingers. A coil of tension spreads through my body, winding tight.

"Come again," he says, sucking on my earlobe.

The orgasm hits me like a big bang. I come for so long my muscles are aching by the time the vice finally lifts. Slowly, he pulls his hand from my underwear, raining kisses on my neck and smearing my arousal on my stomach.

"You're the best thing, princess," he growls in a low voice, "the best thing that's ever happened to me."

The words are the cherry on the cake of my euphoria. I sink deeper into him, falling in love even more as he buttons me up and straightens my clothes. I feel satisfied, cherished, and liberated. Most of all, I feel special. There's nothing Brian wouldn't grant me. I didn't ask for his body or his intimate secrets, but he gave me both.

His warm breath washes over my ear. "Okay?"

"More than okay," I reply with a silly grin.

He chuckles. "I guess that makes you a voyeur." His tone turns serious, all the gentle playfulness gone. "*My* voyeur. Mine alone."

---

*Brian*

PEOPLE ARE FUCKED-UP. They'll talk about Jane behind her back, but not to her face. They'll judge her for loving me while patting me on the back for scoring with a catch like her. I saw it at her friend's house. I see it at the office, although no one knows shit for sure. They can't point fingers. Jane has enough to deal with as it is. I make pretty damn sure I keep my distance at Orion, no matter how hard it is. There will come a time when we take it to the next level, but I haven't yet figured out how to overcome all the hurdles in our way. There are so many of them, I've stopped counting.

There'll come a time when I have to face the music with Monkey, but I don't think about it. All I can think about is Jane. It does something unspeakable to me to see her suffer. I'll rather take a lance in the heart than let her hurt, which is why I'm at the office during lunchtime on Monday when I know she'll be out.

Jane has left to pick up her standard order at the health shop. It gives me the time I need to talk to Toby. She was right about losing the Monroe account. I had a long chat with Alex in Legal. Toby has a meeting scheduled with Mr. Monroe at the end of the month. Toby instructed Alex to go over the contract with a fine-toothed comb, to find any loopholes, and to send him a copy of Jane's employment contract. I hate going behind her back, but she leaves me no choice.

"Come in," Toby says when I knock on his door.

It helps that he has an open-door policy. I don't need to make an appointment for a chunk of his time. I dive straight in. "Can I talk to you about the Monroe account?"

He leans back in his chair and crosses his hands over his stomach. "What about it?"

"Jane and I have a new idea." I pray to God she'll forgive me.

"You and Jane, huh?" He gives me a half-smile.

He doesn't believe me. Maybe it's better I tell the truth. If it's a shit idea and it all goes to hell, at least he won't blame her.

"Me."

He nods, as if to say, *I knew it.* "Sit." He slides down in his seat and kicks the visitor's chair out from under his desk.

The chair rolls to me smoothly. I catch it and sit.

"Let's hear it."

"Freddy has to go digital."

He catches his moustache between his teeth, chewing it for a while. Just when I think he's going to dismiss me, he says, "Go on."

I tell him about my idea for Freddy's own app, and why not a dedicated television show? National television comes cheap, these days.

He hears me out quietly to the end. For another while, he doesn't say anything, and then he nods slowly, riding his chair. "Not bad. Not bad at all. I'll tell you what. I'll run it past Mr. Monroe."

"Thank you."

Damn, I hope it works. I hope it saves Jane's account. If it does, she can be angry with me first and forgive me later.

"You keep on surprising me," Toby says. "I like that in an employee."

"Thank you," I say again.

"Now go study. Straight As."

"Yes, sir."

He grins as I leave his office.

---

## Jane

I CAN'T GET Jasmine out of my mind. Her ordeal keeps on turning in my head. Her situation is awful. There must be something I can do to help. A good start is understanding what she's suffering from better. I'm reading information about agoraphobia and treatments on my laptop at the garden table after I've finished cleaning the cottage. Abby is hanging the washing on the line. Including setting the table, it's part of her agreed weekend chores, even if that agreement came after huge resistance and a lot of arguing.

Opening a new window, I type Jasmine's name and the year of her attack into the search field. A list of headers appears, her name being in the second one. I open the page and read through the article. It gives an account of the assault, but it's what's written toward the end that grabs my attention. The two suspects who were arrested weren't convicted due to a lack of evidence. The only evidence was Ms. Michaels' identification of the men. The attorney who defended the accused pleaded that Ms. Michaels had been in a state of shock and unlikely to have seen the faces of her attackers in the dark. The article links to another one about the suspects. I follow the link and go still. One year ago, the bodies of the men were found in a deserted train tunnel. Both victims had both been shot in the stomach. Due to the nature of the fatal wounds, police suspected a connection to Ms. Michaels, who had been shot in the stomach, with revenge as motive, but no murder weapon or evidence to link a suspect to the crime could be found.

My hands shake as I close the page. Did Brian have something to do with those men's deaths? Did he avenge his unborn brother and his mother? Is he capable of killing? Am I sleeping with a murderer? Guilt churns in my stomach for thinking this about the man I love even as doubt infiltrates my heart.

A blood-curdling scream rips me from my thoughts.

*Abby!*

Jumping to my feet, I run for the washing line. Scream after scream rises from the side of the cottage.

*Abby. Abby.*

My breath is ragged from exertion and fear. I round the corner in a sprint and come to a halt in a cloud of dust. Abby is yelling and sobbing, the heels of her palms pressed against her eyes. A short distance away, stands a cobra.

# 5

---

*Jane*

I act on instinct. Grabbing Abby's collar, I jerk her toward me, away from the snake. He lunges, hissing fiercely. I drag her backward so fast we trip and fall on our butts. The snake lowers its head and crawls into the thick grass around the rock garden.

"Abby!" Getting onto my knees, I twist her around. "Did it bite you?"

My hands go over her body, looking for twin holes. A part of me is eerily calm, while another part is dangerously close to falling apart.

"It hurts, Mom! It burns!" She presses her fists against her pinched eyes.

I give her a shake. "Did it bite you?"

"No!"

*Thank God. Oh, thank God.* "Did it spit you?"

"Yes! Mom, it hurts," she bawls.

My head functions on autopilot. My heart is shocked to a

standstill. I push to my feet and haul Abby with me. "It's going to be all right, honey."

I say it for both our benefits as I guide a screaming Abby to the garden table where I left my phone. Pushing her into a chair, I unlock the phone with shaky fingers, getting the damn code wrong twice. On the third try, I manage to dial Hilda.

"A cobra spat Abby in the eyes," I say when she picks up.

"I'm on my way."

Thank God she's home. Thank God it's not a bite, but Abby can be blind. Refusing to think about it now, I take my daughter's hands and squeeze them tightly in mine.

"Mom! I can't see."

"Hilda's coming. She's a doctor."

Hilda comes running down the hill, her doctor's bag in her hand and a woman in a housekeeper's uniform following on her heels.

"Get some milk," she tells me in a calm voice when she reaches us.

I run into the house, bumping my shin against the corner of the coffee table, but I barely feel the pain.

"You've got to help me," Hilda instructs when I return with a bottle of milk. "Hold her hands down so I can rinse her eyes."

Abby screams louder when I peel her fists away from her eyes. It hurts me with every ounce of feeling inside to pin her arms at her sides while the housekeeper grabs her head and tilts it back. Hilda pries open one eye between a thumb and forefinger and pours a stream of milk into it. Abby fights like a tiger. It's hard to hold her down. Her crying and screaming rips me open. Hilda rinses the other eye and then repeats the milk bath for both eyes.

By the time she's done, Abby is still crying, but not yelling the roof off.

"I can give her something for the pain," Hilda says, taking paracetamol from her bag.

It's a struggle, but we get Abby to swallow down two pills with the milk.

"She needs to get to a hospital," Hilda says. "The hospital best equipped to deal with snake venom is The Willows. It'll be faster to drive her than to wait for an ambulance to come out here. Would you like me to drive you, so you can sit with her in the back?"

"Yes, please," I say gratefully.

The housekeeper motions at my laptop. "You better lock that inside before you go."

"Who's going to steal it out here?" Hilda asks.

Her eyes dart in the direction of the compound where the migrant workers reside. "You never know."

My laptop is the last thing I thought about, but she's right. It's a company laptop and it contains confidential information. I gather my laptop and phone, almost dropping the laptop in my haste. "I'll get my bag."

"I'll bring the car around."

We bundle Abby into Hilda's Land Rover. I buckle her in and take her hand. Hilda's breaking the speed limit, flying over the gravel, but she's handling the vehicle well. Abby has stopped crying and is moaning softly. I'm a ball of anxiety.

*Please, God, don't let her lose her eyesight.*

Hilda glances at me in the rearview mirror. "Did you get a look at the snake?"

I know a cobra. I know the way they stand upright and spread their flanks, but I don't know the different species. This one had a brown body with yellow markings.

"It was definitely a spitting cobra."

"Brown and yellow?"

"Yes."

"Mozambican Cobra."

I don't ask how she knows. I'm too focused on Abby and that after the Black Mamba, the Mozambican Cobra is the most dangerous African snake.

"The hospital will ask you what type of snake it was," Hilda continues. "Call and warn them we're on the way with a spitting Cobra victim."

Letting go of Abby's hand, I fish my phone from my bag and do as she suggested. Thank goodness for Hilda's levelheadedness. All I can think about is how much Abby is suffering.

A team is waiting for us when Hilda pulls up at the emergency unit twenty minutes later. From the way she greets the doctor on duty by name, they know each other.

"You did right to drive them," he says as a male nurses help Abby into a wheelchair. "All our ambulances were out on calls."

"Did you get the info?" Hilda asks, her face tight. "Mozambican Cobra."

"Got it," he says. "Let's go."

They rush Abby to an examination room where the doctor introduces himself as a medical toxicologist. His colleague is an ophthalmologist.

"We're going to take a look at her eyes," the ophthalmologist says, "to determine the extent of the damage."

In other words, if my little girl has permanent vision damage. I clamp an arm around my stomach.

The doctor peers into her red, swollen eyes with a light. "Did you rinse her eyes?"

"With milk," Hilda says.

"A saline solution is better. I recommend using one liter with pressure, but we'll have to sedate her. It's very painful."

The toxicologist is preparing a hypodermic needle. "Next time, rinse the eyes out with running water. Twenty minutes at least."

There won't be a next time. I'll make sure of that.

The nurse holds a clipboard with a disclaimer to me. I take it with trembling hands.

"If you'll be so kind as to sign that and fill out your contact and medical fund details at reception?"

"Of course."

"The nurse will show you the way."

"That's all right," Hilda says, "I'll accompany her."

"Thank you. When you're done, you can wait in the reception area. I'll call you when we've finished the examination."

I hold Abby's hand until they've administered the sedative and throughout rinsing her eyes. When the ophthalmologist applies local anesthetic eye drops for the pain and Abby is calmer, I leave them to finish their examination and allow Hilda to walk me through the hallways and up and down staircases. I fill out the paperwork and send Francois a text to let him know what has happened. A reply comes immediately.

*I'm on my way.*

In the waiting area, Hilda fetches me a Coke from the vending machine and makes me sit down next to her in the plastic chairs.

"Here." She hands me the can. "Drink this. Sugar is good for the shock."

"You knew what kind of snake it was."

She looks past me at the other people who are waiting like us. Waiting for a verdict. "We've had some on the property."

"Some?"

She sighs. "A lot. It's the snake that's the most common in our area."

"The most common?" I ask on the verge of hysteria.

"It's the dam. The frogs and mice attract the snakes."

"Why didn't you tell me before I signed the lease?"

"I thought you knew."

"How could I know?"

"Oh, come on. You're a savvy woman. Where we live is practically the wilderness."

"You should have told me. I would never have rented the cottage if I'd known."

I shouldn't have let Abby hang out the washing. I shouldn't have given her chores. Dear, God. Can I fail any more as a mother? I feel sick. Like vomiting. Bile pushes up in my throat.

"Has anyone ever been bitten on your property?"

She scratches the back of her neck. "A migrant worker."

My gut turns to stone. "What happened?"

"He didn't make it," she says softly.

I don't want to believe it. I don't want to believe someone died on our beautiful, rented property. "Didn't you bring him to the hospital?"

"It was too late."

"Too late? How long do you have if you're bitten?"

"Jane..."

"Answer me, Hilda. How long?"

"It depends."

"On fucking what?"

"Jane, calm down."

"I won't calm down. My daughter could've been bitten. She may go blind! On what?"

"The age and size of the snake. The younger they are, the more potent the venom. Where on the body they bite. The closer the bite is to an area of high blood circulation, the faster it spreads. It also depends on if multiple bites were given. In the case of the worker, he didn't come to us immediately. He rushed to the compound where they stayed. It took the overseer fifteen minutes to drive him back to the house. Twenty was already too long." Her voice softens. "Believe me, this case was an exception. Fatalities are rare."

"Tissue damage is not. Neither is neurological damage. Am I right?"

She sighs. "Neurotoxic effects are slight, but yes, the local tissue damage is serious. It often requires skin grafts."

"We can't stay there. I'm not risking my daughter's life. I want out of the contract. I'm not giving three months' notice, and I want my deposit back."

"Jane, you're not thinking rational, right now."

"I assure you, I've never been more rational."

My phone pings. I glance at the screen in case it's Francois, but it's Brian.

*Where are you?*

Damn. He must be at my place. He was supposed to come over for lunch with Sam. We agreed it was a good time for Sam and Abby to meet. In my panic, everything else slipped my mind.

I type a message to tell him about Abby and where we are.

"I'll let you think about the cottage," Hilda says. "It's not a decision you should make today. We'll talk tomorrow." She pats my hand and gets up. "I'm going to call Gustaf to let him know where I am in case he gets home early for lunch."

"You don't have to stay. Abby's father is on his way. He can give me a lift home. I appreciate that you brought us."

"I want to stay. It's the least I can do."

She's not back yet when Francois and Debbie charge into the reception area. Francois glances around the room frantically. For some weird reason, I can't raise my hand and signal him. I'm simply too tired for even the mundane task, and I want to crawl into a hole and hide in shame. I let this happen to Abby. It's my fault she's in pain. It's my fault she's suffering. God forbid, if she loses her eyesight, I'll never forgive myself.

It's Debbie who spots me first. "There she is."

They rush to my side.

Francois' face is white. "Where is she?"

"In the examination room. The ophthalmologist is examining her eyes."

"What happened?" Debbie asks.

"What I told Francois in my text."

"I know, but how?"

"She was hanging up the washing…" I bite my trembling lip, unable to continue.

"It's all right." Francois touches my shoulder. "It's going to be all right."

I stare up at him, tears blurring my vision. "It's my fault. It wouldn't have happened if I hadn't moved there. I…" I battle to speak past the knot in my throat. "I shouldn't have made her hang out the washing."

Covering my face with my hands, I let the tears flow. I can't stop them. I don't want to stop them, because I deserve the emotional pain. If I could take Abby's physical pain, I would.

"None of this would've happened if you didn't have to move," Francois says. "If it's anyone's fault, it's mine."

"It happened," Debbie says. "Let's focus on dealing with the situation instead of wasting energy on blame."

The toxicologist enters the waiting area just as Hilda steps back from outside.

I jump to my feet, but I can't speak.

It's Francois who asks the question. "Will she be all right?"

The doctor glances at me as if he's waiting for my permission.

"This is Abby's father and his fiancée," I say.

"Yes," the doctor says. "The good news is that there shouldn't be permanent damage. I prescribed an antibiotic ointment."

"Thank God," Francois says.

"Her eyes will be scratchy for a couple of days," the doctor continues, "but it should clear up within forty-eight hours. I suggest letting her rest. She's ready to go home if you don't have further questions."

"Nothing for the moment," I say. "Thank you."

When the doctor walks off, I introduce Hilda to Debbie and Francois.

"I'll let you go," Hilda says. "I know you're anxious to see your daughter. Now that I know she's all right, I'll head back home, unless you want me to wait for you?"

"I'll be fine, thank you."

We say our goodbyes to Hilda and hurry to the examination room. Abby's sitting in a chair with patches of cotton wool over her eyes.

"Hey, honey," I say. "How are you feeling? Your dad and Debbie are here."

"Daddy?"

She holds out a hand, which Francois grips.

"How are you?" he asks.

"I'm okay," she says meekly. "It still hurts."

"It'll be over in a day or two," he replies in a soothing voice.

I want to say how sorry I am, but the door flies open, and Brian all but falls into the room, dragging Sam by the hand.

His face is tight, and his voice strained. "How is she?"

Abby stills. She turns her head in the direction of Brian's voice. "It's all because of you. It's all your fault!"

"Abby," I gasp.

"If you didn't choose the place my mother wouldn't have moved there. I hate the cottage. I hate you!"

"Abby!"

My daughter is distraught. She went through a traumatic experience, but I can't allow her to speak to anyone like this, not even under these exceptional circumstances. It's not how Francois and I raised her.

"It's all right." Brian holds up a hand when I open my mouth. "I'm sorry for what happened, Abby." He nods at Francois and Debbie in greeting. "I'll wait for you outside, Jane."

The door closes with a click behind him and Sam.

"I'm not going back to that place," Abby says.

"I understand, honey. We're moving. I promise."

"Dad, can I stay with you and Debs for a while?"

Francois looks at me. The court granted me full custody. Francois has visitation rights every second weekend, which is the norm in divorces cases in our country. Francois didn't contest due to the third-party breakup of our marriage. Doing so would've meant dragging Debbie into a drawn-out and scandalous court fight. If Abby wants to stay with Francois for a while, I'm not going to stop her, even if it shreds my heart to pieces.

I give him a nod.

"No problem," he says. "I'm sure Debs will be happy to have you."

Debbie hugs my daughter. "Of course, sweetheart. You know your room is always ready. And Dusty will be happy."

"Can we please go?" Abby asks. "I just want to get out of here."

"I'll get a nurse to bring a wheelchair," Francois says.

"I'll drop off some of Abby's clothes later," I offer.

When the nurse arrives with the wheelchair, I say my goodbyes to my daughter and watch her leave with her father and Debbie. It's as if a part of me leaves with her. I don't feel completely whole.

Brian is pacing the hallway of the waiting area, and Sam sits on a chair with her hands clamped between her knees. The minute he sees me, he rushes forward and pulls me against his body. A wall inside me breaks. Sobs shake my shoulders. The shock and horrible experience leave me feeling sick, tired, and empty.

"I've got you," he whispers in my hair, kissing the top of my head.

His arms are warm and strong around me. I submit to his soothing, taking courage from his strength.

After the worst of my tears have subsided, I manage to calm myself somewhat. "I'm sorry for what happened in there."

"You have nothing to be sorry about. Where's Abby?"

"She's staying with her father for a while."

"Jane."

The one words holds so much meaning. It's an apology. It's understanding. Sympathy.

"It's all right." I sniff. "It's going to be fine."

"Come on. Sam and I will take you home."

Home.

I don't know where that's supposed to be.

*Brian*

"You can't stay here."

I hand Jane the cup of tea and sandwich I've prepared for her. Sam sits next to her at the dining room table in Jane's cottage, holding Jane's hand.

"I'm sorry, Jane," my sister says.

Jane gives her a brave smile. "It's all right, honey. I'm sorry about lunch."

I lost a baby brother who hadn't been born, and it ripped my heart out of my chest. I can only imagine how Jane must be feeling.

"Lunch isn't important." I take a seat opposite them. "I don't want you staying here."

"I don't want Abby staying here, either. I'm going to look for a new place. Today, still."

Guilt eats into my gut. "How long is Abby staying with your ex?"

"We didn't discuss it. Probably until I've moved. I doubt she'll want to come back here."

"I don't blame her," Sam says.

"Eat your food," I order. "This is a grown-up conversation."

Sam bites into her sandwich obediently.

"I should stay with you."

Only, I can't. I can't, and it burns a hole into my soul. I can't leave my mom and Sam, and I can't ask Jane to move in with us. There's not enough space for the three of us as it is. I don't earn enough to afford an extension to the house, yet, and I can never move in with Jane.

*I can't.*

Those two little words strangle me. It's as if I'm chained up. Helpless. My life is fucked-up. What do I have to offer Jane? A sword over my head with Monkey's threat and an alcoholic mother who can't leave the house. How can I leave Jane here on her own in a state of shock? I hate it, and there's nothing I can do.

It's the first time my mother's condition makes me feel caged in. I've never resented the situation we find ourselves in until now.

"I'll be fine," Jane says.

I motion at her sandwich. "Eat. You need your strength."

"I'm not hungry."

"Drink your tea, then."

At least she does that.

My phone lights up with a message from my mom. Something's wrong. Jasmine never sends me a text message otherwise. "Excuse me, but I've got to check this."

*The police are here. They want to question you. Tron's been arrested.*

Double damn. Why now? Why today?

Getting to my feet, I round the table and place my hands on Jane's tense shoulders.

"I'm sorry." I can't express how much. "I have to go."

Sam lifts her eyes to mine quickly. "Is Mom okay?"

"She's fine. It's just something I need to take care of."

I kiss the top of Jane's head. "Call me, no matter what. Understand? I'll come back later tonight." I don't give a shit about Clive's animosity. He's going to babysit, and that's that. If all else fails, I'm bringing Jane home with me. I just need to get rid of the police, first.

"Really, Brian, you don't have to. I said I'm all right."

I tilt her head and kiss her lips. "Later." That's not up for discussion, either.

Detective Cowan sits in our lounge when I get home. My mother is on the edge of her seat, her hands wrung together. She jumps up when Sam and I enter.

"You all right?" I ask her softly.

She nods. Her hair is a mess, and she's wearing her velvet robe and slippers. Dark circles mar her bloodshot eyes, but that's the state of her eyes more or less permanently these days. What's new in them is the fear and pain of memories stirred up by Cowan's house call. The first time he questioned me was after my brother's murderers were found dead. No doubt his presence wakes a night best forgotten, like the dead.

I keep my voice gentle. "Why don't you go dress?"

She nods again and escapes to the hallway.

"Sam, have you forgotten your manners?"

Sam holds out a hand. "Good afternoon, sir."

Cowan accepts the shake with a smile. "Aren't you all grown up."

"Go put on the kettle. I'm sure Detective Cowan will appreciate a cup of coffee."

My sister stares at us as she leaves the room. With my family out of Cowan's way, I take my time to study him. He doesn't look different, except for the extra pounds around his waist.

He settles deeper into his seat on the sofa bed, running his arm along the backrest. His jacket falls open, exposing his holster and pistol. "You don't look surprised to see me."

I expected Cowan. I always knew he'd be back. He was just waiting for a reason, and now that idiot Tron gave him one.

Taking the seat my mother has left, I keep my face neutral. "My mother said Tron was arrested."

"So he was."

He studies me, his eyes penetrating, but I know how to hold the gaze of a man with a gun. I know how to look them right in the eyes while their weapons are potent, and I know what their eyes look like when their weapons lay useless on the ground, because I'm not afraid of looking.

"What did he do?" I ask.

"Beat a guy nearly to death."

"Why?"

"Why?" He chuckles. "Trust you to ask that question. It's always about the justification for you, isn't it?"

"Tell me." I shrug. "Don't tell me. It makes no difference."

"He claims the man broke into his shop."

"Theft."

"That's what he says. The dog got to the intruder first, and then your neighborhood watch."

"It's not *my* neighborhood watch."

"It's your neighborhood."

"What do you want with me?" I ask, even if I know.

"Everyone knows everybody in Harryville."

"I don't know who's part of the neighborhood watch, if that's what you're asking."

He smiles. "Of course, you don't."

"Then maybe you should do your job and catch the real criminals like the murderers and rapists instead of sitting here wasting your time."

"Why so angry, Brian?"

"Why aren't you after the other assholes who broke into Tron's place? Or is it your job to protect the perpetrators?"

"It's my job to make sure justice is served."

"Like it was served when my mother's attackers walked free?"

"Is that why you killed them? You think you should take justice into your own hands because the system failed you once?"

"Fuck you. If you'd done your job, those motherfuckers would've been in for life."

"I was doing my job, until someone blew their intestines out. I was on the verge of nailing them for first degree murder of a family of four."

"Sounds to me like justice got to them, after all. Are you moping like a pissy because the glory of *nailing* them wasn't yours?"

"I'm saying if every dick takes justice into his own hands, we're all like them. We're no better than criminals."

"Here's a news snippet for you. When you live in a fuck-ass neighborhood, your cushy, uptown moral arguments aren't worth shit, because it's about survival. It's about your life or theirs."

"Is that why you shot those men?"

Motherfucker. The bastard is clever. He's baiting me, knowing exactly how to rev me up.

"I didn't kill anyone."

"I'm going to find the murder weapon, one day, Brian, one day when you don't see me coming."

"Good luck to you. There's nothing to find."

Sam enters with a tray of coffee just as he stands and buttons up his jacket. "How's your mom keeping up?"

I get up, too. "You saw for yourself."

"She's a fine woman. I'm sorry for what happened to her."

"So am I."

"Here, little lady. Let me help you with that." He takes the tray from Sam and leaves it on the coffee table.

"I'm not a little lady," she says.

I raise my voice in warning. "Sam."

"I guess not." Reaching for a mug, Cowan downs the whole, steaming hot lot in one go and puts the mug back on the tray. "Thanks for the coffee, Sam." To me, he says, "I'll see you around."

Through the window, I watch until his car is out of sight, and then I go look for my mother. She sits on her bed, still dressed in her pajamas.

"Did he go through the garden?" I ask.

"He parked in the street and came straight to the front door."

Good. He didn't discover the cellar where my unlicensed gun is hidden.

"What did you tell him?"

"Nothing. He told me why he was here and then we didn't speak."

"Did you leave him alone at any stage?" I won't put it past the motherfucker to plant bugs.

"No. We sat in the lounge the whole time until you arrived."

"I'm going to see Monkey about Tron."

"He's not home. He's down at the station with his lawyer to try and bail out Tron."

"How do you know?"

"Ingrid called."

I know who else I can go see. "I'll be back in an hour. Can you keep the fort?'

"Yes," she whispers, looking away.

Dammit. I want to bite my tongue. I've just told her in not so many words that she's incompetent and I can't trust her. "I didn't mean–"

"I know. Go. I'll make dinner."


ALBERT AND EUGENE are cleaning out the pigeon coop when I arrive. Albert is a keen participant in pigeon racing.

"What's the deal with Tron?" I ask through the mesh.

Albert chucks a spade-load of bird shit into a wheelbarrow. "The police have been to your place." He spits tobacco from the corner of his mouth.

A pigeon flies down from the perch, flapping its wings. The birds coo from deep in their crops. A smell of shit and wet feathers stirs the air as more pigeons fly to the floor.

"I told Tron those beatings were trouble."

Albert stops scraping the spade over the concrete to look at me. "What was he supposed to do? Leave the door wide fucking open for the thieves with a welcome sign?"

"He should've left it to the police to handle. It's a war now. Those thieves are from the gangs in Sunnyside. They'll be back for revenge."

"They can come. We're ready for them."

"Pa," Eugene says, "Brian's got a point."

"Shut your mousetrap," Albert snaps. He walks over and puts his face in mine. The only thing that separates our noses is the mesh. "You get to pull the trigger, but Tron doesn't get to swing the whip?"

"Nobody saw me pull a trigger. It's speculation. Even if I did pull that trigger, the gangs aren't coming after me. I didn't start a war. Have you ever asked yourself why Monkey is doing this? Maybe he wants to start a war. If there's a war, there's a fight, and if there's a fight, someone's going to win, and someone's got to lose."

He curls his fingers through the mesh. "What the fuck are you saying?"

"Think about it. What does Monkey have to gain if he instigates a fight?"

"Sunnyside," Eugene says.

Albert turns on him, lifting the spade. "I said shut the fucking fuck up, you dickhead."

Eugene cowers, bracing his head with his arms.

"Sunnyside," I repeat, "and we fight the battle for him."

"Are you siding with the police now, Clive?"

"It's Brian."

"What the fuck ever. Answer the question."

"I'm not siding with anyone. I'm just saying you've got to open your eyes."

Albert is not the only member of the neighborhood watch I'm worried about. He recently initiated Eugene into the sinister operation.

"We take care of our own." Albert spits again.

"Like you took care of Jane when you showed us a property infested with Mozambican Cobras?"

"She's not our own."

"She's mine. That makes her every bit our own, same as you, Katrina, and Eugene."

He laughs. It's an ugly laugh with hardly any sound, but it shakes his bony body. "From what I understood, the only woman who's yours is Lindy. Rumor is you're getting married in a year's time. That means you've got to put your dick stamp on her. I don't know anything about uppity-ass bitches, but that woman you're keeping from uptown isn't going to hang around when you dip your dick in another girl's cunt."

I'm gripping the mesh so hard it rattles, sending the birds scattering all over. "Keep your filthy mouth off her." I don't care that he's Eugene's father and that I'm supposed to show respect. "You can be glad you didn't say her name." I swear to God, Eugene would've had to pick Albert off the birdcage floor like the rotten rag he is.

"Go to hell, Clive Claassen," he spits. "You're not fit for anywhere else, you fucking traitor."

"Been there, and it's Brian."

I walk back to my truck with long strides. When I get there, I check my phone. There's a message from my mother saying Tron didn't get bail.

Fuck.

The war has begun.

Whether I like it or not, it's everyone's war, because they won't stop until one side is dead.

*Jane*

AFTER DROPPING off clothes and toiletries for Abby, I return home, feeling only dread. It's late afternoon on a weekend, but I call the estate agent who made me visit the security complexes out east, anyway. I don't want to wait a minute longer than necessary. All I want is for Abby to come home, and therefore I have to find a new home. I don't care where it is or that there's no garden and the view is a brick wall. I'll take the first thing that's available, which happens to be a duplex townhouse in a new development. They're still building all around. The agent warns me there'll be dust and noise, but I promise to be in on Monday to sign the lease. At least there are no pet restrictions, so Abby can bring Dusty. With nothing else to keep me busy, I start packing.

It's long since dark when Brian arrives. I haven't kept track of time. The grumbling of my stomach tells me I haven't eaten, but I don't have an appetite.

"I'm sorry I'm late," Brian says, his gaze going over the open boxes and crockery wrapped in paper. "My mother cooked dinner. It would've been rude not to eat."

"That's all right. We didn't have a date. Who's staying with your mom and Sam?"

He rounds the boxes and stops in front of me. "Clive."

"I'm a big girl. I can take care of myself. I'll understand if you'd rather be home to take care of your family."

"Are you implying you're not important to me?"

"No, but your mother has a problem, and it worries me every time you leave Sam there alone. What if something happens to your mom? Sam's too young to deal with this."

"I said Clive was there."

"Clive can't always be there. I'm sure he has a life of his own."

"I'm fucking winging it, all right?" he says through clenched teeth.

I blink at him. I'm not going to say I don't deserve the outburst. Maybe it's what happened to Abby today that makes me feel extra protective over Sam, or maybe it's that I feel so damn guilty all the time for taking him away from his family that made me push the issue tonight.

Tilting his head toward the ceiling, he rubs the back of his neck. There are lines of tension in his face and a deep frown on his forehead. "I didn't mean to swear at you. That was unforgivable."

I touch his hand. "Are you all right?"

He drops his arm to take my wrist. "It's been a shitty day."

"We can both do with a drink. There's cold beer."

I turn for the fridge, but he doesn't let me go.

"Brian, what's wrong?"

"Nothing." He jerks me against him. "And everything."

His expression is alight with too many emotions to discern. Concern. Love. Lust. It's everything and nothing. What's between us has the power to be amazing, beautiful, and that big, elusive everything I've never had. It also has the power to fall flat like a cake in the oven. No words are needed to explain it, because I feel it. All these fragile emotions can disappear faster than flour scattered to the wind. We can lose it so easily. We're in that delicate stage between everything and nothing, waiting to see if the cake is going to rise or fall flat.

I'm short of breath from fear and exhilaration. "I want everything."

"What?"

His mother, my daughter, I'll take it all. I'll deal with whatever I must for us to be together. I love him. It's the moment he becomes more important than my own life. I've given him my body, trust, and heart, but now there are no barriers left. The last of the walls I've constructed around myself fall away, leaving me open and vulnerable. I'm giving him everything.

My voice is throaty. "Everything. All of me. All of you."

His eyes darken. His fingers tighten on my wrist. He grabs hold of the other one before backing me up to the wall. My body hits the stones with a thud. He pins my wrists at my sides and lowers his mouth to mine, our lips a hairbreadth from touching.

"Then take it," he says in a clipped voice.

With him holding me like this, I can't take anything, but he offers it to me when our mouths finally meet. Our teeth and tongues clash together. It's rough and tender. He devours me with a sweetness I've never tasted. He places my hand on his shoulder and goes for the zipper of his jeans, not bothering to undo the top button. My gaze is drawn down when he frees his cock. His long length juts through the open fly, the head broad and wet with pre-cum. I slip my hand down his side so I can move the hem of his T-shirt up to expose the trail of blond hair that runs from his navel down into his waistband. I sweep my palm lower, not touching his cock, but weighing his balls through the thick fabric of his jeans. Golden hair cushions the base. It's strangely erotic, seeing him naked through only his open fly.

Bunching my dress in a fist, he pushes it over my hips. The crotch of my panties is damp. He moves the elastic aside with a finger and runs the tip through my slit. Satisfied that I'm wet, he bends his knees, positions his cock, and drives home in a hard thrust.

The impact knocks the air from my lungs. My body shifts up the wall as he pulls out and thrusts again, harder this time. He's splitting me in two, penetrating too deep, but pleasure is already gathering in my lower body. Gripping my thigh, he pulls it around his back, opening me wider. He sucks the skin of my neck, kissing and nipping his way to my jaw while he pounds into me with a pace that soon has my knees go weak. He's jostling my breasts and body. He grips my hips with bruising force to keep me in place while he fucks me like this is our last moment. I don't have enough strength to defy him, not that I want to.

My pleasure is building. There's friction on my clit where he penetrates me, but before it can accumulate into something substantial, he pulls out and pushes me to my knees. His cock rubs against my lips. I open to take him.

"Taste your cunt on me," he says, spearing his fingers through my hair.

He goes straight for my throat. I barely have time to swallow. My eyes water, and I try to breathe through my nose as he takes me deep. When he gives me air, I lick over the head and down the underside of his cock. My taste on him is like rain before the storm. His taste is powerful, like the wet earth after the rain.

He makes a grumbling noise in his chest. "Goddammit. Yes."

I'm hungry. Eager. I want more. I reach for the button of his jeans, but before I can undo it, he rips himself from my mouth, gripping the base of his cock hard.

"Fuck. Fuck."

In a second flat, we've reversed positions. I'm pushed up against the wall once more and he's on his knees, his teeth and tongue on my pussy. It's too much. I'm too close. When he clamps his lips over my clit and sucks, I come violently, shaking in his hold. The aftershocks are barely over before he flips me around with my cheek pressed against the stone bricks and spreads my legs. I'm expecting him to push in from behind, but he's smearing my wetness around my anus.

"Not like this." I start to wiggle. The position is not ideal.

The slick head of his cock is already nudging my tight entrance.

"Brian."

"Shh."

He pushes up a little, breaching my barrier. It hurts, but not as much as I expected. It's a pain I need, a darkness I embrace.

Painstakingly slow, he buries himself deeper. My body is soft from the climax, making his passage easier. He's breathing hard. There's a fierceness on his face as I glance back at him. Another thrust makes me moan in a mixture of ecstasy and agony. Towards the end, it's harder to take him.

"You're mine, Jane." Another inch. "No matter how. No matter why."

He shoves home. I cry out. My muscles tense involuntary. Our bodies are flush together, his balls pressed against my pussy. I can hear the crunch of his teeth as he grits them hard.

"Jesus, Jane, you're tight."

I try to relax with deep breaths, but it's impossible when he starts moving. He's careful, but his length is grueling.

"Say it," he says with a thrust of his hips. "Tell me who you love."

"You. I love you."

His pounding turns harder. My nipples scrape over the rough surface of the wall through the thin fabric of my dress. The breath leaves my body with every shove until I'm nothing but erotic gasps and a dark, forbidden kind of need.

"Brian."

It's a plea. I can't take more but I need so much.

His hand moves between my body and the wall. Cupping my sex, he sinks two fingers inside. My back arches from the sudden and instant pleasure, giving him my ass at a different angle. If at all possible, he penetrates me deeper. My scream must've been heard all the way to the main house. The pleasure starts again, more intense, this time. I'm too full. His cock and fingers work in sync to bring me to a second orgasm, one that starts from a darker part and that I instinctively know is going to shatter me. It's when his thumb moves in circles on my clit that the first spark starts. It burns closer and closer. My senses are scrambled. I can't tell pain from ecstasy or breathing from drowning. I close my eyes. Brian is punishing my body. He's fucking my ass with brutal force, his fingers in my channel no less forgiving. His thumb is relentless on my clit. It feels as if he's going to push me straight through the wall. My legs won't carry me, any longer. Only his body holds me up as he demands even more.

"Give it to me, princess."

I'm helpless to stop it. I only hope I'll survive. I don't have enough air left to cry out. It's building, building, until I'm sure I'll drown. It goes up and up, and I'm five years old in a rollercoaster and scared to death.

"B–Brian!"

"I've got you. Let it go."

I can't, because my pleasure is a monster that won't be dictated. Heat diffuses in my lower body, burning down to my folds and clit. It spreads through my thighs to the back of my knees and the soles of my feet. If it's meant to prepare me for what's coming, like the swell of a tide before the freak wave, it fails miserably. Nothing can prepare me for the pleasure that finally rocks me. It sizzles through my insides like an electric torrent, locking every muscle in place. Vaguely, I'm aware of Brian cussing madly. I'm much more aware of how hard his fingers grip my hip, and how his cock seems to swell and pulse in my ass. He jerks, crushing me against the wall with his weight. His hips roll, and his cock stabs one last time, and then he collapses over me, bracing his hands next to my face.

One by one, my muscles relax. If Brian didn't wrap an arm around my waist, I'd be sliding to the floor. He kisses my nape, whispering tender words and telling me to take a deep breath and relax.

"I'm sorry," he says with genuine regret before he pulls out of my ass.

I hiss at the burn of his cum on the skin he fucked raw. There's a rustling of fabric and pieces of clothing dropping to the floor. I'm not capable of agreeing or protesting when he scoops me into his arms and carries me to the bathroom where he swiftly undresses me. He keeps one arm around my waist while he turns on the water and waits for it to warm. There's no place to sit, except for on the floor, and that's what Brian does, pulling me into his lap. He washes my hair and body, his touch gentle, and after he's cleaned himself, he lifts me to my feet and makes me bend over with my hands resting on the wall.

"Can you stand like this without falling over?" he asks.

I don't have to answer. My legs are shaking too badly. I've never been fucked so hard. I've never come so hard. He holds my waist again, making sure I don't slip on the tiles, and removes the shower nozzle from its holder to point it at my ass. I gasp when the first jet of water hits my dark entrance.

"Sorry." He kisses my back. "I have to wash the sperm out. It'll help for the burn."

I let him tend to my most private parts until the water starts running cold. He first wraps me up in a towel and then himself before carrying me to the bed. Lying on his side, he pulls me tight against him. I snuggle deeper, absorbing his heat and the comfort of his arms. There's a quiet accord between us while the night outside is loud. Crickets chirp in a choir of agreeable harmony while frogs croak out of tune. A lonely bird calls from somewhere, strange for this hour of the night. Maybe a lizard is stalking its nest. It's the hushed discord, the words that aren't spoken, that breaks the peace.

*Don't go.*

An hour or more passes before Brian quietly gets up. I clutch the pillow to my chest. If I pretend to be sleeping, will it be easier? Will it be easier to hear the sounds he makes as he sees himself out than hugging and kissing him at the door, letting the full force of the loneliness he'll leave slap me in the face? Finally, I can't bear it. I pull on a robe and walk through the dark house. He's dressing by the light of his cell phone in the lounge, picking up pieces of clothing from the floor. I was so out of it, I don't even know when he undressed. All I remember was his cock through his fly, his body clothed, and my soul naked.

He pauses when he sees me. "I didn't want to wake you. You needed the rest."

"What time is it?"

"Just before midnight."

"You have to go."

Regret again. "Yes." In the blue light of the phone, his expression is pained.

"Stay for another hour. I'll make us something to eat."

"Are you hungry?"

"Starving."

He walks to me barefoot and wraps me up in his arms. "Didn't you have dinner?"

"Not yet."

"Jane." His voice is angry. "You didn't have lunch, either. You have to take care of yourself."

Going on tiptoes, I kiss his cheek. "Keep me company. Please."

His eyes soften. "What do you feel like?"

"I have steak in the fridge, and I can throw together a salad. Will you join me?"

"I can always eat."

Taking his hand, I lead him to the kitchen that is littered with half-packed boxes and uncertainty.

Tonight, I've gained one more hour.

---

*Brian*

JANE IS STANDING in front of the pan, a spatula in her hand.

"Food's ready," she says just as I put the salad on the table.

Taking the spatula from her hand, I serve the steaks on our plates and leave the dirty pan on the stove before I pull her onto my lap.

She smells of fried meat and fat, and I find it oddly disturbing. I don't want the dirty smells of the world clinging to her. I don't want my secrets to soil her, but it's too late. I've dragged her under the day I wrapped my hands around her waist to lift her onto her pull-up bar.

I hug her tighter and nuzzle her temple. "I don't like that you work so hard. You should've let me do the cooking."

"You call frying a steak hard work?"

"It's not just that." I motion at the boxes. "You don't touch another one until I'm here to help."

"I'm not made of glass."

"I know. Still."

"Still, what?"

"I want to take care of you. I *need* to take care of you."

She kisses my cheek. "You are taking care of me."

Keeping my arms wrapped around her, I cut her meat into

pieces, pierce one with the fork, and bring it to her lips. It gives me huge joy to do this, to take care of her. More than I can explain.

"Your food's getting cold," she says.

"My food will be just fine. Open."

She obeys, letting me feed her until her plate is empty. While I eat, she makes tea. I know what she's doing. She's delaying the inevitable goodbye. Fuck knows, I don't want to go. I want to be with her every minute of every day. I want to be with her in the office. I want everyone to know, but there's a lot of sewerage water that needs to run under the bridge before than can happen.

When the tea is gone and the dishes done, I order her back to bed.

"I'll see you out," she says.

"I'm not done with you."

Her cheeks flush a little. "I'm not sure I can take more, tonight."

Guilt rides me hard for the way I've lost control. "I know you can't. Go to the bedroom and bend over the bed."

She watches me nervously. "Why?"

Taking her hand, I lead her to the bedroom and leave her by the bed while I go through her bathroom cabinet. I return with a tube of vaginal anesthetic cream.

"Oh," she says when she sees the tube.

She bends slightly at the waist, watching me from over her shoulder. Putting a palm on her lower back, I push her down all the way and lift her robe over her ass. Her ass cheeks are creamy and soft. Just seeing them makes me want to plant my dick between them again, but I know she's sore.

"This'll be cold," I warn.

I lubricate my finger with a generous amount of the cream and sink my finger slowly into her tight asshole that took my cock so prettily. She jerks.

"You all right?"

She nods, biting her lip.

Twisting my finger a couple of times, I make sure I get the

soothing lotion everywhere, before I pull out and give her a gentle slap on the cheek.

"All done."

She yelps and straightens. The color on her cheeks has deepened to a bright red. It amuses me. She'll let me bury my cock up to my balls in her ass but blushes when I rub cream into her with my finger. I pull her robe down and kiss each pretty red cheek before washing my hands and putting the cream away.

When I take her in my arms at the door, our kiss is soft. It's like we're always doing things in reverse, the foreplay coming after the fucking.

"I'll see you tomorrow, princess."

"I'll be waiting."

"Will you welcome me at the door?"

"If you wish."

"With a kiss."

"With a kiss," she agrees.

That's the sweetest promise anyone has made me. No lover has ever waited for me at the door.

---

*Jane*

THE WEEK IS SPENT SIGNING a new lease contract, cleaning the cottage and new townhouse, and packing. It's the second time I move in a few weeks. The shed snakeskin I find between my jerseys only confirms I've made the right decision.

The exams have ended, and school has finished. Abby got special permission to do oral exams, since her vision is still not one hundred percent back to normal. The doctor assures us her eyesight will return. She's still living with Francois and Debbie. I can't wait to bring her home, especially since it'll be Christmas soon, and we agreed she'll spend her first Christmas with her father. I miss her. I want to see as much of her as I can before the holiday.

Brian takes charge of another move, but this time Clive isn't there to help. When I'm not working overtime to save my Monroe account, I'm unpacking. Brian is there every night, unwrapping crockery, washing the plates that have been wrapped in paper, and cooking dinner.

It feels like forever before everything is once more in its place and I can call Abby to let her know her new room is ready. Francois offers to drop her and Dusty off on Friday after work. I gladly accept. It gives me time to cook a special welcoming meal.

I put flowers on the table and let the chocolate mousse set in the fridge. The schnitzel is just done when the bell rings.

Rushing to the door, I open it wide, but there's only Francois.

I peer over his shoulder to where his car is parked in the driveway. It's empty.

"Where's Abby?" I ask.

"With Debs."

"I don't understand."

"We need to talk." He walks past me into the house.

I follow him sheepishly into the lounge.

He faces the window with his back to me for what seems like the longest time before he turns.

My stomach tumbles and drops like a stone. "Francois, talk to me. What's going on? Why isn't Abby with you?"

His expression is grave. No, beneath the mask he's furious. "Abby says Brian touched her. Indecently."

# 6

---

*Jane*

My legs threaten to cave in. I grip the chair back hard. "What?"

"You heard me." Francois' arms hang passively at his sides, but underneath the calm there's a quiet storm brewing. Those are the worst ones–the quiet storms–because they're unpredictable and hit where and when you least expect.

I'm trying to wrap my head around what he's said, but the words don't make sense. Not Brian. Never. But this is my baby girl.

"They've met once." One time. I trusted Brian. I *trust* him. Was I wrong?

Francois' tone is even, giving away nothing. "Did you leave Abby alone with Brian?"

"For twenty minutes."

He gives me a strange look.

"I was in the kitchen," I exclaim. "They were on the deck. There were only a few meters between us. The doors were open, for God's sake."

"Could you see them?"

"No."

"Then twenty minutes were too long."

I round the chair. "What did she say?" My body is shaking, but the trembling of my heart is worse.

"I'd rather she tells you herself."

"Why didn't you bring her? I need to talk to her. This is my daughter, Francois."

"In the light of what's passed, I don't think it's a good idea that she comes home to you."

My limbs turn cold. A sick feeling makes my stomach heave. My voice is calm, but I can feel the hysteria creeping up on me. "You can't keep her away from me."

"You can see her tomorrow evening at our place. She's in bed, now. Debs gave her something to help her sleep."

My lips feel numb. "When did she tell you?"

"Just before we were supposed to leave."

*Why didn't she tell me?*

"We'll see you tomorrow," he says. "Make it at six."

He doesn't wait for a confirmation. He walks around me and out of the room. The click of the front door confirms his departure.

I can't move. I'm stuck to the spot. I feel too many things to discern one from the other. Guilt. Shock. Disbelief. Don't I trust my own daughter? Was I blind? Self-loath and more guilt.

Slowly, my heart starts beating again. Life returns to my body, amplifying the sickness I feel everywhere. I'm hot and cold. I'm nauseous. Grabbing my face in my hands, I drop down onto the chair.

I know Brian. He single-handedly raised his baby sister. He'll kill anyone who touches Sam. I can't believe this of him, not because I love him, but because I *know* the kind of man he is. How can I tell my daughter, my only child, she's a liar? No matter what happened, she's the victim. Even if she's lying, she's still the victim, because she wouldn't be lying if she weren't suffering. The reason for her suffering may be a different one than what she claims, but she's suffering all the same.

This isn't only about truth and lies. This is about choice. This is about picking a side. Abby is making me choose, and in that she gives me no choice, because Abby always comes first.

There's wetness on my cheeks. Have I been crying? I touch my fingers to the moisture. Tears. The shock passes into a frenzy of anguish, making me tremble worse. Francois is going to take Abby away from me. That was what I saw in his face—the quiet storm, the silent, careful, meticulous premeditation. I jump to my feet. I'll fight like a rabies-infected feline before giving up my child. I won't let him do this.

Pacing the floor, I try to think, but my thoughts are like scrambled livewires, my emotions too out of control to allow my brain logical functioning. I need someone who can think with a level head. I just need someone, and that someone can't be Brian. I can't speak to him until I've spoken to Abby. I want to hear it from her before I confront him, because no matter what I believe, I'll have to confront him. I've picked Abby's side, and that's what standing by her demands.

I fling into action, switching off the oven where I was keeping our dinner warm and grabbing my bag. On the way to the door, I catch a glimpse of myself in the mirror. I'm a mess. I don't recognize the hollow, white face with the smeared mascara. I don't stop to fix it. I lock the door and get into my car. I have to send Brian a text to tell him not to come over. My hand shakes as I type out the message. We've been inseparable during the last few weeks, seeing each other every day. If I don't give him a reason, he'll worry and come straight over. All I say is that I'm spending time with Loretta, and then I drive to her house. She's the friend I need to see me through this. She'll give me the truth and hold my hand while I cry through it like when Evan died, when I gave up my dreams, and when I thought I couldn't go on.

Tears blur the white lines on the road as I drive. I don't know how I make it, but I eventually pull up in front of Loretta's house and announce myself at the gate. The big gates swing open, letting me in. Before I get out of the car, I wipe away as much of the mess on my face as I can, but it's no use. My tears won't stop. I'm devastated. I'm guilty. I'm a failure. I'm frightened. I don't want to lose my child.

The closer I get to the door, the more I'm falling apart. I'm barely holding myself together when I ring the bell. There's a clacking of heels before the door opens. Loretta stands on the doorstep.

Where do I start? Suddenly, I'm at a loss for words. It's as if everything is trapped inside, and I can't let it out. We just stand there and stare at each other. It's then that it strikes me that Loretta is at a loss for words, too. This isn't like her.

The silence is awkward. What am I supposed to make of it? I can't read her face. Is that pity, indifference, or regret in her expression?

*Say something, Lottie.*

Finally, I just blurt it out. "Abby said Brian…" Oh, God. I can't say it.

"I know."

Why is she standing in the door like that, keeping it halfway open? Why doesn't she let me in?

"You know?"

"Francois called Ralph."

"He told him?"

"He needed advice."

My voice is shrill. "What advice?"

"Jane…"

She always calls me Janie. What the hell is so hard for her to say? I want to shake her and tell her to stop this charade, but something in her demeanor holds me back.

"What's going on, Lottie?"

"I'm sorry, but we can't see you any longer."

Can't see me how? Where? I can only look at her in confusion.

"With what happened," she says, "Ralph feels it's better that we cut the ties."

Cut the ties. With what happened. Slowly, her words sink in. "I see."

"I'm sorry."

She doesn't look it. Not one bit.

It was the warning she gave me when she saw the marks on my wrists. The barbecue sealed the deal. The bomb Abby dropped is only the excuse.

There's nothing to say. I feel like an imposter, a beggar on her steps. I shouldn't let it affect me, but it does. This is what mourning a friend feels like. It's Debbie and Francois and Loretta and Ralph on the inside of the big circle, and me on the outside. When I see the truth for what it is, I recognize the look on her face I couldn't place. Animosity.

I'm not brave when I turn from her, because I'm not walking away. I'm fleeing. Before I'm down the step, she's already closed the door. At least there's no one to witness my defeat as I walk the long, humiliating path to my car.

I drive on autopilot. I don't know where I'm going until I sit outside Dorothy's house. Taking my phone from my bag, I dial the only person I have left.

"What's wrong?" Dorothy asks.

I don't even deny it. My voice is shaking with tears. "I'm outside."

"My house?" she shrieks.

"Yes."

"Do you–?"

"I don't want to come in."

"Wait there."

A moment later, her gate opens, and she walks toward my car, dressed in heels and a suit. She's only carrying her phone and keys in her hand. She opens the passenger door and slides into the seat.

"Are you going out?" I ask, taking in her attire.

"Yes."

"I'll come back tomorrow."

"It's only dinner. It can wait. What happened?"

The tears push up like a fountain. I can't stop. In a blubbering mess of crying, I tell her the whole story, including what happened with Loretta. She listens quietly, not interrupting once. When I'm done, she presses a number on her phone.

"What are you doing?"

"I'm calling a friend who works in social services."

"What for?"

"Advice."

I stare through the windscreen at the dark night as she relays what I told her to the person on the other end of the line. It's a long discussion.

"There'll be an investigation," she says when she finally hangs up. "It's a serious allegation. If found guilty, Brian will have a criminal record for life. Guilty or not, he'll be branded. People will perceive him as a pedophile."

I tilt my head to the ceiling. "Dear God." I haven't even thought that far.

"What is Francois planning on doing?"

"I'm not a hundred percent sure."

"Will he try to get custody of Abby?"

She read my mind. "Maybe."

"You need a witness when we go to Francois' house tomorrow, just in case he tries to push you into a corner or manipulate you. Anyway, you're in a vulnerable state. You need emotional support. Whatever happens tomorrow, it'll be your word against Francois' if he decides to fight you in court, and from the way things are standing right now, your word doesn't look too glorious. It's a bitch, I know, but people are going to judge you."

"For sleeping with a younger man. For bringing Brian into Abby's life."

"I'll come with you."

"Dorothy–"

"No arguing. I'll meet you there so you can't *forget* to pick me up." She takes my hand. "Come inside. Please. Sleep over. Let me fix you a warm drink."

"Thanks, but I need to be alone." And Benjamin must be inside.

She regards me for a moment. "I understand." She opens the door and gets out. Leaning back into the car, she says, "We'll get through this."

I didn't believe her when she said that the first-time around, and I don't believe her now, but I'm grateful that she's there for me.

"Did you tell...him?" I can't speak his name.

Her expression saddens. "I didn't tell Benjamin it's you."

"Thank you."

"You're welcome."

I don't start the engine until she's closed the gate. When I drive through the posh neighborhood, I'm thankful for the silence that swallows me and for the darkness that hides my faults and shame.

---

*Brian*

THERE'S a message from Monkey to say I'm expected for lunch the following weekend to discuss the engagement party. I ignore it. I have enough on my plate with work and exams. I'll deal with it when the time comes. On top of that, Jane calls in sick on Monday morning. She doesn't reply when I call from the office but sends a text message to say she was sleeping and I shouldn't worry. Right. Like that's going to happen. I offer to come over after work and cook her soup, but she tells me she'll be with Dorothy and will speak to me the next day. I don't like it. I need to take care of her if she's ill, but this is the freedom I promised myself to give her. Besides, she's been through a tough time. She can do with a friend, and even as I like to think I'm all she needs, women need their girlfriends.

The reason I'm at work when I should be studying is because Toby wants to see me about my ideas for the Monroe account. If he's going to tell me it's a pile of horse shit, it's better Jane isn't here. She won't be pleased. If, on the other hand, my proposal is enough to save her account, we'll have something to celebrate, tomorrow.

I enter his office and close his door.

He takes off his hat and drops it on the desk. "Sit down."

Is it a good or bad sign? There's no smile on his face, so I can't tell which way this is going to go. My gut is twisted in knots when I take a seat in front of his desk. It's like I'm back at school, awaiting punishment in the headmaster's office.

Toby crosses his ankles on the desk and tips his hands together. "I had a long chat to Mr. Monroe about your ideas. As I told you, I found them interesting. Promising."

It already doesn't sound good. I wait for the big *but*.

"Mr. Monroe loves it," he declared solemnly. "He's ecstatic. It's exactly what he didn't know he needed, to quote Mr. Monroe himself."

*Thank fuck.* I blow out a heavy breath. The tightness in my stomach eases up. "Excellent. Jane will be pleased."

"Jane won't be part of it."

"What?" I shift to the edge of my seat. "What's that supposed to mean?"

"I'm offering you the account."

My throat goes dry. "I made those suggestions for Jane."

"I know." He swings his legs from the desk. "I wanted to break the news to you before I tell her." He holds my eyes with a piercing stare. "She's out."

It feels as if a thousand bats start flapping in my chest. "What does that even mean?"

"I'm letting her go."

My ribcage squeezes as if in a vice. "You can't do that."

"I don't have a choice. It's the shareholders' decision. I did what I could to sway them, but they've made up their minds."

"She's a good worker, and you know it."

"She works hard, but you work clever. Jane is old school. You're the new blood we need."

"I won't do it. I won't steal her account."

"We're giving it to someone else, whether it's you or a new recruit. I'd be sad to see you go, but it won't reverse the decision."

"I'm just an intern."

"With enormous potential. We want you to execute your plans for the brand under my mentorship. You'll finish your studies. When you get your degree, your promotion to full account executive is guaranteed. For now, there's a nice bonus and a salary increase waiting for you. It's an opportunity you can't refuse."

I swallow.

"Your loyalty to Jane only makes me like you more," Toby continues, "but if you say no, the account *will* go to someone else. I'm sure Jane would rather it's you."

Goddamn. This backfired in the worst way possible. It's going to look as if I fucked her over. This isn't what I wanted for Jane. Never.

"I'm breaking the news to Jane tomorrow," Toby says. "What do I tell her? Has she wasted her time with you, or are you going to say yes to an opportunity of a lifetime?"

My mouth is so dry I have to swallow twice before I can speak. "I need to discuss it with her first." I'd rather walk away from this job than hurt her.

"In that case, you're in, because I already know what she'll say. There's a lot of work to be done and little time. I want to make the announcement to the team as soon as possible, why not during our monthly staff meeting tomorrow? It's not ideal to do it over the phone, but I'll call Jane and break the news to her today."

"No," I say quickly. "Let me speak to her first. Let me be the one to break it to her. It's my fault, after all. I should be the one to explain."

At least I can break it to her gently. Losing her job is going to be hard on her, and it's not as if she hasn't dealt with enough shit as it is.

It kills me to ask, "How soon do you want her out?"

"With immediate effect. I'm afraid that's how our business works. I'm already having a severance package drawn up. She'll be cleaning out her desk tomorrow."

"Fuck." I drag my hands over my head. I wish with every ounce of me I could take back my ideas. If I'd any inkling this is how it was going to play out I would've never set foot into this office. I'd give my life to turn back time, but Toby is on his feet and rounding the desk, taking us another step toward the future.

"Welcome on board." He pats my shoulder. "You've got your future made, kid."

*Jane*

IT'S EXACTLY six o'clock when Dorothy pulls up to my old house. I've been outside in my car for an hour. I couldn't make myself knock before, and I couldn't sit at home for another minute. I couldn't eat or sleep. I haven't even showered. I'm still dressed in the same T-shirt and yoga pants from yesterday. At least I've washed my face and brushed my teeth.

Dorothy knocks on my window. "Let's go."

Her manner is firm and brusque. It's what I need. Hooking my arm around hers, I tap into her strength. She rings the bell at the gate. It opens to reveal Francois standing in the door. He frowns when we walk up the garden path.

"What's she doing here?" he asks. "This is a family matter."

"Not since you involved Ralph."

His shoulders sag in defeat, and he steps aside for us to enter. Debbie waits in the lounge.

My voice is barely audible. My heart is wrung out. "Where's Abby?"

"She couldn't face you," Francois says behind me, "not yet."

"She asked me to tell you," Debbie says.

I fling around to face Francois. "I have a right to speak to her."

His expression is void of emotion. "We'll talk first."

Suddenly, I'm glad Dorothy came with me. "Debbie, you remember Dorothy?"

Debbie doesn't accept Dorothy's extended hand. "I thought we were talking in private."

Dorothy drops her hand. "Francois has you. Jane deserves support, too."

"She's a close friend," I say, ignoring the way Francois clenches his jaw.

There's no love lost between Dorothy and Francois. I never thought I'd see them in the same room.

"Have a seat." Francois motions to the sofas.

I only accept because I'm not sure my legs will carry me through this. Dorothy sits down next to me, our arms touching. The contact comforts me.

"Let's hear it," Dorothy says as Francois and Debbie stiffly take their seats.

I'm so damn thankful for my friend, right now. I just want to get to the bottom of this, gather my daughter, and leave. I'll break down later, when I'm alone.

Francois gives Dorothy a cool look before he fixes his attention on me. "In the light of what happened–"

"We still don't know what happened," Dorothy says.

He grits his teeth and nods at Debbie.

Debbie's eyes are narrowed on me. "Abby said Brian put his arm around her shoulders while they were sitting next to each other at the garden table. At first it seemed innocent, but then he..." She glances at Francois.

He gives Debbie's arm a squeeze. "Go on."

"Then he touched her breast and tried to kiss her."

I'm going to be sick. My empty stomach protests.

"How did she react?" Dorothy asks.

"She told him to get his hands off her," Debbie replies.

Dorothy takes my hand. "Why didn't she call Jane the minute it happened?"

"Are you accusing my daughter of being a liar?" Francois asks, his cold anger now barely masked.

"Not at all," Dorothy says. "We just want to understand why Abby doesn't want to confide in her mother."

"She didn't want to hurt Jane's feelings." Debbie shifts her gaze back to me. "Brian is Jane's boyfriend, after all."

"In the light of what's happened," Francois says again, "we don't think it's in Abby's best interest to continue living with you. I'm suing for full custody."

Even if I expected it, the statement knocks the air out of my lungs.

"I want a restraining order against Brian," Francois continues, "and I'm laying charges for child molesting."

At first, I can't breathe, and then the fight flows back into my body in a powerful gush of adrenalin. My voice sounds as brittle as my heart feels. "I won't let you use this to take Abby away from me."

"You don't stand a chance in court," he says, his attitude confident, "not with charges of neglect."

"Neglect?" I exclaim.

"A snake attack and molesting by your boyfriend. We have the home and security Abby needs. Here, she's close to her friends. She has access to a garden and pool."

"Face it," Debbie says, "we can give her everything you can't."

A calm born from fighting instinct settles over me. "A garden and pool don't replace a mother."

Francois adopts a non-negotiable air. "Our decision is made."

Of course, he's confident. Ralph's lawyer buddies probably assured Francois I can't win. War with my ex is not what I want, but I'll do anything to keep my daughter. No battle is big or dirty enough.

"Think carefully, Francois." It's no idle threat. "Is this truly the course you want to take?"

He holds my eyes unblinkingly. "Yes."

So be it. "I demand a paternity test."

# 7

---

*Jane*

The room goes quiet. It's a silence much more devastating than the quiet of Francois' storm. Debbie jerks her head toward Francois. Dorothy drops her head between her shoulders.

Francois has turned into an ice statue. His face is whiter than snow. "You won't play that card."

"What does she mean, *a paternity test?*" Debbie asks in a shrill voice.

I just look at Francois as he looks back at me. It's the bomb that wasn't supposed to drop, the wall between us we've never mentioned or acknowledged. If you ignore something for long enough, you can almost forget it exists. Almost.

"Answer me, Francois," Debbie demands. "What does she mean?"

It's Dorothy who knocks out the first brick. She lifts her head slowly. "Abby's father can be any of three men."

"Three men!" Debbie lunges to her feet. "What are you, Jane? A slut?"

Francois tries to pull her down. "Debs, please."

She rips her hand from his. "I'm assuming you're one of the men," she says to Francois. "Who are the other two?"

"My sons," Dorothy says. "Jane slept with both my sons and Francois in the space of two days."

I've never heard her sound so defeated, not even when Evan died.

Francois is visibly shaking. "You won't do it."

I guess he didn't expect me to ever face those unspoken demons, but there's nothing I won't do to keep my daughter, even digging up skeletons.

"Watch me," I say.

Debbie sounds somewhere between angry and hurt. "Francois, why didn't you tell me?"

A sob from the doorway stills me. It freezes me to my core. We all turn our heads in the direction of the voice. Abby stands in the frame, dressed in her favorite ice cream pajamas. A tail-wagging Dusty stands next to her.

*No. Dear God, no.*

"Who is my father?" Her breath catches on a hitch. "Tell me."

"Abby!" I'm on my feet, rushing over to her.

I want to take her in my arms, but she takes a step back.

"Who is my father, Mom?"

"Francois will always be your father."

"You know what I mean," she yells.

"Abby, honey, I'm so sorry. I'm so sorry. I didn't mean for you to find out..." Like this, I want to say, but the truth is I never wanted her to find out. I never wanted this for her.

"I want to know," she says, fresh tears brimming in her eyes.

"Abby." Francois reaches for her, but she backs away more.

"Don't touch me. I want to know. *I have a right to know.*"

Tears are running over Debbie's cheeks. "How could you?" She points at my daughter. "Look what you're doing to her."

"Francois left me no choice."

"I want you to leave." Debbie crosses the lounge and stands defiantly next to the door. "Both of you." She points at Dorothy and me. "Out."

I face my baby girl, three unbridgeable steps between us. "Do you want me to go? Will it make you feel better?"

She wraps her arms around herself. "I just want to be alone."

"All right. I'm sorry, honey," I whisper.

Dorothy is the only one who Abby allows to hug her. In many ways, Dorothy has been the grandmother she's never had. If Dorothy was only at the house whenever Francois wasn't there, Abby never questioned it. Now she knows why.

Now the world will know.

"Let's go," Dorothy says for a second time that day.

I let her guide me, not knowing where I'm going or where this is taking us. My world is falling apart, but I made my choice. I chose Abby. The next step is one of the hardest I'll ever take in my life.

Dorothy insists on coming home with me, but I manage to convince her I need time by myself. In truth, it's time to face Brian.

At home, I stand on my tiny balcony that faces my neighbor's wall. The only sound that greets me is the traffic from the highway. Fast-moving cars. The air smells of cement dust from the building. So mundane, and yet, so profound. When the police officer knocked on the door that fateful night, I was trying to eat something I could keep down. Dry toast. The bread burnt in the toaster while he told us. Ever since, death smells like burnt toast. Now, the end smells like dust.

I'm at the end, but I know how to go forward. I've done it once. I can do it again. The worst about losing Evan was not being able to say goodbye. I never had a chance to tell him how much I loved him before he left. At least I'll have this with Brian.

---

*Brian*

THE GROUND LEVEL of Jane's duplex is dark. Only the bedroom light upstairs is on. At this time of the evening, she'd be cooking with music playing in the background. Is she still sick? Using my key to enter, I half will her to stand in front of the sink, swaying her hips to a song while she rinses wine glasses. It's a cute thing about her, how she always washes every glass before setting the table. It says a lot about her personality. She's meticulous and committed to whatever she does. If that's what she pours into a task as mundane as setting a table, she's given her soul for her job. Here I am to destroy that.

The smell of roast or lamb chops doesn't come from the oven. I should've picked up take-outs. If I weren't so preoccupied with what I have to tell her, I'd have thought of it sooner. I stop at the bottom of the stairs to gather my thoughts and words.

*I'm sorry. Toby offered me your job.*

*I'm sorry. I didn't mean to steal your biggest account.*

*I'm sorry. I didn't realize my meddling would get you fired.*

*Fuck.*

Dragging a hand over my face, I climb the stairs one by one, feeling each step like a shock to my joints. In the doorframe to the bedroom, I pause. Jane is standing on the balcony, staring into the distance. I don't like it. A heavy feeling of doom pushes down on my chest, stealing my breath. I take a shaky drag of air and walk to her. The carpet cushions my steps, but she's aware of my presence, because she doesn't react when I touch her shoulder.

"What are you doing out here in the dark?" I ask gently.

She turns to me slowly. The light from the bedroom falls over her figure. The look on her face knocks the wind from my stomach. Her eyes are hollow in their sockets, and her skin is so pale I can see a fragile blue vein in her temple. She doesn't only look beaten. She looks broken.

Putting our bodies flush together, I cup her cheek. "Tell me."

"I'm sorry."

*No. Fuck. No, no, no.* I won't let her go. I can't. I swear to God I'll blackmail her, lock her up, kidnap her, whatever it takes, but I won't settle for *sorry*.

"You're hurting me," she whispers.

My fingers are clenched around her jaw. I didn't realize how hard I was gripping her. Softening my touch, I trail a thumb over her bottom lip. My voice is tight. My gut is in a ball. "What happened? What's wrong?"

"It's Abby."

My heartbeat accelerates to a painful hammering. Jane won't survive anything happening to her child. "Is it her eyes? Are they worse?"

Her beautiful, wide eyes tell me no as she stares up at me, catching her lip between her teeth.

"I'm so sorry, Brian."

"It's all right," I blabber. "Whatever it is, we'll fix it. We'll work through it together."

Before I'm done talking, her head is already shaking in denial.

"She said you touched her."

*She said you touched her.*

I haven't heard right. The words don't make sense. They can't mean what I think. Of course, I touched her. Our hands touched when we greeted each other with a handshake. I may have knocked my elbow into her arm when we both reached for the Parmesan cheese. It's Jane's despondent look that gives me the answer.

My heart goes from over-drive to slamming on brakes so hard it feels like whiplash in my chest. Everything inside me goes cold. My core is a block of ice. I drop my hand from Jane's face and take a step back.

"I swear to you I didn't lay a finger on Abby, not in the way she suggests. I'd rather cut off my hand."

"Francois wants to lay charges."

"I don't care," I say in a reckless disregard for the consequences, because charges will brand me as a child molester, innocent or not. "I'm not losing you, Jane. Ever."

Tears shimmer in her eyes. She swallows twice.

Helplessness makes me weak. "You have to believe me."

"What I believe won't make a difference. I had to make a choice."

Of course. Fuck. I feel like dropping to my knees. Only sheer willpower keeps me standing, waiting for the final blow that'll ruin my life with a power nothing else can ever outweigh.

She wrings her hands together. "Abby always comes first."

I want to rip the clouds clean out of the sky and trample fate under my boots. I want to punch a hole in the wall and break every bone in my hand, just so the physical pain will overshadow this gaping, burning slash that cuts my heart in two. Helplessness isn't weak. Helplessness is a monster. I want to slay it, but how can I not understand? Wouldn't I do the same for Sam? The uselessness of the situation makes me tear at my hair. If I could, I'd pull every strand from my head.

Her voice is shaking. Scared. "Brian?"

I stop, registering I've been circling like an animal stalking his own tail. Jane is shivering like a frail ribbon in a violent thunderstorm. Her slender legs are quivering, and her teeth are chattering.

Clasping a hand over my mouth, I swallow the words of pain, denial, and anger. Tonight, I'm walking away–she gives me no choice–but I'm not leaving her with the epitome of my fury at everything that's unrighteous and fucked-up in this world.

One by one, I release my fingers, freeing my words. "I understand. I'd do the same for Sam." I close the distance between us, letting the full length of my body rest against hers. My voice turns hard with intention. "But I'm not giving you up. I'll wait. Ten years. Twenty. However long it takes."

At some stage, Abby will leave the house. She'll grow up. I have to cling to that or go to pieces. I want to smash the chair standing innocently to the side, placed there on its own as if she knew she'd sit here alone. I want to throw the one-man table over the rail and kick it to splinters, but I only fold my arms around Jane and hold her against me.

She sobs against my chest. My heart throbs under her cheek, breaking a little more with each beat as she cries harder. I run my hands over her back.

"Shh, princess."

How do I soothe someone when I'm broken myself? How do I make it right when all I have left is so much despair? I can't even be angry at Abby. I made her mother the older woman. At Abby's age, it must be a hell of an embarrassment. She made no secret of hating my guts. I just never thought she'd take it this far.

Jane's breath hitches on another sob.

"Come." I lead her inside and pull her down on the bed.

The fact that she wants me to stay is enough. She wouldn't have asked if she believed I did those unspeakable things to her daughter.

She's a mess. Her hair is disheveled, and her make-up is smudged from the crying. It's a knife in my chest to see her like this. There's no way I can tell her about the account. Her job, for Christ's sake. Not tonight. I pull a blanket over her since she's still trembling, although I suspect it's not from cold, before I go look in the medicine cabinet for something to calm her. There's nothing save for over-the-counter pills for everyday ailments. I settle on two headache tablets and a triple shot of vodka, the only strong alcohol I can find.

She's still crying when I get back to the bedroom. Her pillow is soaked.

"Shh." I kiss her forehead and help her into a sitting position before handing her the liquor and pills. "Drink this. It'll calm you."

If nothing else, it should knock her out enough to get some much-needed sleep.

She swallows down the vodka and pills without arguing. Jane isn't big on hard liquor. This alone tells me how much she needs relief from her pain. She hiccups and wipes her mouth with her hand.

I lower her back onto the mattress and rearrange the pillow and blanket.

"Will you stay?" she asks in a small voice.

"Yes." Until she's asleep. It'll be better if I sneak off in her dreams. It's less harsh than having to face the wrenching pain of a goodbye spoken in a doorway, of watching someone walk away, until you're the one left behind, standing on your own with nothing but silence and loneliness.

"Don't go to work tomorrow." I stroke her hair. "Stay and rest. You need it. I'll explain to Toby."

She nods, her eyelids already heavy. When was the last time she slept? She looks knackered. At least if she stays in tomorrow, it'll win me another day before having to share my own shitty load of bad news. It's too much to take all at once. No single person can carry such a load. I'll break it to her gently, when she's rested and feeling better. It hurts to even think it, but maybe it'll help her keep her distance from me. Her anger will see her over until I claim her back, because that's the only given in my future at this moment. I *will* claim her back.

Not trusting myself enough to get under the covers with her, I sit on the edge of the bed, clutching her clammy hand in mine until the vodka kicks in, and she finally falls into a fitful sleep. Etching her features into my mind, I place a last, soft kiss on her lips before I walk away.

---

*Jane*

I WAKE up with a slight hangover, even if I'd swallowed down half a glass of vodka. The headache, fuzzy brain, thirst, and queasiness are only dull aches. They're nothing compared to the emptiness in my heart. Brian is gone. His place in my bed is empty. He must've closed the sliding doors to the balcony and the curtains. The room is dark and depressing. More tears find their way to my eyes, but I have to stop crying. I have to face the world, today. I have to face Francois.

Allowing that purpose to drive me, I throw back the covers and get to my feet. I consider getting straight into the shower, but on second thought I pull on my exercise gear. I need to run. I need to maintain a resemblance of a routine. I try not to think about the squat rack Brian assembled in the garage.

Running past the construction site toward the more established part of the residence, I push myself until my lungs feel like combusting and my cramping muscles protest. Still, I carry on. On and on. Running in circles. Close to the main entrance of the complex, my knees buckle. My legs cave in. I hit the grassy shoulder next to the tarmac, going down in defeat. I'm sucking in gulps of air. The over-exertion makes me want to vomit. Turning on my back, I try to get back control over my breathing and body. A passing car slows down and stops. The door opens and a man exits. His face blocks out my light as he hovers over me.

"Hey, are you all right?"

"Fine," I wheeze. "Ran too hard."

"You sure?"

"Yes. Thanks."

"All right, then. Maybe take it easier on yourself."

A truthful answer is not an option.

When he leaves, I take another few minutes to gather myself. I'm okay. I lived through Evan's death. I can survive anything. Rolling onto my side, I force myself onto my hands and knees. It takes tremendous effort to get to my feet, but I manage. It's a small victory. Running is no longer possible. Physically, I've depleted myself. I don't have a choice but to walk the rest of the way home.

After a shower, I feel considerably better. Endorphins from the exercise flood my brain, and my energy starts to return. Since I can't face food, I forego breakfast. I force myself not to think about Brian, lest I break down again. I need my strength to fight for my daughter. I need an action plan. I need the best defense I can get.

Dorothy organizes the lawyer. He listens to my case carefully before confirming that the court can order Francois to take a paternity test in the light of our circumstances. The other *candidates* are under no obligation and can't be forced to undergo a test by court order. Francois must already know this, because when I call to ask how Abby is doing, he tells me he's made an appointment for a paternity test. Thanks to Ralph's contacts, he got an appointment at a private facility for today. That can only mean he'll fight me with everything he's got. Part of me wants it to be Francois for Abby's sake, but another part fears the outcome. I can't lose Abby. Dorothy's lawyer assured me if Francois is Abby's biological father, he has a strong case. The lawyer's guess is that Francois will build a case on arguing that I'm an unfit mother. The multiple sex partners when Abby was conceived, the accusation against Brian, and the cobra attack all count against me, not to mention that Abby's wish in the matter will weigh heavily, since she's over thirteen years of age.

After lunchtime, I'm drained again. All I manage to keep down is a banana and a cup of tea. Not ready to face an empty house, I drive to the office. I'd rather immerse myself in work than sit at home in dreaded suspense, waiting for the outcome of Francois' test. My nerves are shattered. My heart is broken. Work will be a welcome balm.

Erica, the receptionist, gives me an uncertain greeting. Our floor is empty when I climb up the stairs. Through the sandblasted glass walls of the meeting room, people are visible. All stations are deserted, which means everyone is in there. Of course. It's the monthly staff meeting. With everything that's happened, it completely slipped my mind. I can't see the faces through the patterned glass, but Brian won't be in. He'll be studying. It's soothing that no one in that room knows my history or dilemma. I can get lost in the problems of advertising without worrying about the people in the office. Thank God Brian and I didn't announce our relationship at work.

Taking a steadying breath, I push open the doors. All heads turn toward me. A strange silence falls over the room. Then I see him. Brian stands at the head of the meeting table next to Toby. He's wearing a shirt and tie. His handsome face hurts my heart with a force I haven't expected, rendering my knees weak. It's not the uncharacteristic attire that speaks to me, but the way his tanned face pales as he stares at me. What's going on? I look at the other people in the room for a clue. Beatrix averts her eyes. Mable takes a gulp of water. Priscilla has a strange expression of pity. Alex shifts in his chair, and Bernard glances at Toby. Toby is wearing his thin-lipped smile, the one that promises nothing good.

"What's going on?" I ask, taking a step into the room. The double doors close quietly behind me.

"You weren't supposed to be in," Brian says.

Toby clears his throat. "Everyone take five. Jane and Brian, in my office."

He walks out ahead of us. Brian and I follow. In the hallway, Brian puts a hand on my arm. "You said you were staying at home."

"I need to work. I couldn't stand doing nothing, any longer."

I can't place the look he gives me.

"Jane," Toby says, holding his door.

He lets me enter first but doesn't invite me to sit. He stands in front of his desk, facing Brian and me. Did he find out about our relationship? Did Francois let something slip? Or did Francois tell him about Abby's accusations? My heart stutters. If Brian loses this job because of–

"You didn't tell her," Toby says.

Brian doesn't move his eyes from mine. "Yesterday wasn't the right time. I was hoping to speak to you tonight, Jane."

"Tell me what?"

Toby huffs. "This should've come from me. I shouldn't have indulged you, Brian. I take all the blame for this awkward situation."

I tear my gaze away from Brian. "Toby, you're killing me."

"Jane..." Toby licks his lips. "I wanted to tell you first, but this couldn't wait, and Brian believed it was better he tells you. The investors wanted me to make an announcement today."

"About what?"

"We're giving the Monroe account to Brian."

My ears start ringing. I stand perfectly straight, but underneath my dress my legs are wobbling. "What?"

"Mr. Monroe decided to go with Brian's pitch. They're going digital."

He went behind my back? I can't believe it. I glance at Brian, but the truth is there. He's not denying it. He's not trying to hide the remorse etched on his face.

"I'm sorry," Brian says. "I didn't mean to steal the account. I was trying to save it for you."

"As of today," Toby continues, "you no longer work here. I'm truly sorry. I am. I did what I could, but the big bosses want younger blood. New ideas. I hate doing this, but a security officer will escort you to your office and from the building. It's what protocol dictates."

I square my shoulders as much as my broken pride allows. "I understand. Congratulations, Brian. You deserve it."

Toby picks up an envelope from his desk and hands it to me. "Your severance contract. You can have your lawyer look it over before signing it." He comes to me, holding his arms open. "Love you, sugar. It's not personal. Just business. I'll give you a great letter of recommendation."

My lips are numb. "Thanks."

As I can't think of anything else to say, I turn and leave. The eyes of the people in the meeting room burn on the back of my head as I make my way to my old desk. I can't see them, but I feel them. I can feel their pity.

"Jane!"

Brian comes after me.

I don't stop. I can't. I keep on walking until I reach my office, but the door is locked. Embarrassingly, I don't have a choice but to turn and face him. I lean on the door, not sure that my legs will carry my weight.

Brian's expression is pained. "I was going to tell you last night," he says, "but you weren't in a good place."

"I understand. Really."

The security guard exits the stairs.

"I meant it when I said you deserve it." I'm big enough to admit defeat. I can also give credit where it's due.

The guard stops next to us.

I step aside so he can unlock the door. "I'll only be a minute." I don't have much to collect other than a photo of Abby and a few knickknacks.

Brian follows me inside. "Talk to me, Jane."

I scrape stupid lucky charms from client promotions into my bag. "There's nothing else to say."

"I didn't want it. I told Toby I wouldn't take it, but he was going to give the job to someone else."

"It's all right, Brian."

"I reckoned I'll need the money to take care of you if you're going to lose your job."

I can't deal with this. Not right now. "You're cut out for advertising. I'm sure you'll be a big success." I push past him. "I've got to go."

Forcing myself not to run, I go back to the meeting room. My ex-colleagues stare at me expectantly.

"As you know, I'm out of here." I hope my smile doesn't look as tremulous as it feels. "Brian is taking over. I have complete faith in him. He's an invaluable asset to the company. Don't give him a hard time like you gave me when I started."

Hesitant laughter erupts.

"That's short for a departure speech," Priscilla says.

More laughter. The atmosphere in the room lifts slightly.

"That's all you've got to say?" Beatrix teases.

"Thanks for being an awesome team. Take care."

Toby nods at me as I exit. "That was big of you."

"Brian's got a good mentor in you. Take care of him."

The guard and Brian are standing at the door. I try to walk normally even if my heart still urges me to flee. The guard follows a step behind, saving me the humiliation of making it clear to everyone on the ground floor what's happening.

It's only in the parking lot that Brian calls out to me again. I ignore him. I'm fitting the key into the car door when he stops next to me. When I try to open the door, he slams a palm on it, preventing me. He searches my eyes, but I can't look at him. Shame, humiliation, guilt...too many emotions prevent me.

"Talk to me."

Staring at the cracked concrete, I shake my head.

"We agreed, Jane. We agreed we'd always talk. Talk, damn you. Hate me. Shout at me. Slap me. I can take it. Give it to me."

It's an effort to turn my head and face him. I'm so, so tired. "I don't hate you." If anything, I love him even more, and it hurts. It hurts that he went behind my back, but I understand why he did. If I weren't so pigheaded about a brand that had become my baby over the years, I would've listened to him.

"I meant what I said back there. I'm happy for you."

Emotions simmer in his eyes. "I'll resign."

"Don't be an idiot. You'll throw away the opportunity of a lifetime." *And you need the money to take care of Sam and your mother.*

"That's it?" he asks, his remorse morphing into anger. "You just lost your job. Don't stand there and tell me it's all right. I know you're upset."

I can't tell him about the case Francois is building against me, or that losing my only source of income has just made Francois' case even stronger. It's not his fault. I won't lay that kind of blame on his shoulders. I can only tell him I feel nothing but love for him, because I have to let him go.

Cupping his cheek, I drink him in. The stubble on his jaw pricks my palm. He smells like soap and a slightly too strong aftershave.

"I love you, Brian." Closing my eyes, I savor the words and say them again. "I love you." *I'm so sorry for ruining your life.*

I let the closure of goodbye settle in my heart, enforcing it with my guilt. It's harder than I could've ever imagined. It's like a piece of me dies. This time, he doesn't stop me when I open the door. He doesn't speak or move as I start the engine and put the car into gear. I don't want to look in the rearview mirror, but I can't help myself. My eyes are drawn to the figure standing in the mirage of heat that rolls over the concrete. Tears well up in my eyes. A hysterical sob surfaces.

*Don't cry. Don't cry.*

It's no use. I can't stop. His image blurs behind my tears. Is losing everything the price I'm paying for falling in love with Brian? If I hadn't met him, I wouldn't have moved to the cottage and a snake wouldn't have spat Abby. My daughter would still be living with me. I wouldn't have found Brian a position at Orion and Toby wouldn't have given him my job. If Brian didn't help me realize how unimportant the material things in my life are to my peace of mind, maybe I would've fought Francois with a drawn-out and expensive battle in court. Maybe I'd still have my designer house. Yes, I can lay all the maybes on Brian for coming into my life, or I can admit that Abby loves Francois more and Brian is better at my job than me. I can argue I would've been better off if I'd never met Brian, but that's not true. Isn't owning your pain the same as owning your decisions and every taboo that comes with them? As I clear the gates and his figure is brutally cut off from my vision, I know with certainty that if given a choice, I'd be the oldest cliché in the book. I'd do it all over again.

———

It's not until the following day that Francois calls. I grip the phone hard, but I can't bring myself to answer. Four, six seconds pass. The call goes onto voicemail. I've been making myself sick with worry, pacing all night. I haven't eaten or slept. I'm on the brink of collapsing. I know better, but I'm incapable of taking care of myself. Sleep evades me. Food makes me vomit. I want to know, but I'm scared. Staring at the phone, I finally gather enough courage to press the redial button.

"I've got the results," Francois says.

That was fast, thanks to connections. I close my eyes and hold my breath.

He utters a shaky sigh. "It's not me."

My heart comes to a stop. Adrenalin makes me feel nauseous. It's the shock of both relief and dread. I get to keep Abby, but I can't think about the meaning of the test.

*Please, God, let it be Evan.*

I'm shaking so badly I have to sit down. "I'm sorry." How hard this must be on Francois.

"Me, too." He gives a wry laugh. "The house of cards comes crumbling down."

None of this would've happened if he hadn't left. We'd still be married, and Abby would be blissfully unaware. I'd still pretend to be happy. I'm sorrier than I can ever say about what's happened, but I'll never regret it. The events led me to Brian. It's the aftermath that's a dirty disaster.

"How's Abby taking it?" I ask.

I should've been there for my daughter. Keeping her from me

isn't something I'll easily forgive Francois for, even if my heart is aching for his suffering. After all that's happened, I can't make myself hate him. We were friends, if nothing more. That counts for something. He loves Abby with all his heart. No matter the biology, she's always been his daughter.

"Not well," he replies, "but she wants to see you."

"You can bring her home." With the outcome of the test result, he doesn't have a choice. "It's over between Brian and me. She doesn't have to worry about him being around."

"It doesn't mean I'm not laying charges."

"I know." I just hope Brian will be able to forgive me, one day. "When can you drop Abby off?"

"In an hour?"

"I'll be waiting."

Needing to keep busy, I make cottage pie. It's Abby's favorite from when she was little. I drink two cups of sweet tea to settle my nerves and have something in my stomach before they arrive.

The doorbell rings on the hour. Abby stands in the doorway, her face forlorn. Francois remains a step behind with Dusty. His hands are shoved into his pockets. He's rattling the coins in there as if he can't keep still.

I take Abby into a hug. This time, she lets me.

"Would you like to come inside?" I ask Francois.

"Debs is waiting in the car."

"All right."

Abby turns to him. "Will I still see you this weekend?"

Francois goes down on his haunches to put them on eye level. "The test doesn't change my feelings for you. You're still my daughter." His voice shakes. It takes him a moment to gather his control. "As we said, your room is always there."

She throws her arms around him. "I love you, Dad."

"Love you too, baby."

He blinks tears away before he gives me a hasty nod and hurries down the path to the garden gate.

I put my arm around my daughter and lead her into the house. Dusty follows, sniffing as he goes.

"Would you like to see your new room?"

She shrugs. "I guess."

"I realize there's much to talk about. We'll get through this. I promise you."

She pulls away from my touch. "I want to know."

"Abby." I was hoping, praying, she wouldn't go there, but I knew better.

"I want to know, Mom."

I reply with a tired sigh. "I understand." I'd feel the same if I were in her shoes. "There are other things you need to know, honey."

She gives me a wary look.

"Let's go to the kitchen. I'm making pecan nut pie for dessert. There's cottage pie for lunch if you're hungry."

She shakes her head but follows me to the kitchen. After settling Dusty in the basket I left in a sunny corner, we sit down at the counter I've converted into a breakfast nook. Dusty doesn't stay long before he starts exploring again. I pour two glasses of iced tea and put one in front of her.

"Did your dad tell you anything about when you were conceived?"

"We only spoke about the test results."

Taking a deep breath, I steel myself to go down memory lane to a place I'd sworn I'd never revisit.

"Before your dad and I got together, I was engaged to someone else. His name was Evan."

"Dorothy's son."

"Yes."

"Why didn't you marry him?"

"He died."

She watches me with rigid concentration, not moving or blinking.

"The night he died was his father's birthday. There was a party at the house. I went with Evan. Close to midnight, Evan was called out on an emergency job. He was a plumber, you see. I decided to stay and wait for him, so I hung out with his younger brother, Benjamin. We were in the same class at university." I swallow, choosing my words carefully. I want to relay this as undramatically as possible. "Benjamin and I ended up sleeping together."

"You slept with your fiancé's brother?" she asks with disbelief.

"Yes."

"What did Evan do?"

"He said he needed to go out to cool down. I think he was afraid of hurting his brother. He was very angry when he left." My voice trembles at the recollection. "So angry he crashed his motorbike."

"That's how he died?"

"Yes."

"Wow. That's tough. I'm sorry, Mom."

"So am I. More than you can ever know."

"Then my biological father can be Evan or Benjamin."

"That's right."

"When did Dad come into the picture?"

"We got together two days after Evan's death. I was very sad, and Francois was there for me."

"Why didn't you tell me?"

"It's not a pretty history. For obvious reasons, both Francois and I tried hard to forget."

She studies her hands. "I'm sorry for what happened to you."

"I'm sorry for not telling you sooner. Before the divorce, it didn't seem worth upsetting your life. I'm even sorrier you had to find out the way you did."

"Dad knew?"

"Yes."

Her eyes brim with tears. "Who else knows that I was a mistake?"

I cup her cheek. "Oh, honey, you're not a mistake. You're the best thing that's happened to me."

"Who else except for Dorothy and Dad, Mom?"

"Only Loretta. We were best friends. I confided in no one else." She pales. "Do you think she told Jordan?"

"I don't know, but you have nothing to be ashamed of. I love you, and I'm proud of you. I'll never give you up for anything."

"Not even for Brian?"

"We're not seeing each other, any longer."

"You broke up with him?"

"Yes."

"Are you sad?"

"You come first, honey. Always. I love you so much." I add carefully, "Do you want to talk about Brian and you?"

"I already told Debs and Dad everything. I don't want to talk about it, anymore."

"Okay. We don't have to talk about it until you're ready."

"Has Benjamin agreed to a test?"

Thank God she can't see how every bone in my body is rattling. "I wanted to speak to you first."

"Will you ask him?"

"If that's what you want."

"It's what I want."

"Then I'll speak to him."

Nodding, she hops off the chair. "Can you please show me my room? I'm really tired. I'd like to rest."

Concern flares in my chest. "How's your eyes?"

"Fine. My vision doesn't blur any longer. It's just been a rough week."

"Of course. Come, I'll show you."

She calls for Dusty, who appears from under one of the armchairs.

She arrived with no bag, but most of her clothes are still with me, and I stocked the bathroom with everything she'll need.

Upstairs, I show her the two bedrooms and bathroom.

"This one is yours." I open the door to the sunny room. "Do you like it?"

"Yes," she says unenthusiastically. "Thank you."

"You're welcome."

"Can Dusty stay in my room?"

"Sure. Come down when you're hungry. I'll keep the food warm."

Closing the door, I give her the space she needs and take a moment to find my balance. I'm utterly grateful my baby is home, but a piece of my heart is missing. I've lost my joie de vivre, but all it takes to carry on is putting one foot in front of the other. I go back to the kitchen and finish the pie. Then I call Dorothy.

"How are you?" she asks.

"The test is negative."

"Dear God."

I give her a moment to digest the news. This is huge. She's a grandmother to someone other than Benjamin's son. She must've toyed with the idea as much as I have through the years, even if we never allowed ourselves to say it out loud. Maybe she respected my decision not to talk about it too much. Maybe she believed it was in Abby's best interest. Maybe she was scared, like me. Maybe she felt guilty.

"Is Abby back with you?"

"Yes."

"How's she taking the news about Francois?"

"Not well."

"Jane, I'm sorry."

"I'd like to speak with Benjamin, please."

She sucks in a breath. "I always knew it would come to this. I always hoped you'd find it in your heart to talk it over, but not like this."

I don't reply. What is there to say?

"I'll get him for you," she says with resignation.

When his voice comes on the line, I have to close my eyes at the repulsion pushing up in my chest.

"Hello, Jane."

"I need to see you."

"I know. Come over. I'm not leaving for rehearsal until six."

"Today? My daughter just got back. I was thinking next week." Abby can do with another week before we go through the next traumatic experience.

"Today."

The line goes dead.

My throat is dry. My heart is beating too fast. I fill a glass with water from the tap. I'm staring through the window as I down it, seeing nothing but the past. Facing Benjamin will be facing what happened. There's a good reason I've been avoiding him all these years. Not only will I have to face the awful truth, but also Evan's death all over again. The *reason* why he died. I don't realize how hard I'm gripping the counter until a nail breaks, tearing into the skin.

"Dammit." I open the tap and hold my bleeding nail under the stream of water.

"Are you okay?" Abby asks from the door.

I school my features before I turn back to her. "Yes. I just broke a nail. Are you ready for lunch?"

"I'll try to eat something."

"Good."

I dish up a hearty portion and set her a place at the table before filling Dusty's bowl with kibbles.

"Aren't you eating?" she asks.

"I had a big breakfast," I lie. The truth is I may vomit if I take one bite before facing Benjamin.

"Do you miss him?"

"What?"

"You're staring into space," Abby says. "Do you miss Brian?"

I cup her hand from across the table. "I have a lot on my mind, that's all. It's nothing to worry about."

Like finding a new job. Like settling in this house. Making a home of it. Like finding out who Abby's father is.

I can't take Abby with me to Dorothy's house, not when confronting Benjamin, and I'm not welcome at Loretta's. Asking Francois to look after Abby for the afternoon when he's just dropped her won't seem right. He'll really think I'm not a fit mother, but I don't have anyone else to turn to.

"I'm going to see Benjamin," I say.

She looks up from a forkful of food. "To ask him to take the test?"

"Yes. Do you mind staying with Debbie for a while?" I add, "If she agrees."

"Of course not. I'm sure she won't mind."

I pat her hand. "Eat up. I'll call her after lunch."

The locket I gave her for her birthday catches the light. I trace the engraving on the heart. "This suits you so well." Catching it between my fingers, I press on the mechanism to unlock it. The pendant falls open to reveals two miniature photos, perfectly aligned. Francois and Debbie.

What this does to me, I can't begin to describe. How could I have failed so badly when I love her so much? Where did I go wrong?

"Yes, it's pretty." She pulls it from my hand and closes it.

It's as if a needle twists under my nail. The pain of my own daughter's rejection is unbearable. Am I doing the right thing by keeping Abby? Is this the best for Abby or me?

Putting those questions away for later, I focus on what needs to be done today. One thing at a time. That's how we'll get through this.

. . .

DEBBIE AGREES READILY enough to let Abby stay for the afternoon when I explain where I'm going. Just before teatime, I stop at Dorothy's house. She meets me at the door with a hug.

"Come." She takes my arm. "He's in the study."

We walk down the hallway, our steps muffled by the familiar Persian carpet.

At the door, she pauses. "Would you like something to drink? Maybe a cup of tea?"

"Yes, please."

I don't want tea, but I sense Dorothy needs something to keep her busy. When she's making her way to the kitchen, I knock and enter.

Seeing Benjamin standing behind his late father's desk almost makes me stumble. It's like a punch in the stomach. He hasn't changed much, except for the grey hair creeping into his sideburns. He's dressed in a dark suit, holding a glass of amber liquid. His black hair is slicked back, and his face is still as smooth as candlewax. His slender frame is relaxed, but his green eyes are chilling. Cold. He's always been the opposite of Evan in everything. Evan was tanned, muscled, and good with his hands. His disposition was carefree and fun-loving. Benjamin is the silent, brooding, artistic one.

I close the door with a click, leaning against the wood for a moment to find my courage.

"I expected you," he says. "When Francois left you, I knew it would come to this."

"To what?"

"Pushing me into a corner when you no longer have a family to protect."

"This is for Abby. She wants to know. She has a right to know."

He puts the glass down on the desk. "It's not going to happen."

My fear and discomfort make way for anger. "I'm not asking."

He smiles. "Are you threatening me?"

"If you don't go willingly, I'll get a court order."

We stare at each for an immeasurable moment. We both know what getting a court order implies. I'll have to tell the truth of what happened that night. The world will know why Evan really died, that the fight I had with my fiancé as the newspapers reported was only a smokescreen. This is how far I'm willing to go for Abby. I'll even break my promise to Dorothy.

"You see," he picks up an envelope and rounds the desk, "I had the foresight to predict this exact moment." He pushes the envelope into my hands. His voice is eerily soft. *"It's not going to happen."*

"What is this?" Bribe money?

"Open it."

His smug look warns me not to, but I don't have a choice, not if want to know why he looks like he's just announced checkmate.

Lifting the flap, I pull out a stack of photos. They fan out in my hand, some dropping to the floor. At first, the images don't register. Slowly, the reality kicks me in the teeth.

*No.*

It's an image of me in sheer green lingerie, tied to my bed in the most compromising position. Nothing is spared. One breast is spilling over a bra cup, and the crotch of the panties is pulled aside. My most private parts are on display. My make-up is smeared, and my hair is a mess. I look fuck-ruffled and cock-whipped. A whore. There's no other word for it. Shame engulfs me. If I've been feeling sick earlier, I now feel like dying. Of all the people to see me like this, Benjamin is the worst. He saw me naked once, but the photo feels like the biggest violation of all. It leaves me more vulnerable, more shattered than the time he touched me, because he stole something that was special to me and defiled it. He stole every good impression I've had of Brian and disillusioned me. That's the hardest part to take. *That* and having him witness my mortification as realization washes over me.

Brian betrayed me.

I've been such a fool.

Even as my insides cringe and my heart slows to a painful thump, I refuse to show Benjamin what the image does to me. I flip through the rest of the photos. Each is of the same scene, of me with a different expression. Ecstasy. Screaming as I'm coming. My ass being spanked. Brian's cock is visible, but not his face. I force myself to go through the pictures, one by one. The most humiliating are the ones where I'm simultaneously being fucked by a vibrator and penis. Brian's penis. The blood drains from my head, leaving me lightheaded. I'm sick to my stomach. I can't breathe. I can't speak.

Anger laces every molecule in my body as I look back at him, anger and the worst kind of betrayal. A lover's betrayal. It feels as if my guts are being shredded. The fortuneteller's prediction crashes into my memory, as clear as yesterday. *A lover's betrayal. Be careful who you trust.*

"Where did you get this?" I ask, my voice steady despite how the rest of me trembles, already knowing the horrific answer and praying to God it isn't so.

His smile is mocking. "I think you know."

I bend to pick up the photos from the carpet, taking my time to collect each one and slipping them back into the envelope. Facing him with a calm I don't feel, I say, "Are you blackmailing me?"

"I have a family. I'm a world-famous musician. I'm not about to sacrifice my career for a scandal, or my wife and son for your daughter's ease of mind. If you get a court order or spill as much as a word about that night, these go public. I have more photos. I have films. I have you in every fuckable position possible. The world will see what a slut you are. You can say whatever you want about me, but *you* seduced *me*. We'll see who they believe."

Slipping the envelope into my bag, I turn for the door.

His words follow me out. "Have a nice life, Jane."

I don't go to the kitchen to tell Dorothy I'm leaving. I walk straight to my car and start the engine. I know where I have to go.

# 8

---

*Brian*

The Digital Media exam went as well as it could with everything that's turning in my head. I'll pass, but it won't be the A Toby wants. At least it was the last exam for the year. I can't stop thinking about Jane. I can't stop wanting or needing her. I can't focus on anything other than what she must be feeling and thinking. Life is a time bomb about to detonate. I'm doing a mental countdown, waiting for the cops to knock on my door and question me about Abby. That's all I can do. Wait. My hands are chopped off.

Life doesn't pause to give me time to deal with my shit. It goes on, and I do what must be done. After my exam, I pick up Sam from school. It's holiday. She's in high spirits, but I only feel despair. I make her a salad for lunch before driving her to her friend's house near the Hartebeespoort Dam with her new party clothes. They're going to do a dress rehearsal for tomorrow night's party to try out their hair and make-up. The drive to the dam takes a good hour. I'm not back in

Pretoria until four o'clock. It's already peak hour traffic due to the people who leave work early on a Friday, but I'm planning on putting in some extra time at the office to get my mind off my problems. I can't even think about my love life for the fear of going ape shit crazy.

It's wrong to take the chair behind Jane's desk. It's wrong to sit in her space. It's wrong that Abby accused me. How I met Jane is wrong. The why is the biggest wrong of all. I knew I was going to steal her from the moment I saw her photo. Everything is wrong, except that we're made for each other. We fit together so perfectly, I feel I've grown into the man I became just for her, for the moment we met. We were born for each other at the wrong time, two planets in an orbit we can't break. I'm out of solutions. There's no choice but to take the coming blow and wait it out until Jane is once more free. I'll wait however long it takes. Into forever and hell, no time or place is too long or far.

My head is swimming with dark thoughts and how to survive like a living dead man for the next ten years when my door opens, and a woman I've never seen before enters. She has a stylish hairdo, and her dress looks expensive. A yellow ostrich leather handbag matches her shoes. I judge her to be in her sixties, but she may be older. She's one of those well-preserved women whose age is hard to guess.

"Brian Michaels?"

Out of habit, I get to my feet. "That's right."

"Dorothy James. I'm a friend of Jane's."

The James stops me even before she gets to the friend part. "As in Evan James?"

She takes a seat without being invited. This woman has presence, and she's not afraid to call the shots. "I'm Evan's mother, yes, but I'm here to talk about Benjamin."

My gut turns inside-out. Not moving my gaze from hers lest I miss an important clue, something that'll tell me what the hell this is about, I lower myself into Jane's chair. I'm not saying anything.

There's no need to implicate myself until I know exactly how much *she* knows.

"I gather you care for Jane," she says. "At least, that's the impression she gave me."

Care is putting it lightly. I'd give my life for her. "You discussed me." It sounds angry, but I'm pleased I was important enough to Jane to have made me a topic of conversation with her friend.

"We spoke about you, yes. She loves you very much."

"I know." It's the one certainty that keeps me sane.

"If you care for her as much as the impression she gave me, you'll tell me if Benjamin bribed you to sleep with her."

I shoot like a rocket from my chair. "What?" How the fuck did she find out? I can't imagine the dandy confiding in his mother. And if she knows... My blood freezes. My voice is chilling to my own ears. "Does Jane know?"

Her expression turns pained, as if I'm a child who's greatly disappointed her. She reaches inside her bag and pushes an envelope toward me. "I found these today."

Picking up the envelope, I pray it's not what I think it is. I lift the flap and peer inside.

*Fuck. Jesus, no. Christ.*

The strength leaves my body. I sink back into the chair, taking the pack of glossy images out. "I assume you looked at these?" I flip through them with mounting fury.

"Not everything," she says modestly. "You need to tell me how much Benjamin paid you for those," she motions at the pictures in my hands, "and how you orchestrated the scam."

"Nothing," I grit out. "He paid me nothing, and there is no scam. What I feel for Jane is real."

"Tell me how you met Benjamin."

"I don't have to tell you anything." I'm not giving her ammunition to shoot me down before I've spoken to Jane.

"I don't think you realize what's at stake, Mr. Michaels."

164

"Enlighten me," I say, crumpling a photo of me fucking Jane from behind in my fist.

"I'm going to tell you a story about Jane, and I need you to hear me out to the end. From the moment Evan brought her home, she was like a daughter to me, only better. Daughter and friend. Evan met Jane via Benjamin, who was in Jane's class. Only a mother will know that both her sons were head over heels in love with the same girl. Benjamin never said it, but it showed in the subtle ways he hurt Evan from the time Evan started dating Jane. He felt Evan stole her from him. Their engagement made Benjamin crazy. He was enraged. On the day Evan announced it, Benjamin smashed every glass in the kitchen. Jane and Evan weren't there to witness the violent display, and I didn't want to spoil the little of the relationship left between my sons, so I cleaned it up and said nothing."

This is news. I reel as an insight hits me. Benjamin's revenge was born from jealousy, not from concern for his brother.

"On my husband's sixtieth birthday," she continues, "we had a party at the house. Evan got called out to an emergency plumbing job, and Jane decided to wait for him. I didn't want her to go back to the dorm where she stayed on campus so late at night, so I told her to sleep over. I was occupied with our guests, and Jane hung out with Benjamin. He offered her a drink, only..." She looks toward the window with the view, staring at it for a couple of seconds as if she's searching for something, maybe her courage, before she faces me again. "It was drugged."

My veins ice over. I can't speak for the fear of breaking the confession, and I've got to hear what happened. I need to know if I'm going to murder Benjamin in cold blood.

"Evan got back in the early morning hours. We'd all gone to bed, already. I presumed Jane had retired to the guest bedroom."

Premonition fills my gut. I will her not to say it, but I know what's coming.

"Evan found Jane in Benjamin's bed. To say he was furious is an understatement. The argument woke up the whole house. When my husband and I got to Benjamin's room, Evan was punching him so hard I thought he was going to kill him. My husband had to drag him off his brother. Evan didn't stop until Benjamin admitted the truth. He'd drugged Jane and slept with her in a jealous fit."

I feel Evan's rage. It's coursing through my body, defrosting the ice in my veins and turning my blood to boiling. I'll finish what Evan didn't, breaking that coward's neck.

She gives a sad shake of her head. "I don't know if Benjamin did it to spite Evan or because he didn't want Evan to have her if he couldn't. Maybe he thought in his warped state of mind he'd convince her there was an attraction between them. Whatever the case, the damage was done. Evan said he needed to get out of there to clear his head, or he'd kill Benjamin. We were all so focused on the fight between Evan and Benjamin, we forgot about the real victim. Jane. I'll never forget that picture, how she sat motionless in bed, clutching a sheet to her naked chest. She said she couldn't remember anything."

My hands shake under the desk. I have to wring them together not to punch something.

"My husband took Benjamin to clean up the blood and bruises while I took care of Jane. Evan and Jane had been dating for a while. She was on birth control, so I wasn't worried about pregnancy. I..." She blinks several times. "I begged her not to lay charges. The implications... I said the beating Benjamin had taken had been enough of a punishment. Jane was more preoccupied with Evan than justice. We waited for hours for him to return, but it was a police officer who knocked on the door." Her expression is haunted. "The rest you can guess. I had lost one son. I wasn't prepared to lose both. I asked Jane not to go to the police. Instead, she took the blame. She said they had a fight before Evan left in a fury, and the media jumped on the opportunity to brand her as the scapegoat for getting her fiancé killed. She loved Evan too much to let Benjamin's sins soil his name. She loved me enough to let me keep a son who did something unspeakable to her and his brother. Not a day goes by that I don't feel the weight of that guilt on my shoulders."

"If you feel so guilty," I snarl, "why didn't you tell the truth?"

"Jane was devastated when we got the awful news. The doctor had to give her tranquilizers to calm her. I was busy with the funeral arrangements. My husband and I didn't want to drag it out, we just wanted it over. Jane went back to the dorm. Francois was a student at the same university Jane attended. When she was at her most vulnerable, he took advantage. Four weeks later, Jane discovered she was pregnant."

My breath slams into my ribs as the meaning penetrates my mind.

"The doctor said the tranquilizers probably interfered with the oral birth control. In cases of severe emotional shock, it's also not unknown for oral contraceptives to be ineffective. It was the last thing we expected. She decided to keep the baby, and Francois married her. She dropped out of university to have Abby, and to pay the bills when Francois was still studying. Babies are expensive, and she was too proud to accept my help. She said it would've felt like a bribe."

My tongue is tied. I can't wrap my head around the facts that are spinning around my brain faster than a spindle. Swallowing to wet my dry throat, I force out the question burning foremost in my mind. "Who's Abby's father?"

"It's not Francois. He did a test and got the results this morning."

Comprehension dawns. "It's Evan or Benjamin."

"When Abby made accusations about you, Francois wanted to sue for full custody. Jane will always fight tooth and nail for her daughter. No sacrifice is big enough. That's why she insisted Francois took a paternity test. I was with her when she confronted him. Abby overheard the conversation and demanded to know who her biological father is. Jane came to the house to ask

Benjamin for a paternity test. By law, she can't force him to take one, unless she tells the truth about what happened."

"He's using the photos to blackmail her into keeping her mouth shut."

"He's trying to protect his family and career."

My anger escalates again. I'm on the verge of exploding. "Are you protecting him?"

"Not any longer. Not when I found these." She points at the damnable photos. "I was making tea, and when I got back, Jane was gone. It's not like her to pick up and leave like that. I knew something was wrong. I threatened Benjamin with telling the truth myself until he showed me the photos and told me what he'd done. My son knows me. I don't make threats lightly. That's why I'm going to ask you one last time what Benjamin paid you to get these photos. I'll double the offer, and then I need you to destroy each and every one, or I swear to God I'll destroy *you*."

Jesus Christ. Jane thinks I betrayed her. In a way, I did, but not like she thinks. "I told you. He paid me nothing. He made an offer, but I didn't accept. Meeting Jane was a consequence of that offer, but that's where it ended."

"Then how do you explain the photos?"

"I can't, but I will. I'll find out, if it's the last thing I do." I jump up and push the envelope into the back of my waistband. "Where's Jane? I need to speak to her. I need to explain." Urgency runs through my blood. I need to get to Jane.

"I don't know. I was hoping you would."

"I'll find her," I say as I rush past her.

She grips my arm. "She's in a fragile state. You have no idea how much Jane has lost in the short span of a few months. Her husband, her home, her daughter, her job, her best friend..."

"Loretta?"

"With the charges Francois wants to lay against you, Loretta and Ralph decided they couldn't be associated with Jane."

Those fuckers. The jealous bastards weren't Jane's friends, anyway. No loss there, if you ask me.

"Do you have feelings for her?" Dorothy asks. "And you better not lie to me."

"Yes." The word is heavy. Final.

Slowly, she releases her hold. "I don't know why, but I believe you. Maybe it's because you erased the pain Evan left. Will you call me when you find her?"

"Give me your number."

I program her number in my phone and call my mom to ask if Jane had gone looking for me at the house. From how I know her, she'd want answers, and then she'd kick my balls in.

There's no time to waste. I'll find Jane. I'll explain. I'll beg. Then I'll deal with Benjamin James. I made him a promise, and I don't break my promises.

---

## Jane

DEBBIE'S EXPRESSION is shocked when she opens the door. I don't know if it's my face or how I push past her into the house without waiting to be invited, but she backs away, her eyes huge.

"Abby fell asleep in front of the television."

"I'm not here for Abby. Not yet." I walk down the hallway to the master bedroom.

She runs after me. "Where are you going?"

I jerk open the door and assess the space.

"Francois' playing golf," she says, her voice alarmed.

"I'm not looking for Francois."

From the angle of the photos, they were taken facing the bed. I scan the wall. There's a painting, a dresser with a vase, and an air vent. Dragging the chair from the dresser against the wall, I climb on top for a better view. Sure as hell, there's a red light in the ventilation hole. Son of a bitch. The security equipment. Brian installed it all. He had keys to the house. He knew the code to the alarm. I let the hurt convert to anger. Right now, anger will get me farther, or I'll curl up in a ball of agony.

"Jane, what are you doing?"

"I'll be back for Abby later."

I walk out of the house and get back into my car. The keys rattle in my hand when I turn the ignition. My phone rings. I glance at the screen.

Brian.

Rejecting the call, I drive to his house. I hope he isn't there.

Jasmine opens the door, clearly surprised to see me.

"Where's Sam?" I ask cautiously. I don't want her to witness this.

"At a friend's house."

"Is Brian in the cellar?"

"He's at work."

I hold out my palm. "Give me the keys to the cellar."

"What do you–?"

"You heard me. The keys. Now."

I practically bulldoze her to the kitchen. Too flabbergasted to protest, she takes a set of keys from a hook on the wall and hands them to me.

"Thank you."

Leaving through the back door, I half-run, half-stumble to the cellar. I lift the heavy trap door and let it fall open with a thud. Unlocking the grid, I flick on the light and let myself down the stairs. I'm shivering with cold rage. I start with the books neatly stacked on the shelf, knocking them all down. I feel under the shelf and behind the flat screen mounted on the wall. I rip the cushions from the sofa and turn the sofa upside-down. I scatter the electronic equipment organized in boxes over the floor. I don't know what I'm looking for, but if there's evidence that Brian did something too unspeakable to voice, I'll find it.

I grab the remote and push on every button, switching on the television and flipping only the legal cable stations. I open Brian's laptop, but it's locked with a password. I try everything from Sam's name to his birthdate, and finally my own, but nothing works. He's got a camera feed on me. I know it. I feel it in my gut.

Gritting my teeth in frustration, I give up on the electronics and start looking for photos. I pick up every fallen book and fan the pages. Nothing. My gaze falls on the book on the coffee table, the one he last used for studying. Expecting to find the same–nothing–I stretch the spine and shake it upside-down. Something falls from the back, fluttering to the floor. Dropping the book, I snatch up the picture, and then I freeze.

My stomach drops. My shoulders shake. I clamp a hand over my mouth. It's a photo of me at a product launch. I know, because I've only worn that dress for that one event and never after. I know, because I'm standing outside the exhibition hall we rented. It was exactly one month *before* I met Brian.

The photo trembles in my hand as I stare at it, willing it not to be, but it's real. The evidence is incriminating. It's devastating.

"Jane!"

I jerk my head up toward the door. Brian's face hovers over the hole. His gaze flitters over the destruction around me, and then zones in on my face. His expression is guarded, which tells me everything the photo has already told me.

Slowly, he descends, as if he's stalking a bird that can fly away at any moment. He doesn't speak. He stops in front of me, every muscle locked tight, and waits. No apology. No admittance. He's waiting for me to make the first move.

I fist my hands at my sides. I don't want to show him how much he's hurt me, but I can't keep the agony from sounding in my voice. "You lied to me."

The familiarity of his intense gaze as it bores into mine kills me.

"I never lied to you, princess."

"Don't you dare call me that."

"I never lied to you, Jane."

"No? Then answer my question. Tell me the truth. I don't want explanations, only yes or no. Did you plant cameras in my house?"

"Only for security."

"I said yes or no," I grit out. I don't want excuses or justifications. I just want the naked truth, cut down to the bone.

He clenches his jaw. "Yes."

I let the truth slice me, allow the pain to sink in and burn. I need this if I'm to sever him from my life. It's like cutting off my arm, but I'd rather live without him than with lies.

Steeling myself, I ask on a whisper, "Did you film me?"

His jaw moves from side to side. A muscle ticks above the joint. "Yes."

"Show me."

"Jane–"

"Show me."

I want the full lash of the betrayal. I don't want him to spare me. It needs to ache enough to set me free from him.

With a slump in his shoulders, he types a password on his keyboard, letting me see it. An image of me cooking in the kitchen flicks to life on the screen. It's from not so long ago, when I was preparing the cottage pie. He pushes a button on the television remote and the same image fills the big screen. There's no sound, only the sickening clear color movie of stolen moments.

"Was swimming in my pool by accident?"

"No," he says, his face tight.

Damn, it hurts hearing him admit it was a set-up all along. I take the envelope from my bag and empty it on the coffee table. "Did you give Benjamin these?"

His nostrils flare. "No."

"Do you work for Benjamin?"

"No, dammit."

I push the photo I found in the book in his face. "Then explain this."

"He gave it to me."

"Did he offer you money?"

"Yes."

"How much?"

"I didn't take it."

"How much, Brian?"

He remains stubbornly silent.

"Why, Brian? Why you? Are you a gigolo?" My laugh is wry. "Boy, you sure had me fooled."

"It's real, Jane. Every second of it."

"Everything is a lie! *Us* is a lie."

"We're real."

"Don't you dare lie to me."

He reaches for me. "I know it's hard for you to trust me right now, but you have to let me explain."

I backtrack before he can touch me. "I don't have to listen to anything. Did you know he was going to blackmail me?"

"He told me it was revenge."

"For what?"

A pained look filters into his eyes. "For cheating on his brother."

"God." I let the soft laugh of hysteria escape. What a work of art. Revenging *my* cheating with *him* on Evan. "Is that what your scam was all about? Revenge? I suppose you had it all planned–the raunchy sex, the cottage in the middle of snake valley, my job, my *daughter?*"

"Don't." His eyes turn hard. "I know you're hurting, but don't accuse me of things I'd never do to you."

"I'm done." I pick up my bag and throw the strap over my shoulder.

He grabs my wrist as I pass. "We're going to talk about this. We have an agreement, Jane. We said we'd always talk."

"There's nothing left to talk about."

"I'm not giving you a choice."

"I do have a choice. It's walking out that door."

His phone rings with the ringtone he uses for Sam.

"Fuck."

I'm trying to twist out of his grip, but he doesn't release me as he fishes his phone from his pocket and answers. He listens in strained silence, uttering a string of swear words before saying, "Stay where you are. I'm coming for you."

I jerk on his hold. "Let me go."

"So that you can walk away?"

"I don't ever want to see you again. When I walk through that door, we're done. Do you hear me? You don't come near me again. I'll get the restraining order Francois wanted."

Something like desperation filters into his eyes. Where the brown-amber hue always seemed warm, it now glitters cold. "I'm sorry." Regret infuses his tone. "There's too much at stake to simply let you go. I love you too much."

"Don't you dare say that to me!"

Not letting go, he uses one hand to flip the sofa upright.

"What are you doing?" I shriek when he pushes me down on the sofa, restraining me with the weight of his body.

Locking his fingers around my wrists, he lifts my arms above my head and slams something around them. It locks with a soft click. I jerk my face up. I'm restrained in broad leather cuffs that are fixed to the wall.

"I had something more kinky in mind when I installed these." He plucks on the cuffs, testing their hold, and runs a finger along the inside of one. "Not too tight, but you won't be able to pull your hands free, so don't try. I don't want you to chafe your skin."

"You're insane." I try to knee him, but his weight is as effective a constraint as the cuffs.

"Where you're concerned, I guess I am."

Running his palms down my arms, he pushes to his feet, easily avoiding the kick I'm aiming at his knee.

"Release me, Brian."

"I'm going to get Sam." He picks up the throw from the floor and drapes it over my legs. "I'll be back in two hours."

"You can't leave me like this."

He's already backing up to the stairs. "I'm not letting you go before we've talked."

"Brian, please." He won't don't it. It's a sick joke.

"Try to relax," he instructs sternly. "If it gets too claustrophobic, focus on your breathing. You're going to be fine."

"I beg you, don't."

"Sorry, princess."

"Brian," I scream in anger.

"I'll leave the hatch open for air."

"Brian, come back," I yell as he climbs up the stairs.

My begging is to no avail. He drops the security gate in place and locks it.

It seems as if his voice comes from far, as if I'm Alice in the rabbit hole and he's already light-years away. "I'm locking you in so no one can get to you. You'll be safe."

"If you're locking me in you can free my hands." I'm close to sobbing, but keeping it in. I won't show him how scared I am. What he's doing is only making matters worse. Being held against my will adds to my humiliation and pain.

"I can't risk you calling someone, and I don't have time to remove every electronic device down there. I'll be back before dark."

His face disappears from my vision.

He did it.

He's keeping me against my will.

## Brian

SHIT. *Shit.*

Of all the days in the year, Sam's so-called friends had to pull a stunt on her today. I'll wring those little bitches' necks when I get there. I set the phone on hands-free and dial Sam's number. She's still crying.

"How are you holding up, piglet?"

"I–I just want to come home." She hiccups.

"I'm on my way. Put Lynette's mom on the phone."

"Hold on."

There's a lot of sniffling going on before a woman replies.

"Mr. Michaels? I'm so sorry. I had no idea what Lynette and her friends were up to. Rest assured, they're all grounded, and the party is off."

I should fucking hope so. "How bad is it?"

"I'm afraid Sam's clothes and hair are ruined. My husband and I are washing the paint off her legs and arms with turpentine now, but I'm afraid..." Her voice is small. "I'm afraid she'll have to cut her hair. It's a strong oil-based paint we used for the exterior of the house. I called my doctor, just in case, but he said unless she has a skin reaction there's nothing to be worried about. We'll pay for the hairdresser and to replace the clothes, of course."

"Money is the least of your problems," I grit out. I dodge a truck that skips lanes. "Where were you when it happened? Why weren't you supervising them?"

"It happened outside, in the shed. I can't apologize enough."

"Try apologizing to Sam. This party meant the world to her."

"I know," she says softly. "Again, I'm sorry. I wish I could make it up to her."

"Just tell her I'll be there in an hour, and don't take your eyes off my sister. I don't trust your daughter."

"Of course," she whispers.

I end the call and grip the wheel hard. All I can do for Sam is give her a lecture about true friends and the nasty people of this world. It won't be the last time. Like bullies, nasty people are everywhere, no matter how old you get. There will always be the Benjamins and the *friends* like Loretta who turn their back on you in your hour of need.

As I approach the tunnel just before the dam, a drop of water explodes on my windscreen. I glance up at the sky. Thick clouds are milling overhead. Darker ones are threatening in the distance.

"Shit."

It looks like heavy rain is on the way. I'm already in a long line of cars in the single, one-way lane, waiting at the traffic light to traverse the tunnel. As there's only one lane, it's interchanging. We have to wait for the traffic from the other side to cross and the light to go green before it's our turn. More drops splash on the windscreen and windows. I switch on the wipers and turn on a local radio station that broadcasts weather and traffic updates.

In the space of three seconds, the heavens open up, and the water comes down in torrents. The sun is gone, and the day turns dark. Lightning flashes menacingly. A spectacular electric storm erupts across the sky. Flashes of light run vertically, horizontally, and in every other direction while the lashes of sound follow a moment later.

It looks like the storm is moving toward the west. *Jesus, fuck.* I go colder than a hail storm. If the storm hits Pretoria West, the cellar is bound to be flooded. I need to get through this tunnel and find a place on the other end of the narrow mountain road where I can make a U-turn, but I'm helplessly stuck in traffic.

The light switches just as the announcement comes over the radio. Cloud-burst and it's heading west.

My heart kicks into over-drive. "Come on. Come on."

I will the cars to move faster, but we're driving at a snail's pace. *Please, God.*

Another few hundred meters and we come to a complete stop. At this pace, I'll never make it. Yanking my phone from the console, I check the screen. No bars. There's no reception in the tunnel.

Drumming my fingers and tapping my foot, I wait it out for another few minutes. It's taking too long. We're not moving. I pull onto the shoulder of the road, leaving enough space for cars to pass, cut the engine, and pocket the key. There are too many car thieves around to leave it in the ignition. Running along the side for the exit, I go forward instead of backward, as there's no way to turn around. If I'm going to go back where I came from, I need to catch a lift from the opposite side of the tunnel.

The air inside is excruciating hot due to poor ventilation. It smells of coal and smoke. The sounds from the outside are muffled, but I can hear the assault of the rain like a distant drumming. The tunnel is long. Despite the storm, my skin and lungs are on fire. I exit at full speed, sweat dripping down my face. Rain pelts my face and arms. It stings. Water washes down my back and soak my shoes. I'm drenched in a second flat.

I tap on a car window. The driver wounds it down a fraction.

"What's going on?" I ask, blinking drops of water from my eyes.

"A truck jackknifed in front of the zoo entrance," the man says. "It's the rain. The road is flooded. The tires can't grip in this much water. Traffic report says it's going to take a while to clear."

Mumbling thanks, I rush farther up the road, combatting the full force of the storm.

God help me, if I don't get to Jane, she's dead. The cellar will be under water in no time. With all the gutters and ditches running to the hole that sits in the lowest point of the lawn, I give it no more than an hour. I'll be lucky if I make it back in time.

Adrenalin bursts through my body, compelling me forward. I'm like a wild animal. A short way up ahead, there's a kiosk with a covered picnic area. I run for my life. For Jane's life. Under the protection of the roof, I yank my phone from my pocket and dial Eugene, praying he's at home. The phone goes straight onto voicemail. Shit. I dial Albert. No connection. We have a bad network service out west, and whenever it's raining it's almost non-existent.

Uttering curse after curse, I try Clive as a last resort. At least he answers.

"Where are you?" I shout over the rain.

"Fishing with my uncle at the Vaal River. Where the fuck are you?"

Shit. Shit. I cut the call. There's no time to explain. I scroll to Dorothy's name and hit enter.

"Did you find Jane?" she asks.

"Where are you?"

"Germiston."

"Germiston?"

"I'm just about to go into court."

"Court?"

"I'm a graphology expert witness for a fraud case."

She won't make it, either. It'll take her more than an hour to drive to Pretoria, and who knows how long she'll be in court?

"I need a favor. My sister, can you pick her up from the Hartebeespoort Dam? It'll take a while. The road's blocked due to an accident. You may have to follow the traffic broadcasts to know when it's been cleared."

"I heard about the storm on the radio. It's pissing down cats and dogs here, too. What's going on?"

"I'll explain later. I'm going to get Jane. Just tell me if you can pick up my sister. I wouldn't have asked if it weren't important."

"All right."

"I'll send you the address and a telephone number. She's with friends. Tell the mother I had an emergency, and I'll speak to her later."

My fingers shake on the screen as I send Dorothy Sam's number and the address where she is. Then I dial my mother.

"What's going on, Brian? Jane was in a state this afternoon. She took the keys to the cellar."

"Mom, listen to me. Jane's in the cellar."

"What?"

"Jane's in the cellar. The hatch is open. It's going to flood. You have to go outside and close it." At least Jane will have enough air to breathe until I get back.

"No, no, no. Brian, no. Why doesn't she just come out?"

"The security gate is locked, and she's handcuffed to the wall. I've got the only keys."

"Brian." Her voice starts to tremble. "What have you done?"

"Mom, please. I need you. I've never asked you for anything. I just need this one thing from you. Please."

"Brian, I can't. I can't. I can't."

"She's going to die in there." My own voice quakes with tears. "It's easy. Close your eyes. Visualize it. You're going to pull on your raincoat and walk outside. See it in your mind, how effortless it is. You're going to walk down the steps, cross the yard, and close the hatch. That's it. There's nothing to it."

"I don't know," she keens.

"For me. I'll never ask anything of you again."

"I can't."

"Of course, you can. You're a strong woman. You can do anything you set your mind to."

She starts crying harder. "Please, Brian."

"Don't cry, Mom. Come on. Show me how strong you are. Please don't let Jane die. You can stop it."

"All right." She drags in a shaky breath. "All right. I can do it."

"That's better. Of course, you can."

"All right. I can do it."

"Go, Mom. I'll be home as soon as I can."

I cut the call, hoping and praying and dying with every breath of air I take, knowing Jane may not have the luxury of breathing for long.

Having taken care of the phone calls, I scan the area. A group of bikers are sheltered under the roof, waiting for the storm to pass. I rush over to the first guy.

"I need to borrow your bike."

He looks me up and down and laughs. "Yeah, right." Turning his back on me, he continues his conversation with his friend.

I look around. There's a curio shop on the opposite side of the road with a bank teller sign in the window.

"I'll give you ten thousand." That's my Christmas bonus and Sam's private school fees. It's everything I've got.

Slowly, he faces me again. "Are you fooling with me?"

"It's an emergency." I point at the curio store. "There's an ATM in the shop. We can withdraw the money now."

"If this is some hoax to attack me when you've got me alone, you'll die slowly and painfully."

"It's no hoax."

He pulls away his leather jacket to show me a pistol in a body holster. "It better not be."

We cross the street and enter the shop. At the cash dispenser, I insert my card, letting him see my secret code. My withdrawal limit is two thousand. I hand him the stack of bills as well as my card and the receipt with my balance.

"You've seen my code. You can withdraw two thousand every day. Give me your address and I'll return your bike as soon as I can."

He takes the cash and card. "You're for fucking real?"

Taking out my phone, I hand it over. "Put your number in. I'll call to get your address."

"Okay, bro," he says with a small shake of his head. "But that bike ain't worth ten grand if you're thinking of stealing it."

"I'm not."

"You can't go out in this weather. Gotta wait it out. Roads are too slippery. The mountain road is dangerous on the descent."

"I don't have a choice."

He pockets the money. "Your call, man."

After he's given me his number and the keys for the bike, I take off like a maniac. I go against the static traffic in the tunnel on the shoulder of the single road, racing home in the pouring rain and thunder for all I'm worth.

---

## Jane

THE SKY IS GRUMBLING and dark. I yank on my constraints one time too many. My skin is raw where the leather has chaffed it. I've twisted my wrists in every direction, but it's no use. The cuffs are a tight fit. My arms are aching from being bound above my head. My back cramps from the awkward position. I shift again. The throw drops to the floor. My legs break out in goose bumps from the cool air. The temperature has dropped since the clouds started building.

Images of me play over and over on the television screen. They come from the feeds on Brian's laptop. Thankfully, there's none from the bathroom, but enough of me stripping in the bedroom. As long as the evidence unrolls in front of me, anger keeps me afloat. I haven't given in to my tears. I'm determined not to. I won't show weakness.

According to the time on his laptop, it's been almost an hour since Brian left. I've had a lot of time to think. I've been gullible, naïve, and foolish to fall for a man like Brian. I should've known. Still, how can something so perfect not be real? What we shared must have meant *something*. It has to. If our so-called relationship was nothing but acting, it will destroy the little that's left of me. I'll have nothing to take away with me. No true memories.

Something wet splashes on my cheek and knee. Raindrops. I look up just as the rain starts pouring. It's like taking a bucket of icy water in the face. Gasping for breath, I try to shake the water from my eyes. I have an incredible urge to wipe my face. The helplessness of my situation only makes it worse. The best I can do is wipe my face on my arms.

In a matter of seconds, I'm soaked. Darn it. It's a cloud-burst. These summer storms habitually last a couple of hours. If I'm lucky, it'll be over soon, but the rate with which the floor fills with water alarms me. It must be at least a centimeter deep, already.

Without warning, a small waterfall gushes down the stairs. Another flow erupts from the other side of the trapdoor until a ring of water is pouring steadily and way too fast into the room. My breath hitches on a gasp. The water is running toward the lowest point, and I'm at the bottom of it.

The power. I don't want to risk being electrocuted. The plug point is to the right of the sofa. I can just reach it with my foot if I stretch my arms and legs. I cry out in pain as the cuffs eat into my skin. Thank God I'm wearing flat heels. It takes several kicks before I finally manage to knock the plug out of the wall. The cellar goes dark. Only the deafening downpour and the lash of thunder remain.

Pens and notepads start drifting in the water. The books I've strewn over the floor rise to the surface, only to sink again as they absorb the water. Soon, the water is at the cushion level of the sofa. My shoes come off and float away. How fast can a small room like this fill up? A hysterical laugh bubbles from my throat. As soon as it's out, it's as if the cork on my panic pops.

I'm going to die in here.

"Help!"

I scream my throat raw, knowing damn well no one can hear me above the rain and this far out in the garden. When the water rises to my waist, I start crying shamefully. It's not for my life that I'm mourning. It's for Abby. I may never see her sweet face again.

The raindrops come down so hard now I have to close my eyes to the sting. It hurts my skin. I'm cold to my core. Shivers wrack my body. The water teases the collar of my dress. I'm kicking with my legs to say warm, but eventually I'm too exhausted. When the water reaches my chin, my lower body rises involuntarily. For a while I manage to float on my back, but then I rise above my arms and the water rushes into my nose. I kick down, choking and coughing. I want to look up and see something, anything, but there's only water and more water. I tilt my head back, keeping my nose as high as I can, until my mouth is underwater. I'm not making it out. With all the fight left in me, I drag in one last breath.

# 9

*Brian*

That I make it back to the house alive is a miracle. I leave the bike in the street and jump the gate, not wasting time opening it. The sight in front of me rocks me to my core. My mother is sitting on the top step of the back porch in her pajamas, rocking back and forth.

She didn't do it. Fuck, no! She didn't close the hatch.

I sprint like a possessed man. I don't feel the drops battering my body or the wetness of the clothes clinging to my skin. I'm only aware of the water running in ditches toward the hole in the ground. I stumble over a tuft of grass and go down, face first. For the few remaining meters, I drag my body through the mud, in too much of a frenzy to even get up. When I reach the grid and peer down, my world comes to an end. Jane's head is under water. Books are drifting around and over her. I can't see her face. I can't fucking see her face.

I dig the keys out of my pocket, my fingers shaking almost too much to unlock the grid. Throwing back the grid, I shout to my mother, "Call an ambulance."

It's dark down there. I bite the waterproof utility flashlight on my keychain between my teeth and jump straight down. Something sharp hits my shin, but I'm only vaguely aware of the pain and red color that tints the water. Holding my breath, I keep my eyes open in the freezing water. In the light from the torch, Jane's face stares back at me, pale and lifeless. Her blue eyes are open, and her lips are the same shade. It's angelic and terrifying. Gripping her face, I pinch her nose shut and part her lips with mine to blow air into her mouth. Nothing. Not even a flutter of her eyelashes. I work fast to unlock the cuffs. Her body floats up as her arms fall free. Cradling her to me, I dip her head back and blow more air through her lips while treading water. My brain takes over, fighting my heart not to fall apart. I refuse to give up. I haul her over my shoulder and drag us both up the stairs and onto wet soil. My actions are mechanic. I did a first-aid course in school. I know how to do mouth to mouth. I pump her chest with the heels of my palms and blow air into her lungs, over and over.

"Come on."

*If there's a God, take me, but not her.*

Pump, pump. Blow. Pump, pump. Blow.

Nothing.

"Come on, Jane. You're not giving up on me. I'm not letting you go."

Pump, pump. Blow.

A gurgle. A cough.

She gasps and chokes. A river of water tumbles from her lips.

*Thank God. Thank you. Thank you.*

Turning her on her side, I let her empty her stomach and clear her lungs. She'd swallowed shitloads of water. My hands are all over her. I need to be sure she's all right. Alive. Her skin is so cold. So white. She's convulsing and shivering. Her breath is ragged, as if she can't get enough oxygen. Rubbing my hands over her arms, I drag her to my chest.

My tears mix with the rain that washes over her face. "I'm sorry. I never meant for you to get hurt." I mean that on so many levels. "I love you." I kiss her icy lips, rocking her in my arms. "I love you."

She's covered in mud and exposed to not only the rain, but also the lightning that rips through the sky. I have to get her inside. I have to get her out of these soaked clothes and warm. A siren blares in the distance, fast gaining in volume, but I'm oblivious to anything but the woman in my arms, the woman who almost died because of me.

I stumble to my feet, keeping her limp body hugged to mine. The safety of the house is only a few meters away, but it feels too far. An ambulance stops in front of the gate. Two paramedics in raincoats pushing a stretcher open the gate and rush our way. Even as one of the men reaches for her, I take a step back. It's an instinctive reaction. I can't let her go.

"Sir," the man says, holding out his arms, "we're going to help her."

There's an urgency in his tone that makes me look down at her beautiful face. Her head is tilted back at a strange angle. Her eyes are closed. My princess. Ruined.

When they reach for her again, I don't resist. Letting her go is like cutting my heart out with a nail clipper.

"Unconscious," the one man says to the other as they lower her onto the stretcher.

"Pulse weak," the other replies.

The first is covering her with a thermal heat blanket. "Sir, what kind of injury did she sustain?"

I can't tear my gaze away from Jane. "Drowning." When they both give me questioning looks, I point to the cellar. "She was stuck in there. It got flooded."

They're running back toward the ambulance with me jogging next to the stretcher.

"How long has she been under the water?"

"I don't know. When I got here she was already under."

"How long ago did you get here?"

"Ten minutes. Fifteen?" It feels like forever.

"Her name?"

"Jane Logan."

They open the back and lift the stretcher inside.

"Oxygen. Monitor her vitals."

"Hypothermia. Cardiogenic shock. Risk of brain damage. Sending it through to the hospital now."

I make to climb in, but one of the men pushes me back. "Are you related?"

"No."

"Sorry, sir. You'll have to meet us at the emergency unit. Hospital policy."

"Where are you taking her?"

"Pretoria West."

"Will she be all right?"

"We're going to do everything we can."

The guy who pushed me adopts a sympathetic demeanor. "It's a good idea to inform her next of kin."

The other medic bangs his fist twice on the window that separates them from the front. "Good to go."

The doors close, and the vehicle takes off. For a moment, I'm frozen to the spot, and then the five million implications of the situation punch me in the gut, but only one brings me to my knees.

I can still lose her. I might have still killed her.

A classmate's brother survived a near drowning only to die twenty-four hours later of complications. I know the risks. I'm standing on my knees in the road, not sure if I'm praying, crying, or dying. Maybe all three. I hate myself so fucking much. I should've never touched Jane. I should've never given in to my sick obsession. If I'd left her alone, none of this would've happened. If I'd let her walk away, she wouldn't be in the back of an ambulance, fighting for her life. I'm no good for her. I'm worse than scum. She deserves a million times better.

It takes everything I've got and more to drag myself to my feet. I have to call her next of kin. Francois and Abby. Dorothy. The walk back to the house is the longest I've made in my life.

My mother is whining and still rocking herself on the step when I climb the stairs.

"I'm sorry, Brian."

I place a hand on her shoulder and squeeze. "It's not your fault. It's all mine."

I'm dead inside when I walk into the house. It's over. Something died in that water today. From the deepest place in my gut, I know I can never have it back. A piece of Jane is gone to me. A piece of me is gone to myself. Our love drowned. It wasn't strong enough to withstand the onslaught of my lies. My deceit. Maybe everyone was right. Maybe our love never stood a chance.

---

*Jane*

MY CHEST and throat hurt as if a truck has driven over me. I feel bruised inside. The skin where the cuffs chaffed it is raw. Every muscle is stiff, as if I'd exerted tremendous physical effort.

Dorothy is the first to enter the hospital room. "Oh, Jane." Her eyes fill with tears as she grabs my hand between hers and falls down in the chair next to the bed. "What happened to you?"

"The doctor says I'll be fine." My voice croaks like a frog's. "I was lucky."

"What happened?" she repeats.

I don't want to talk about it. Not with her. Not with anyone. "Abby?"

"They're on their way. Do you need something? Can I get you anything?"

"Thanks, but I'm all right. If all the tests come back normal, I can go home tomorrow."

"Tests?"

"They ran renal function tests. The ABG levels and ECG are normal, and the chest radiography looks good. There's no evidence of pulmonary edema."

"Oh, my God." She presses my hand to her lips. "I hope there's no permanent damage."

The worst damage can't be detected by medical tests. It's the kind that is both permanent and irreversible. It hurts my heart more to think about Brian than the physical pain in my body.

"When Brian called to tell me you're in hospital, he said you were locked in a cellar that got flooded. Did he lock you in there?"

"Dorothy, please. I don't want to talk about it."

"You can tell me. I know about the photos."

"What?" I say with a gasp.

"This isn't the best time to bring it up, but we have little time. They'd only let me see you for ten minutes. I know what Benjamin did. I confronted Brian."

"You did what?" A flash of pain bursts through my head at the sudden outburst.

"He said he didn't do it."

"You believe him?"

"Don't you?"

All evidence points to him. He gave me the answers I wanted. He did what he did.

"When I left Brian this afternoon, he was going looking for you. What happened, Jane? Please talk to me. I need to know if Brian did this to you, because if he did, he's going down. I swear that to you."

I sigh, feeling it in every aching muscle. "I went to look for proof that Brian secretly filmed me. Brian found me in his cellar.

He wanted to talk, but Sam called with some kind of emergency. When I tried to leave, he locked me in. He wanted to force me to listen to whatever he had to say after fetching Sam, but then the rain started."

Her mouth tightens. "I see."

"He didn't hurt me on purpose, at least not physically."

"He shouldn't have done that."

"No, he shouldn't have, but we're not going to talk about this with anyone else. Do you understand, Dorothy? I don't want anyone to know why it happened."

"You mean you don't want anyone to know Brian seduced you for money, if that's still what you believe."

"I don't think I can survive the humiliation."

"Jane…" Her eyes plead with me. "I think you should give Brian a chance to explain. What he did–if what Benjamin says is indeed true–is wrong, but that man has feelings for you. True feelings. Deep ones. No one can act *that* well."

"Just, stop. Please?"

"I understand you're hurting. I know how hard you fell for him. Maybe in time, despite all his wrongs, you'll let him finish what he wanted to say."

"I can't talk about it anymore. Not now." Maybe never.

She swallows. "Benjamin is going to take the paternity test."

The news stuns me into silence.

"I told him if he doesn't do it," she continues, "I'll tell the world the truth myself. You won't have to worry about the photos. I made him destroy each and every one, including the original paper and electronic files."

Thank God for that. I squeeze her hand in gratitude.

A nurse enters. "Time's up. Ms. Logan's daughter is here."

Dorothy pushes to her feet. "I'm here for you, no matter what."

"I appreciate that."

As Dorothy leaves, Abby flies into the room.

"Mom!" she says on a sob, running to the bed and falling over me.

Her hug is tight and beautiful. Tears of gratefulness to have been gifted more time with my precious girl build behind my eyes.

"Easy," Francois says from the foot of the bed. "Your mother might be hurting." He gives me a quiet smile.

"I'm fine," I say with a laugh of relief.

Abby and I cling to each other, her tears wetting my hospital robe.

"I love you, Mom," she sobs.

"Shh, honey." I stroke her hair. "It's going to be all right."

She pulls away to look at me. "What happened?"

My eyes meet Francois'. That's the question everyone is asking. "An accident."

Like I told Dorothy, no one else needs to know about the photos or why Brian really came into my life. The two people who share our dirty truth–Dorothy and Benjamin–can keep secrets. I know that from experience.

"Abby's got something to tell you," Francois says. "I'll give you two a minute."

When he's gone, Abby sits down on the edge of the bed. She wipes her cheeks with the back of her hand.

"What is it, honey?"

"This is kind of embarrassing for me."

"You know you can talk to me about anything."

"I know, it's just… I'm scared you'll judge me."

"I'm not going to judge you. I'll always love you, no matter what."

"I don't want you to be angry."

"Abby, just say it. I won't be angry about something you did or say if you're genuinely sorry and making amends."

She inhales deeply. "I…I lied about Brian."

Enormous relief washes through me, but it doesn't come as a

surprise. Wiping away her tears, I ask gently, "Why? Why did you tell such a lie?"

"I guess I was embarrassed that he's only seven years older than me." She bites her lip. "I didn't want him to be your boyfriend. Can you imagine what it would be like if you marry him and he becomes my stepdad?"

"You don't have to worry about that, honey. I'm not going to marry him."

"I want you to, if that's what you want," she says quickly. "I know you miss him. I could see it in your eyes. I was wrong and selfish, but I was just so angry at you."

"Angry? Why on earth?"

She averts her eyes. "I was angry that Dad left you."

"That was his choice."

"I felt if you'd tried harder he wouldn't have. I know you never loved him."

"Oh, Abby. It's not that I didn't love him. I just loved him in a different way. If your dad is with Debbie, it's because he found someone to love him the way he wants."

She sniffs. "She's cool."

"Debbie's good to you."

She lifts her eyes back to mine. "When we got the news, I thought you were going to die. I thought I'd never be able to tell you, and I just felt so, so guilty." There's desperation in her voice. "Can you forgive me?"

"Yes." I pull her into an embrace. "I'm glad you told the truth." She still needs to understand the consequences of her actions. "Brian's life could've been ruined for the lies. Those aren't allegations to take lightly. Please don't ever lie again. You can always tell me what's bothering you."

"I'm sorry," she sobs. "I really am."

"You'll have to apologize to Brian. You owe him an explanation."

"I know. Will we be okay if I do?"

"Yes. We'll be okay. We're good."

"Okay," she says against my neck.

Francois sticks his head around the doorframe. "There's someone else here who'd like to speak to you, Jane. Time to go, Abby. We'll check on you again tomorrow."

Abby hugs me tight for another two seconds, squeezing the air out of me. It hurts, but I'm not going to tell her to stop.

"Love you, honey." I kiss her cheek. To Francois I say, "Thanks for letting Abby stay with you while I'm in hospital."

"Are you kidding? Debs and I aren't happy about what happened to you, but we're always happy to have Abby."

I offer him a grateful smile.

The man who enters as they leave is wearing civilian clothes, but I know he's a detective. He has a certain air about him and something searching in his eyes.

"Ms. Logan, I'm Detective Cowan. The doctor said I may ask you a few questions. You don't mind if I take notes?"

I steel myself as he takes a smartphone from his pocket. The question is rhetorical. His gaze is penetrating and disturbing.

"We've already questioned Mr. Michaels, but I'd like to hear your side of the story."

My heart clenches at the mention of Brian's name.

"Can you tell me what you were doing at Mr. Michaels' house, or more specifically, in his bunker?"

"I was waiting for him to come home."

His gaze slips to my bandaged wrists lying on top of the sheets. "Cuffed?"

I resist the urge to slip my arms under the covers. "Yes." There's no point in denying. The doctor would've been obliged to give him a report of my injuries.

"May I ask why you were cuffed?"

"As I said, I was waiting for him to get back."

"Cuffed?" he repeats.

I meet his gaze head-on. "Our love life isn't vanilla, Detective Cowan."

He taps something on his phone and looks up. "It was like a submissive kind of thing."

"Yes."

"To cuff and leave you?"

"Yes."

"You gave your consent to that?"

"The objective of being cuffed is about the illusion of not giving consent, otherwise there's no point. I gave my consent to the kind of relationship we share."

"I see. At what time did he, eh, cuff you?"

"I think it was around four-thirty when I arrived at his place."

"For how long were you supposed to wait?"

"Two hours, roughly."

"What do you get out of it, waiting in what must be an agonizing position for two hours?"

"That's a personal question."

"I'm just trying to understand your motive for allowing this. I'm not familiar with BDSM."

"If you want a lesson in BDSM, you should consult a professional practitioner. I don't know anything about BDSM, either. We've never felt a need to label our sex life. We practice what we both enjoy in the bedroom. Is that a crime?"

"Negligence can be. If you'd died, Mr. Michaels would've been charged with manslaughter." He puts away the phone. "Ms. Logan, I've been on Brian Michaels' case for little over a year. It's not the first time he's under investigation. Did you know he was a suspect in a double homicide? If Mr. Michaels did something you should tell us about, now is the time."

What Brian did was wrong, but I don't want to give the detective ammunition to incriminate him. Brian's deceit hurt like hell, but my emotional pain isn't a reason to send him to prison. Restraining me against my will, now that infuriated me. What was Brian hoping to achieve? Why was justifying himself to me so important if money was the objective of sleeping with me all along? The only reason I can fathom is that money wasn't his only objective. There must've been something real in the facade. This is what I hold onto when my heart threatens to break irreparably. This is the only piece of solace I can salvage from the wreck of emotions we created, and I cling to it for life and death. It's what gives me the will to carry on. Not everything was wasted. Not everything was false. No, there had to be something real.

If I was vengeful, I could avenge Brian's deceitful actions by telling the detective he held me against my will, but the godawful truth is I still love him too much. I can't see him convicted for a crime he didn't intend. He couldn't have known about the rain. It doesn't justify his actions, but he didn't try to murder me.

The detective gives me a long look. "Mrs. Logan?"

"It was an accident."

"We found mostly books, electronics, and…" he coughs, "… photos when we drained the bunker. Is there anything we should be looking for?"

My face grows hot up to my hairline, thinking that he saw those photos. "No."

"Right, then. I'll leave my number with the nurse. If you remember anything that may be helpful, give me a call." He inclines his head, and then he's gone.

Silence descends on the room. The only noise is a strange buzzing in my ears. Dorothy comes back later with enough snacks to last me a year, pleading with me again to give Brian a chance to explain when he comes to visit me, because surely he'll want to see for himself how I'm recovering after what happened. I'm not sure how I feel about a visit from him, but it's something I didn't need to badger myself over. It's a visit that never comes.

## *Brian*

THE HOSPITAL CHAPEL is not a serene place. It's a small room with a simple cross filled with people's anguish and pain. The air smells of disinfectant, a stringent reminder of the diseases and conditions we're here to combat with our prayers while the doctors do what they can with science. Even the diluted light that filters through a stained-glass window is infected with the desperation that clings to the space.

There are two other people kneeling in front of the cross. I've passed the praying stage. I've passed anger and self-blame. I'm at the point of bargaining with God or the devil. It doesn't matter which. I'll take any deal I can get. I just want Jane to be like she was when I found her. Perfect. It doesn't matter to me if she's perfect, broken, or damaged. I'll love her all the same. I just don't want to be the reason for ruining her. I don't want to be the reason her body or mind dies. I can't live with that.

The nurse from Jane's floor enters the chapel. I rise from my seat. Knowing Jane wouldn't want me near her–for good reason–I asked the nurse to inform me of any news.

Her smile is broad. "She'll be fine. All the tests are looking good. We're just waiting for the renal test results, and we're monitoring her for the risk of developing pneumonia, but if all looks well she can go home tomorrow."

I grip the bench in front of me hard. Relief makes me sway on my feet.

"You can see her if you like."

"Thank you."

With a nod, she's off.

I have no right to ruin Jane more than I already have. The best I can do for her is to stay away. I'm setting her free from her invisible prison, even if it's killing me. The agony is hell. I deserve no less. I gambled and lost. The price was her love. No, I'm not going to visit Jane, but the urge to see her is too big. If I hang around her room, maybe I can catch a glimpse when the door opens. She doesn't need to know I'm there. I just need to reassure myself that she's fine. With that resolution in mind, I take the stairs and exit on the second floor. As I round the corner, I almost bump into Francois. Abby is at this side.

"Brian," he says, inclining his head in greeting.

"Francois. Abby."

They're probably having a restraining order issued against me as we speak. I'm about to walk a circle around them when Francois grips my arm.

"Abby just spoke to her mother. She has something to say to you, too."

Abby looks like she's going to bolt, but Francois puts an arm around her, grounding her to the space next to him.

"I, um..." Abby licks her lips and starts to cry. "I'm sorry I lied."

The confession catches me off guard. "Why did you?"

"I was embarrassed and angry."

"Angry about what?"

"My parents' divorce. You. Everything."

A lot of her feelings make sense to me. I can understand a teenager's turmoil with what's being going on in her parents' lives. I suppose she came clean because of worry over her mother. Fresh guilt eats at me for what I did to Jane. On the upside, if Jane ever had any doubts, at least she has no more reason to distrust me because of the accusation.

"All right, Abby. Apology accepted."

"Really? Just like that?"

What right do I have to be angry about Abby's lie when my actions nearly killed her mother? "Just don't let it ever happen again."

She sniffs and averts her eyes. "Um, thanks, Brian."

"As her punishment," Francois says, "Abby is not only grounded for a month, but she's also doing voluntary work at the animal shelter. I owe you an apology, too. I hope you'll be generous enough to accept it." He pats me on the shoulder. "I suppose you're eager to see Jane."

He has no idea.

They're hardly gone when Detective Cowan exits Jane's room. He questioned me when he arrived at the hospital just after a doctor had stitched up my shin. My mom called to say the detective had been at the house to inspect the site of the accident shortly after I'd left. He questioned her, but she said she didn't know anything, which is true, in a kind of a way. Cowan finally has the reason he needs to lock me up. All he needs is Jane's statement. She only has to tell one, crucial piece of truth, that I tied her up against her will. I'm not unfamiliar with the law. I'll be facing kidnapping and assault with the intent to cause grievous bodily harm charges. I steel myself for what's to come, not that I don't deserve it. I'll happily take my punishment. What's a whole lot more devastating is knowing I'll never see Jane again. The knowledge that I turned her trust and love into loathing is a harder punishment than any jail sentence.

Cowan stops when he sees me. "You're one lucky bastard, Michaels." He shakes his head as if in disgust or disapproval. "I don't get it. Why does she cover for you? What does she see in you?"

Jane covered for me? It's like a knife in my chest, strengthening my guilt.

His smile turns too broad for my liking. "Never mind. I don't need her confession. The forensics team found something much more interesting in the sludge. They found a pistol. I bet when the forensics come back, the bullets we found in those murder victims are going to match."

*Shit, no.* I've been too distraught about Jane to think clearly. I should've thought about the gun I'd so carefully hidden behind a cut in the upholstery of the sofa. I should've destroyed the damn weapon, but I was too worried I'd need it again, one day, and unlicensed firearms don't come easy or cheap. After everything, this is what's going to put me away. My own, damn negligence. My obsession with Jane.

He's got me. This is checkmate.

He watches me closely, like I'm a map he can read. "Last chance, Michaels. If you've got something to say, now's the time."

I know exactly what I have to say. "I want to cut a deal."

# 10

*Brian*

Cutting a deal with Cowan means selling a part of my soul, but it's the only way I see out. It's the only way I can get rid of my baggage. If I don't accept the terms, I'll keep on sinking under, deeper, dragging everyone I love with me to the murky depths of my future. If I go to jail, there'll be no one to take care of Sam and watch over my mom. Cowan won't stop harassing Jane until she confesses the truth. This is why I'm sitting in Monkey's lounge on Sunday afternoon, wearing a wire. This is why I don't have a choice but to play along, making a commitment I don't mean.

Lindy is sitting next to me on the sofa, her hands folded between her knees and her back stiff. She's pissed off with me, but that's the least of my concerns. Sweat trickles between my shoulder blades when I think of what'll happen if Monkey discovers I'm ratting on him. He'll make sure I suffer, chopping me to pieces, starting with my fingers and toes, but it's not me I'm worried about. It's Sam and my mom.

There's an awkward silence in the room with Monkey glaring at me and Lindy giving me the silent treatment. It's definitely not your usual engagement celebration. Ingrid, Lindy's mom, flitters into the room with a tray of champagne glasses. I get up to take it from her.

"Thank you, Brian." She beams. "You can put it on the table. Monkey, why don't you pour?"

Monkey grunts but gets up to loosen the cork on the champagne chilling in the ice bucket. The cork comes free with a loud pop, going straight up and bouncing from the ceiling. The champagne boils over before he can aim the bottle at a glass.

"Well, then," Ingrid rubs her hands together, "shall we make a toast?"

Poor woman. She's trying hard to make this into what it's supposed to be, but an ostrich can never be an eagle, no matter how hard he pretends he can fly.

She lifts her glass. "To the love birds."

Monkey gulps down half of his glass and belches. "Did you get the ring?"

My voice lacks enthusiasm. "Lindy can pick whatever she likes."

Lindy gives me a dirty look.

"A practical young man," Ingrid says, obviously trying to cover up that there's no love lost from my side. "We'll go shopping this weekend. Won't that be fun, Lindy?"

With a future father-in-law like Monkey, I don't have to worry about giving the women a budget limit. Monkey will pay for whatever his daughter wants. I don't give a shit that the ring she'll wear on her finger won't be bought with money *I* earned. No pride lost there, either.

"Lunch is almost ready," Ingrid says. "I'm sorry your mother can't be here, Brian." Her face pales a little as she realizes what she's said. Hastily, she adds, "What about Sam? Why didn't she come?"

"She's still not comfortable with her new look. The short hair is a bit of a sore point."

"Simply awful what those girls did."

I fume a little. Ingrid means well, but Sam's not her business. Of course, the whole school knows about what happened, which means the whole neighborhood knows, too.

"We need to discuss the engagement party," Ingrid says in an over-enthusiastic tone.

I wish she'd stop trying to make up for what everyone else is lacking. It's only making the atmosphere worse. As she dives into the color scheme and catering, I tune out of the conversation. My mind drifts to Jane. Everyone in Harryville knows about the *accident*. News spreads fast. Monkey didn't take it kindly. It doesn't look good for his daughter that I had my lover handcuffed in a bunker. Every time I think about Jane, it's as if my heart goes through a mincer. How she must hate me. My only defense is to push the thoughts away and repeat the mantra I have on replay in my head since the accident–she's better off without me. It doesn't change how I feel, though. I'm never going to stop loving her.

The meal is an ordeal. My companions' eating noises put my disorder to the ultimate test. I have to dig my nails into my palms to endure it. Lindy's eyes rest accusingly on my champagne, which I haven't touched. After dessert has finally been served, Monkey and I retire to his study for cognac and cigars while Lindy and Ingrid clear the table.

It's business time. It's the moment I've been waiting for and dreaded. He goes into a long explanation of what he expects from me. In one year's time, the minute Lindy and I are married, I'm to leave my job and get involved in the *business*. I ask enough questions about the illegal side of his business to feign interest without seeming over-eager for information. It's like balancing on a tightrope. My shirt is drenched in sweat by the time we're done, but thankfully it's a hot day, and I can blame the weather. At least

Cowan will have some of the information he needs to start the process of putting an end to Monkey's dealings.

"We better get back to the women," Monkey says. "Ingrid will have coffee ready." At the door, he grips my shoulder. "I hope you're going to make a better performance at the engagement party. I'm being lenient with you today, seeing what happened with Sam and that woman you had chained up in your basement for whatever sinister reasons. I won't be lenient when my daughter faces a hall full of people. Understood?" He slaps my shoulder and without waiting for a reply says, "Good. I'm glad that's settled. One more lukewarm show and I cut off your left nut. Once you've given us grandchildren, I'll cut off the right one, too."

---

### Jane

DOROTHY HOLDS my hand as we enter the doctor's office. We take the only two seats. Benjamin takes a stiff stance to the left. The atmosphere is fragile, like glass. The tension is unbearable. My ribcage tightens. It's been a week since I'm out of the hospital, but I still get these sensations that I can't breathe. I wake up in a cold sweat at night, dragging ragged breaths into my lungs. It's as if the air burns me when it finally fills my body. The familiar fire starts spreading through my chest as my throat clogs up. I close my eyes and practice what I've been doing for the last seven days, simply pulling in the next breath, and the next, until the sensation of suffocating passes.

"We have the results," the doctor says needlessly.

That's why we're here. Why I'm here is for Abby. She's outside in the garden with Francois and Debbie, waiting. We agreed it was best if she's not in the room when the doctor shares the result. He looks between us, locking eyes with each person before dipping his gaze down at the report in his hands.

"Ready?" the doctor asks.

I'll never be ready for this. The repercussions of Benjamin being Abby's father are huge. What if Abby wants to get to know her *real* father? Benjamin will never agree. He has too much to lose. I don't want my baby girl to be hurt more than she already has.

Dorothy's fingers squeeze around mine as the doctor opens his mouth.

"It's not Mr. James."

Not Benjamin. His shoulders go slack, as if the air has left his chest.

Dorothy sucks in a breath. Her voice trembles with tears. "Oh, my God."

Abby is Evan's. Evan and I made a baby. *Thank you, dear God.* I close my eyes, letting relief break and put me back together inside. On the outside, I keep it together. It's Dorothy who cries softly, but they're tears of joy. She has something left of her dead son, after all. Evan didn't leave us completely alone.

The doctor shuffles the papers into a file and pushes it over the desk. "If you'll excuse me." He gets to his feet, our cue to leave.

I'm glad for his clinical attitude. It makes the situation easier to handle. Dorothy, Benjamin, and I pause in the empty reception area. The atmosphere is awkward. There are no social polite or small talk for circumstances like these I can fall back onto. I give up wracking my brain for something suitable to say and simply go for what needs to be done.

"I'd like to tell Abby alone."

"Of course," Dorothy says. "The two of you have a lot to talk about." Dorothy looks at Benjamin. "Shall we go?"

"I'll catch up."

Dorothy gives an uncertain nod, but she exits the room, leaving me alone with Benjamin. I both appreciate and dread the opportunity. The questions bottle up inside me. Neither of us speaks, and then we talk simultaneously.

205

"Did you–?"

"Thank you–"

"Sorry."

"No, please continue."

"You go first," I say.

He wets his lips. "Thank you for not going public with this."

"That wasn't the objective."

"I know you did it for Abby, but you could've easily gotten back at me by telling the truth."

"I would've if you were her father."

"Then that's another reason to be glad I'm not."

"Since we're being so brutally honest, if I ask you a question, will you tell me the truth?"

"I owe you at least that much for your discretion."

"Did you offer Brian money to seduce me?"

"Yes," he says solemnly.

I didn't think it could hurt worse, but at the verbal admittance my world splinters a little more. A few more cracks, and I'll never be able to glue it back together.

"I did offer him money," he continues, "but he didn't accept it."

It takes a while for the meaning of his words to settle. *Brian didn't take the money.* They're a balm on my cut-open heart, but they can't fill the fissures. They can't patch up the mistrust that works both ways. It doesn't change why Brian ended up in my pool on a hot summer's night. Brian lied to me from the start. As for my wrongs, I believed he destroyed my trust, when in reality I didn't trust him enough. When it mattered, I was ready to believe the worst of him. I didn't want to listen to what Brian had to say in his cellar that day, because then I would've had to forgive him, and I'm not ready to forgive him. Forgiveness hurts too much. Forgiveness means making myself more vulnerable than I already am. Forgiveness will be the proof that my love for Brian is bigger than everything else, that he'll always hold the power to hurt and destroy me, and that my feelings render me at his mercy.

"If Brian didn't supply you with the photos, who did?"

"When Brian declined my offer, I paid someone to break into your house and install the camera in your bedroom."

"How did he get in? Brian installed an alarm."

"It was before Brian installed it. It wasn't difficult. He picked the lock on the sliding door to the deck."

"Why did you lie about it? Why did you tell your mother and me it was Brian?"

An air of despondency settles over him. "The truth? I don't know, Jane."

"You don't know?" He ruined my life–twice–and *he doesn't know?*

"I suppose I was angry. Brian was to ruin you, not fall in love with you."

"Why? What have I ever done to you?"

"What have you done to me? You fell in love with my brother when *I* brought you home. I brought you home to meet my parents. I brought you home for *me*. You were supposed to be with *me*, Jane. *Me*. Evan had no right to steal you away."

"This is still about Evan? My God, Ben. He's been dead for years. Does it ever occur to you the one who got done in was me? You *drugged* and *raped* me. How demented must you be to still want to hurt me?"

"What can I say? Old vengeances die hard."

"We were never more than friends. I never gave you false hope."

He utters a wry laugh. "You hurt me, and you don't even know how much. You don't even know how much I suffered. You'll never know. I only wanted to give Evan a taste of what I was going through."

"You've done your worst. I hope you can live with yourself."

He stares at me for a moment. "You don't want to know what I'm living with. Not really."

"You're right. I don't."

"Will I have to keep on looking over my shoulder, worrying about the tabloids?"

"No. You have my word."

"How can I be sure you won't change your mind?"

"I don't want a scandal for Abby. She's suffered enough. What's done is done. It's over. In the past."

"At least that's one thing we agree on. Neither of us needs a scandal."

I hesitate. I still have so many questions, but dare I delve deeper than what I already have? Can I handle the truth? Finally, my need to know wins out. "How *did* you meet Brian?"

"By fluke. I was having lunch between rehearsals at the restaurant opposite the theater when he walked in. From the attention he got, I thought he was a good candidate, plus I could see from his clothes he needed the money."

I want to own every piece of the pain. I don't want to be spared anything. That's why I need to ask. "Did he decline your offer immediately or did he...?" My voice drops an octave. I have to clear my throat to get the question out. "Did he consider it?"

"I could see he was thinking about it, but he didn't want to bite. I gave him a photo of you and my email address, but not my name. I told him to think about it. A few days later, he contacted and threatened me. He'd figured out who I was."

"He threatened you?"

He chuckles. "He said he'd cut off my fingers or something in that regard if I came near you."

That sounds like the possessive, protective Brian I've come to think of as mine. I reject the thought. I'm too raw to think about the future, yet, or where these facts leave us. I haven't heard from Brian since the accident. I owe him an apology for not giving him the benefit of the doubt. I owe him that chance to talk about what has nearly destroyed me, but are his feelings even the same? Does he still love me? Did he ever love me? If he does, why hasn't he come to see me in the hospital? Why hasn't he called, even if just to ask how I was doing? I can't bear to think of the answer. For now, I prefer to focus on the easier subject of logistics.

"I haven't told Francois about the camera," I say. "You need to have it removed."

"That will be hard to do without explaining why my guy needs access to his house. On top of that, the alarm is back on. You don't have to worry. I swear on Evan's grave, I won't access it."

"That's not good enough."

He sighs. "Fine. I'll find a way. My contact can say he's from Rentokil, and that he's checking for rats because the neighbors have an infestation."

"I want proof that it's been removed."

"Stalking isn't in my nature. I said I'll have it taken out, and I will."

"I don't trust you."

"All right, I deserve that."

"You have a week. I'll inspect that hole personally, and if the camera is still there, I'm telling Francois."

It won't be difficult to find a moment to check their bedroom when I drop off Abby. I can say I need to use the bathroom. I'll be in and out of the room before they know it. I'll have to be careful, though. Debbie asked me what I was looking for on the day I stormed into their house. I crossed my fingers behind my back and said I was checking if the maintenance guy had painted over the grid after fixing the air vent fan.

"Fair enough," he says after a short consideration.

I have nothing left to say. "Goodbye, Benjamin."

I'm three steps away when he says to my back, "I'm sorry, Jane."

It's late, but it's something. If I can start working on this first step of forgiveness, maybe I'll get there in the end. I don't want a life of blame and vengeance. What I yearn for most is peace.

"If it makes you feel any better," he says, "I've been living with Evan's death on my conscience for every minute of every day."

I glance at him from over my shoulder. "It doesn't make me feel better."

"The guilt never eases. It's only bearable when I pretend it's not there."

I can't tell Benjamin how to slay his ghosts. He'll have to make his own peace.

"What now, Jane?"

"What do you mean?"

"You said you won't talk to the tabloids. Are you going to the police?"

"No."

We all paid a terrible price for Benjamin's sins. I'm not going to allow those sins to haunt me more than they already have. Besides, if I go to the police the news is bound to end up in the tabloids. It's not what I want for Abby.

"Then we're done?" he asks, hopeful.

I can't look back at him. He's already a part of my past. "I'm done."

When I walk through the door, it's as if a weight lifts off my shoulders.

Dorothy waits outside, looking pale.

"Are you all right?" I ask.

"I'm battling to digest the news. Oh, my God, I have another grandchild. Evan's grandchild."

"I know. Abby loves you. She'll be happy." I'm happy.

"This is the biggest gift. Oh, Jane, can you forgive me?"

"There's nothing to forgive."

"If I hadn't asked you to lie, you would've taken the paternity test sooner. We would've known this thirteen years ago."

"We know now. It's enough."

We stop talking when Benjamin exits.

"I'll wait for you in the car," he says to Dorothy.

"He's going back to Venice on Monday," she says when he's gone. "He cancelled the rest of his performances."

For the first time in my life, I don't care where Benjamin will be. I'm no longer worried about running into him on the street or looking into a pair of black eyes that will force me to face the past.

She holds me back before we reach the garden access. "What about you, Jane?"

"What about me?"

"When are you going to talk to Brian?"

I can't answer, because I don't have the answer. How much time is enough?

"He's been at the hospital," she says. "I saw him when I came back in the evening. The nurse said he'd been sitting in front of your door through the night. He still cares about you."

This is news to me, and I'm not immune to the hope it carries.

"I know you don't want to talk about him, but there are things you should know. If it's any consolation, on the afternoon of the accident Brian was stuck in the Hartebeespoort Tunnel on the way to pick up Sam. He asked me to fetch her from her friend's house so he could go back for you. When I ran into him in the hospital, he said he left his truck in the tunnel and paid some random biker ten grand to borrow his bike. He did everything in his power to get to you on time."

"Dorothy, please stop."

I don't want to think about that afternoon, but she's relentless.

"He wouldn't have left you like that if it weren't for what happened to Sam."

"What happened to Sam? Was she all right?"

"Some girls from school ruined her party clothes by dumping a bucket of paint over her. The clothes were unsalvageable, and the poor girl had to cut her hair. The hairdresser tried, but she couldn't get the paint out."

"Oh, my God." Poor Sam. "If I ever get my hands on those girls, they'll be sorry they ever thought up the evil plan."

"Don't worry." She gives me her signature smile. "I suggested they all cut their hair to show Sam how sorry they are."

"Did they?"

"The lot of them."

"You're terrible."

"I'm happier." Her expression turns serious. "I'm happier now that I have a part of Evan back." She grabs my arm. "I want you to be happy, too. You deserve it more than anyone I know."

"I will be. I just need time."

"Speak to Brian," she calls after me as I walk through the door. "He deserves another chance."

I drown out her words. I'm too focused on Abby's tense face as she stands between Francois and Debbie. The locket catches the sun, reflecting the late afternoon rays. It's then that I know what I have to do.

---

THE NEWS HITS me like a bulldozer. I feel sick. Dorothy regards me with sympathy from across the newspaper on my kitchen table. Just to punish myself, I read the announcement again. Brian and Lindy got engaged the day after I was discharged from the hospital. Forty-eight hours. That's how long he waited, and that was after he promised me there was nothing between him and Lindy. I should've known better. Why would a young, drop-dead gorgeous, sex-savage guy be single? Why would Brian be interested in someone old enough to be his mother? Of course, he had a young and pretty girlfriend. You don't simply get engaged from one day to the next. Despite my humiliation and self-directed anger, I feel genuinely sorry for Lindy. No wonder she projected invisible daggers at me at Eugene's birthday party. Humiliation and anger I can deal with. The devastation I push onto the backburner. I have no right to feel pain. Pain warrants sympathy, and I deserve none, not when I've been stupid, naïve, and blind.

I fold the newspaper neatly so that the announcement is hidden on the inside.

"Did you read the part about the party?" Dorothy asks softly.

Two-hundred people at the Irene Country Club. This coming Saturday. Every word is imprinted in my mind, but I only say, "Mm."

I was *there* with Brian. He allowed me to make a fool of myself. Brian, Eugene, Clive, and Lindy, they all deceived me. Why did he parade me around at Playback? Were they all in on the joke? Dusty lifts his head from his basket and whines, as if he feels my pain.

Dorothy clicks her tongue. "I'm sorry you had to find out like that."

Dragging my fingers through my hair, I hold my head between my hands. "How could I not see it?"

"Love is blind."

"Don't rub clichés in my face." Or more rightly, don't rub my love in my face. It only makes it worse.

"When I saw this, I couldn't *not* tell you."

"You did the right thing."

"I believed him when he said he loved you."

I give a wry chuckle. "Don't beat yourself up over it. So did I. He's good, I have to give him that."

"Yet," she gives me a piercing look, "there was something."

I push away from the table. "Tea?" I need to keep busy before I crumple into a ball. That *something* was all I held onto, and now that there's nothing, I have to face that the most profound love of my life was meaningless. A farce.

Before she can answer, Abby skips into the room.

"Oh, hi, Dorothy. I didn't know you were here."

"You can call my grandma if you like," Dorothy half-teases.

I smile to myself. She'd really like that.

"It'll feel weird," Abby says.

Dorothy brushes an imaginary hair from Abby's shoulder. "I'm just joking with you. It's still such a novelty to me."

"You must have guessed," Abby says in the honest way children do.

Dorothy gives me a guilty look. "It was easier not to think or wonder about it." She waves a hand, as if wanting to wipe the past away. "I'm glad it's official, now."

Dorothy and Abby have always gotten on well. Not much is going to change in terms of their relationship, except for that official stamp Dorothy mentioned.

"Are you hungry?" I ask Abby.

"I was looking for you to ask you something."

"Go ahead."

Abby glances at Dorothy. "It can wait."

"Don't mind me," Dorothy says, "I was just leaving."

She gives Abby a kiss on the cheek and hugs me. "Call me if you need to talk."

I show Dorothy to the door and go back to the kitchen to see what Abby wants to talk about.

"I was thinking…" Abby flops down on the chair and fiddles with the frayed ends of her shorts.

"Go on," I encourage.

"Will you mind very much if I…"

"Abby, it's all right. Just say it."

She takes a deep breath. "I want to stay with Debs and Dad, if that's okay with you."

To let her choose is a decision I made when I told her who her biological father is. The photos she carries inside her locket already gave me an inkling as to what her answer would be, but the request still knocks my world off its axis.

She's babbling, her words tumbling from her lips too fast. "I want to be there for the baby, when he's born, and my friends live around there. It's not that I don't love you, and if you need me–"

"Honey, it's fine." Logically, I understand her decision. Inside, I'm shriveling like a dying plant.

Her voice is hopeful. "Really?"

"Of course. You can spend weekends with me, and holidays, and come back to live with me whenever you want."

"Thanks," she whispers. "I'm glad you understand."

I open my arms. "Come here." I hug her against me. "You'll always be my baby girl. Never forget that."

She smiles against my chest and pulls away too fast. I'm not ready. I don't think I'll ever be, but this is a crucial part of being a parent. It's a crucial part of love. It's knowing when to let go.

---

### Brian

OF COURSE, Jane removed each and every camera I've installed. The whole security system is gone. I don't have access to her any longer, not even remotely. The fact that she's so unprotected burns a hole in my stomach. I have a good mind to drive over there and install the whole nine yards again, but my pushiness is what got us into this mess for starters. My pushiness is what almost got her killed. I paid a hacker to get me the medical report. I couldn't go on until I knew she'd be all right. The near drowning did some serious damage. Technically, she died twice. *Twice*. Once alone, abandoned and cuffed in freezing cold water, and once in my arms. I resuscitated her the first time and the paramedics the second. Just thinking about it makes me shake all over again. It makes bile rise in my throat. It makes me break out in cold sweat and puke my guts out, time and again, but I can't stop reliving it.

According to the checkup report, Jane is physically all right, but I don't know how she's doing emotionally, and it's driving me insane. I called Dorothy, but she won't tell me shit. What makes it worse, is I can't go near Jane. I set her free, cut her loose from the destruction I brought, but I can't even check on her, not while I'm in this volatile mess with Monkey and having to make my engagement to Lindy look authentic. I've got to make it appear as the real deal, not only for Monkey's sake, lest I want him to cut off my nuts and feed my body finger by finger through a mincer, but also for Cowan. This is the cover I need to infiltrate Monkey's organization as Cowan's rat. I've got my work cut out for me. I never thought I'd be a rat, but if that's what it takes to protect my family, keep out of jail, and get out of Monkey's blackmailing claws, that's what I'll do. No matter which way I look at it, I don't have another choice.

For now I dance to Monkey's tune, starting with moving into a spare bedroom in their house. He says he wants me close to teach me the business, but it's to keep an eye on me, which makes ratting all the more difficult. I'm a walking mess, worried that he'll discover the wire and not only kill me, but also torture my mother and sister to death. Cowan promised me Sam and my mom will have protection if anything happens to me, but he knows as well as I do, the whole police force isn't enough protection against Monkey and his goons. He's too powerful. I won't rest peacefully in my grave until that fucker is locked away for good.

The living situation complicates matters. I'm not there for Sam and my mom at night. I can only check on them during the day. I refuse to let one of Monkey's guards sleep over. I don't trust any of them. Lindy has already pointed out she's not willing to let my mother move into the big joke of a castle Monkey is having built for us on the highest part of the mountain that divides Waverley and Pretoria North. It's a wedding gift. So much for family love where my future wife is concerned. Anyway, my mother couldn't leave our old house even if she wanted. I already knew what I had to do on the day Jane almost died. On the day she clinically *did* die. It had nothing to do with my future living arrangements and everything with my mother's physical and mental health. What happened with Jane made me realize we couldn't carry on like this, which is why I booked Jasmine into a fancy institution that deals with cases like hers. She resisted. It wasn't easy to convince her, but she eventually agreed when I threatened to have her declared incompetent and forcefully removed to her new, temporary home. It was damn tough. I don't like bullying her, but my mother is too hardheaded for a gentle nudge. Thanks to Cowan, I got custody of Sam. I put her in the hostel of her private school until things calm down on this end. It's safer for her there. I still work for Toby, but Monkey has made it clear he expects me to leave my cushy job and throw my full weight into his business when I'm officially his son-in-law. To that extent, my training starts with immediate effect. I spend as much time at Monkey's office as at Orion, if not more.

I'm exiting Monkey's workshop office when Clive saunters over from across the road. I was supposed to have a look at the legal side of the business–the orders of motor parts and new vehicles–but I was taking photos of the illegal books and ledgers on my smartphone. Sweat rolls down my temples and back. I'm tense. If anyone suspects something and is bright enough to check my phone, I'm fucked. I haven't had time to send the photos to Cowan so I can delete them. Clive's untimely arrival irritates me. It means I have to postpone getting rid of the dangerous evidence in my pocket.

Clive slaps me on the shoulder. "What's up, bro?"

"Busy. What are you doing here?"

"Monkey said he's got a job for me."

I tense more. Clive doesn't want to get mixed up in this shit. I don't want to see him take a fall when Cowan takes the whole lot down.

"You don't look happy," he says. "What's the matter? Afraid someone else will take a slice of your pie?"

"You don't want a job with Monkey."

"Fuck you, man."

He tries to push past me, but I grab his arm.

"Listen to me, Clive. Stay where you are or get a better job elsewhere. You don't want a part in this."

"Says the man who's just joined the band. What's your problem with me, anyway? You're suddenly too good for the likes of me?"

"That's not it." I hesitate to admit this. I don't want Clive to get suspicious. "I worry about you."

He snorts. "I'd rather worry about the party if I were you." He jerks free and dusts his leather jacket where I'd gripped him. "I'm bringing Eugene in, too. You may think you're too good for us now that you're bagging Lindy and Sam's going to that fancy girls' school, but at least Eugene and I still stick together."

I clench my teeth. "Don't do it, Clive. You're not doing Eugene a favor."

He puts his face in mine. "He needs a fucking job, or his old man is going to throw him out. Albert says he can't stay any longer if he doesn't pay rent."

"I'll find him something. I'll find you something. Give me a couple of days."

"You're a shit-ass friend." He sneers. "We're in, whether you can deal or not." He continues toward the office, but halfway there he flings around again. "Anyone else would've been happy for his friends. You're a selfish asshole."

Biting my tongue, I tilt my head back and let out a heavy breath. From what I've seen, Albert already has one foot in Monkey's business. It was only a matter of time before Eugene followed, but I was hoping it wouldn't come to that. Maybe I can still talk sense into Eugene.

A whistle from the road pulls my attention. Lindy stands next to her car, curling her finger at me. I take my time, which pisses her off. She's tapping her foot when I reach her.

"Get in," she says.

Is this a damn joke? I need to get rid of the photos on my phone. "No time."

"It wasn't a request, muffin."

I clench my jaw so hard I'm about to pop a joint. "Don't call me that."

"I'll call you whatever I please. Now get in. We've got an appointment at the tailor. You need to try on your suit."

I was going to give it a skip. I don't give a damn about the suit for Saturday's party. She must know how I feel, or she wouldn't be here.

She throws me the keys. "You drive."

---

*Jane*

WHAT THE HELL am I doing here? It's to get closure. That's so lame, not even I believe it. No, it's to punish myself, to slice my heart open even wider and rub more salt in the wound. It's not anything as noble as bleeding out the hurt to get rid of the pain once and for all. It's a sick need to see for myself that Brian's betrayal went deeper than I could've ever imagined. It's flogging myself for my naïve trust. It's facing the truth. It's admitting that *something* I was so desperately clinging onto, the something that would've justified everything I lost for loving Brian, doesn't exist. Until I've seen it with my own eyes, I can't move on. Until I've seen Brian and Lindy together, the hope Benjamin rekindled when he told me Brian didn't accept the money is alive in my chest. I'm here to lay down my hope.

Moving deeper into the hall, I grab a glass of champagne from a passing waiter. With two hundred guests, it's not difficult to blend in and go unnoticed. Like everyone else, I'm wearing a cocktail dress. On the outside, it's pretty. Inside, I'm a bloody mess. I look around the huge room, but Brian is nowhere to be seen. I swallow down half of the champagne. It tastes like nothing, until I see her. Then bitter yeast burns in my stomach and acid pushes up in my throat. Lindy and an older woman, who I presume to be her mother, stand in the center of a group. The women are chatting animatedly, admiring her outfit. She's wearing a coral-pink evening dress embroidered with crystal beads, and her hair is twisted in a French roll. There's a glow on her cheeks, and her eyes are sparkly. As radiant as she looks, I feel as dirty and used.

The music stops and a thick-set man in a tuxedo goes up behind a podium on a small stage.

"May I have your attention?"

The chatter dies down.

"As you know, we have a special announcement to make. Tonight, my sweet darling girl–no longer such a girl–is getting engaged."

Loud clapping erupts.

"I'm not a man for long speeches, so I'm just going to call Lindy and Brian up here."

My heart starts pounding so hard the beat reverberates in my temples. There's a stir in the crowd and a black blur as one of the many suited men moves toward the stage, but there is only one man like him. Brian's appearance catches me off guard. It's not the torn jeans and T-shirts I got used to. His hair is combed back, and he's wearing a tux like the man who can only be Lindy's dad. Brian looks ravishing. He looks ten years older. Sophisticated. Dangerous.

I press my clutch bag so hard between my arm and ribs that the clip painfully indents my skin. Brian hops onto the stage in one easy stride and takes his rightful place next to Lindy. She beams up at him. There's familiarity in the look. It speaks of trust and time spent together.

"With no further ado…" Lindy's father says, nodding at Brian.

Brian, the man who loved me with his hands, mind, kink, and words, the man who seduced me into giving up everything for a false fairy tale, takes a ring from his pocket and slips it onto her finger.

Cheers and whistling sound around me, but I'm deaf to everything except for the silent words she mouths to Brian, the same words Brian said to me not so long ago. The words I returned.

This is as much as I can take. I've seen what I wanted to. Fighting my way through the crowd, I swallow back tears. I drop the glass in my haste, but I don't care. It's then that Brian lifts his head and scans the crowd with a furrow between his blond brows, as if he senses the intruder that gatecrashed their party. His gaze moves left, right, and connects with mine.

*Shit.*

I push harder, trying to open a path to the main exit, but Brian jumps off the stage and rushes effortlessly on the outskirts of the hall toward my escape route. He's going to cut me off. I change direction, going for a side-door. Around me, the people seem oblivious to my flight. I don't stop to gauge Lindy's reaction or to see if she's spotted me. I almost trip over the threshold. Catching myself with flailing arms, I run over the patio. Nightlights illuminate the garden, so I choose the dark golf range, covering a good distance of short-trimmed grass before I hit a patch of trees.

"Jane!"

It's him. His footsteps are soundless on the grass, but I can feel him as sure as I can't see him behind me in the dark. He can't witness my humiliation. I have to get away. What *was* I thinking?

His breath is on my neck before his fingers clamp around my upper arms. The momentum of his body crashing into mine sends me face-down to the ground, but his arms are around me before the impact hits, cushioning my fall. My breath is nevertheless knocked out. His weight on top of me doesn't help. The panic that seized me since my near drowning threatens to turn into a full-blown attack. I fight and wiggle, clawing with my nails in the dirt for leverage.

His breath is hot on my ear. "Shh. Keep still."

For a moment, the command grounds me. It allows me enough control to master my breathing. The damp from the grass soaks through the fabric of my dress. My knees and elbows sting from grass burns.

"That's it," he says. "Easy, princess."

Princess. It's a name you call someone either with disdain or affection. *She thinks she's a princess. She's my princess.* How dare he call me that after slipping a ring on another woman's finger?

His hold loosens. He gets to his feet, pulling me with him. I'm compliant until he steadies me, and then I break free and make another run for it. I don't get far. His body envelopes mine from behind, slamming my chest into the trunk of a tree. The air leaves my lungs with a humpf this time. He grabs my wrists and pins them next to my face.

"For fuck's sake," he growls against my neck. "Will you keep still? You're going to hurt yourself."

I laugh almost hysterically. As if I can hurt more than I'm already hurting.

"You think that's funny?" he grits out.

His hips are flush against mine, letting me feel the steel length of his erection. He's pressing too hard. My breasts are pushed flat against the tree. The rough bark grazes my nipples and bites into my palms. My hipbones are crushed against the wood, and the apex of my sex rubs against the trunk through my clothes. My heart starts speeding up. My breaths turn erratic. Shamefully, my folds turn wet and swollen. I can hide many things from him, but not this, not my raw, unfair, traitorous desire. I hate him for having this effect on me almost as much as I hate myself.

His fingers tighten around my wrists. "Goddammit. Damn you, Jane."

"Let me go."

He rolls his hips, lodging his hard-on between my ass cheeks. "What are you doing here?"

"Oh, you mean I wasn't invited?"

He punches his hips up, driving me harder against the tree. "Do you have any idea how dangerous this is?"

It's the only thing I'm certain of. His closeness is toxic, but my body craves his poison. Yes, this—our bodies rubbing together—is the biggest danger of all.

He drags his nose along my neck and groans. "Jane."

My body responds, shivers running over me and accumulating in the aching spot between my legs. We're both panting, but not from our running stunt.

I try to jerk my arms free. "Let go."

I yelp when he nips my shoulder before soothing the spot with his tongue.

"Why did you come here, princess?"

"To finish what you couldn't. To look you in the eyes when I tell you goodbye."

He stills. Not even his chest rises or falls with a breath. "I'm never saying goodbye to you. I set you free, but you came back to me. This changes everything."

I huff another laugh. "God, Brian. Does your betrayal know no end?"

"You trust me, remember?"

The notion is hilarious. My laugh is hollow. Ugly. Like me. Like everything that's withering and dying inside. "Give me one good reason why I should still trust you."

"Because I love you."

If he'd driven a pincushion full of needles through my heart, he would've hurt me less. Those words slash me open and fill me with bitter sadness. It's a notion of what could've been, and it's entirely cruel. It's like showing a dog a bone and snatching it away before he can latch onto it. My pride is trampled. My dignity is crushed. All that is left is agony and the humiliating truth pulsing between my legs. I can't even win this last battle in our raging war.

"Yeah, right." It's my anger speaking. "You blew your reason, because I don't believe you."

He sucks in a breath. It's loud, trapped between us. "You don't mean that."

"It wasn't real."

*It wasn't real.* I believed our love was *it*, once-in-a-lifetime, The One, soulmates, and it *wasn't real*. That's what hurts the most.

The noise he makes is between a growl and a groan. He thrusts his hips, sliding his length along my crack. "Is this real enough for you?"

"No," I spit out. It's lust, plain and simple, in its crudest form.

"You want proof?" he hisses. "You want me to remind you what our reality feels like?"

Gripping both wrists in one hand above my head, he bunches my dress up over my hips. The cold night air assaults my thighs and buttocks. I lock my legs tight, hiding the evidence of a different kind of betrayal, my body's betrayal, from him, but he pushes his knee between my legs and rips the underwear from my hips. The rough sound of fabric tearing only makes me wetter. Oh, God. I don't want to give in, but I'm already halfway there. My body both jerks away from and toward his touch when he drags four fingers over my slit.

He smears my wetness on my inner thigh. "This is fucking real."

When he pushes a finger inside, not gentle and loving, but uncompromising and completely, I cry out, pushing my hips back to take more.

"This is real," he grits out, nuzzling his nose along my neck.

I can't stop a moan from slipping into the night, carrying a hint of the truth he's so desperately seeking. How much more of myself can I lose? Nothing. There's nothing left. He's already taken it all. There's no point in defending a fortress that's long lost. I sag against him as his thumb finds my clit. I'm helpless to stop it. I'm so much weaker than I thought. A tear leaks from my eye as he flaunts my vulnerability, showing me how defenseless I am against his touch.

"That's it." He gives it to me harder, just the way I like. "Come for me. Show me."

It doesn't take long. I shatter to pieces, shaking with my orgasm and shame. Aftershocks run through my body, keeping me primed. Through the haze of pleasure that fogs my mind, the sound of his zipper registers. The slick head of his cock nudges my folds.

"Tell me this isn't real," he whispers against the shell of my ear, "and I'll stop."

I can't do anything of the kind. Of all the weapons I'm willing to use to defend myself, I can't use this untruth. Our love may not be, but our lust is real. It's the last shard of light I have left, the last piece of driftwood to cling to as the storm rips me deeper into a dark and tremulous sea.

"Thought so," he says triumphantly.

Pinning me in place, he rams into me, filling me with a scream and everything I can't have, everything that's no longer mine. He lets go of my wrists to clamp a hand over my mouth while he holds me to him with an arm tightly wound around my waist. My cries are muffled in his palm as he pivots his hips with a grueling rhythm, splitting me in two, breaking me into pieces. He's so deep it hurts. Every thrust pushes me closer to ecstatic pain. He no longer has to hold me down. I'm clawing at his arms and ass, needing him harder. Deeper. All the way to my broken soul.

Covered in mud and grass, we fuck like animals. There's no place for pretty pink gowns and tenderly mouthed words in what we're doing. We're raw and basic, stripped to our barest truths. He fucks me while I scream into his hand, treating me like a dirty whore and precious princess, giving me the devastating illusion of being the center of his world. But right now, we are the center of each other's worlds. Our pleasure is intertwined, wound tight as he batters my heart and loves my body.

The air changes, becoming darker and more depraved as our lust spirals out of control.

"More," I pant into his palm. My release is close again, but I can't slip over.

His cock swells inside me at the plea. Grabbing the short ends of my hair, he tilts my head back, exposing my neck. His lips are all over mine before he clamps down on the tender skin where my neck meets my shoulder. He sucks on me like I'm a medicine for his madness, and then he yanks his cock brutally out of me. My pussy clenches in protest. He uses his fingers to smear my arousal around my asshole. Before I can tense up, the head of his cock is spearing my dark entrance. It hurts and burns with a fierceness that makes me scream louder and him snuffing out the sound harder. He catches my cries in his hand as he shoves in all the way, taking everything I've got. For a moment the burn is all I register, but then his fingers are inside me and his thumb is on my clit. Incredible sensations of pleasure and pain collide to form something more explosive and scary. I whimper as the darkness overtakes me, driving me to needs I fear, but he cradles my back against his chest and whispers, "I've got you."

That's when I let go. The orgasm hits me from all sides. White spots explode in my vision. I don't realize how badly I need air until he lets up his hand that covers my mouth and part of my nose. My nipples rub against the rough bark as he drives deeper and harder until his cock jerks and his hips cushions mine. Warm jets of cum erupt in my ass. His body falls over mine, his chest covering my back. His breath chases down my neck and spine. We're both breathing too hard. We're both doing the ultimate wrong while everything between us feels so right.

The very reality he wanted me to feel slashes through me as he carefully frees his cock. What have we done? Cum dribbles from my ass and down my thighs, giving me the answer. I'm boneless. He has to hold me up while he searches the ground for my torn underwear. He uses the ruined thong to clean up as best as he can between my legs, but the scrap of fabric is not enough to wipe away all the evidence. Slowly, he turns me, letting my back rest against the trunk. My eyes are accustomed enough to the dark to see the turmoil in his as he searches my face.

"Jane..."

God, we're a mess. We're dirty and disheveled. My dress is still hitched up over my hips and his cock is hanging half-erect through his open fly. His cum is sticky on my legs, the ache between my thighs and in my ass still fresh.

"Jane, I–"

A voice interrupts from nearby. "What the fuck?"

Brian goes rigid. I freeze. He jerks down the fabric of my dress, hiding my body with his.

"Oh, God," Clive says, stepping into our line of vision. "You did not just fuck Jane. What the fuck is wrong with you? Monkey and Lindy are looking for you."

At the mention of her name, my body tenses. More shame fills me until I feel nothing but disgust for myself.

Brian's hands tighten on my hips as I go from legless to taunt.

"Shut the hell up, Clive."

"You better get back there," he says, shooting arrows, and daggers, and needles at me. "I covered for you, saying you had too much to drink and are vomiting your guts out in the bushes. It's only a matter of time before Monkey himself comes out here looking for you."

"Jane…"

It's the third time he says my name, and this time it's laced with regret. I didn't expect anything else, so why does it hurt even worse than before?

Gathering the last scraps of whatever dignity I have left, I straighten my dress. "Goodbye, Brian."

His jaw bunches. He clenches his fists, but he doesn't say anything. He doesn't try to stop me when I hobble over the grass, feeling the sting of his passion in the most forbidden places of my body. All I can do as I feel their eyes on me, betraying and judging eyes, is walk away with my head held high until I get to my car.

Unlocking the door with trembling fingers, I fall down in the seat. Wild sobs shake my shoulders. Messy tears soil my face, dripping into my lap. I'm such a sucker for punishment. The only thing I accomplished was proving to myself and Brian that I'm not over him, not even after what he did. I'm an idiot. A pathetic creature. I'm the woman Brian fucks like an animal, not the one he puts a ring on. At least that part sank in.

The fairy lights of the party blurs in my vision as I start the engine and turn the car toward the gates. I can't see well enough through the shower of tears to find the road even if I wanted, but I have to get away. I want to go home where I can curl into a ball and hide from my feelings and the world. I'll have a good cry, and then I'll get up and move on. I'm alive when I could've easily been dead. I'm not wasting this second-chance life that has been gifted me. Not even for Brian.

# 11

*Jane*

S omething nags at me in my sleep. It's not the slow-dying ache in my body from Brian's rough fucking. It's more like a mental nudge, like a little voice telling me I forgot to lock the door or switch off the oven. I glance at the alarm clock. It's two in the morning. Turning on my back, I try to discern the reason for my unease. The pain of last night is a fresh wound, but it's too all-consuming to account for the splinter of anxiety that pulled me from my sleep. I saw what I went to see. I got what I wanted. That kind of pain drenches your body and soul. It encompasses everything until you exist inside of it, and it becomes as much a part of you as your need to eat and sleep. It's like an ache that never goes away, but your body learns to live with. It becomes your new pain threshold, pushing the bar up to an unequalled high. You feel within the black hole that becomes the universe of your heart. That's why something else registered in my subconscious mind. Did I lock the door? I'm sure I did. My mind is playing tricks on me. Still, I can't shake the feeling.

Throwing the covers aside, I swing my feet to the floor. The tiles are cool. It should be welcoming. My townhouse is too warm inside with all the windows closed, but I can't stop being cold. I've been shivering since I left the country club. I rub my palms over my arms and pull the T-shirt I'm sleeping in over my ass before going downstairs. Enough light falls from the digital panel on the fridge through the kitchen door into the hallway to find my way. From the bedroom upstairs, the alarm clock ticks. The fall of the second hand is amplified in the silence that huddles like emptiness in the house. The smell of last night's wasted lasagna TV dinner hovers in the kitchen as I pass the door. What didn't end up in the bin ended as vomit in the toilet.

I pad over the cold floor to the front door. The keys are on the table in the entrance where I'd left them. I'm about to test the doorknob when a hand covers my mouth from behind.

My scream is lost in the smell of leather. Adrenalin surges through my body as a meaty arm wraps around me, lifting me off my feet. I fight for my life. Twisting, biting, and kicking, I struggle like a mad person. A bite of pain nips into my arm. I faintly register the butcher's knife clutched in my assailant's hand, but not even the small cuts the wrestling earns me is enough to keep me still. I throw my head back, butting him in the chest. He doesn't even grunt. In a sickening shift of our axis, we go down to the ground. He lands on top of me with his full weight. Sharp pain explodes in my head as my cheekbone hits the hard floor. It feels as if every bone in my body is crushed. Panic sends my mind reeling. I can't breathe. He's cutting off my airflow. Not this. Not drowning and him pinning down my body. *Please, God.*

The weight eases marginally, and then I'm jerked around. The pressure is only relieved for a second before he replaces it, this time by sitting down on my abdomen and pinning my arms to the floor with his knees. It hurts enough to send tears to my eyes. He's going to crush my wrists. His hand is still pressed over my mouth, but he frees my nose, letting me breathe. My jaw aches from biting down on the leather to no avail. The glove is thick. He's tall and muscled. I'm no match for him. Plus, he's got a knife. Pleading is my only salvation. I search his eyes through the balaclava mask. What I find makes my stomach drop. His pupils are dilated. His eyes are cruel. He's enjoying this. Begging won't work on him, because he doesn't have an ounce of compassion. The grin of his sickly full lips confirms the hunch. Still, I owe it to myself, to the vow I took to grab this second chance with both hands, to try.

"Please," I mumble into his hand, "don't hurt me. You can take what you want."

Money. My body. What difference does it make when your life is at stake?

He shakes his head slowly. He's not here to take. He's here to hurt me.

*Oh, God.*

The minute the realization sinks in, he lifts his hand. The knife is a flash of metal that slices through the air. There isn't even enough time to scream. I want to stare him in the face when he deals me my fate, but my eyes close involuntarily as the blade comes down in my line of vision. Too close.

A blinding pain sears my cheek. I go still from the sheer intensity. The agony freezes me, hurling me into a state of mental and physical shock. I pry my eyes open. I need to measure the danger. My fate. The knife lifts and dips again. Another slash. My skin burns as if it's on fire. Warm liquid runs over my jaw and chin. A metallic smell fills the air. Bile pushes up in my throat, but my stomach is empty.

He grips my jaw with jarring strength, forcing me to meet his eyes. When he places the knife on my chest and reaches for something in his pocket, I will myself to fight again, even if it's only to call for help. I force the cry to my lips, but no sound escapes, except for a hollow whistle of wind. The barren sound is lost before it reaches my lips. He holds a smartphone up to my face and snaps a photo. The flash blinds me.

His voice is gravelly. "This is a message from Lindy. Stay away from Brian."

When he lets go, my head hits the tiles with a clack. Stars explode behind my eyes. My lungs heave as he lifts off me. His boots fill my line of vision. A drop of blood drips from the tip of the knife onto the floor. Without a second's pause, the boots advance soundlessly to the door. The door opens, the hinges not making a squeak, and then he goes, leaving the door open.

I grapple for breath, sobbing dry tears and gasping like a fish out of water.

I'm alive.

I can see. He didn't take out my eye.

He didn't rape me.

Rolling onto my stomach, my face lands in something warm and sticky. I drag my body through it, my progress slippery but made easier by the blood as I crawl down the hallway and up the stairs. It's only in the bedroom that I gather enough strength to get to my knees. Grabbing the phone from the nightstand, I dial the emergency service. As the call connects, I catch a glimpse of myself in the full-length mirror. There's a flapping gap where my cheek used to be, and through it I can see my jaw and teeth.

---

*Brian*

I JUST GOT off the phone with my mom when one of Monkey's goons walks into the study and drops an envelope on the desk.

"From Lindy," he says with a mocking smile.

My irritation flares. I talk to my mother every morning to see how she's doing, and today isn't a good day. All I need is to be left alone. Especially after last night. After Jane. She came back to me. I still can't believe it. After all that's happened, she still feels something for me, or she wouldn't have been there. I know she's hurting, but I'm about to set it right. This morning. Right now. As soon as Monkey's guard gets out of my face. I just have to be careful, that's all. I can't drag Jane into this mess. In the meantime, I feel like punching someone. Maybe the goon facing me with that stupid grin. The man's saving grace is that he walks away without a word.

There's nothing after Jane. I know it as sure as I'd known it the day the ambulance drove her away. It's fresher now that I know she still wants me. Rawer. Will this hell I'm living ever become bearable?

I rip the envelope open. An unwelcome spell of déjà vu settles over my senses. The last time I accepted an unassuming, humble brown envelope was in Jane's office, and the content tore my world apart. It destroyed Jane's. A single photo drops out. As I flip it over, what's left of my world crashes. I jump to my feet in cold rage, fury pumping through me.

*No, no, no.*

One minute I'm in Monkey's study, and the next, I'm in Lindy's bedroom. The house is quiet. Her mom's gone shopping, and Monkey is at the office. The housekeeper is downstairs, vacuuming. We've finished our exams. It's holiday. Lindy's home. Her eyes grow large in the mirror of the dresser as I go straight for her. She jumps up. A hairbrush drops from her hand to the carpet. She backs up to the wall, but I'm already on top of her. I close my fingers around her throat and lift her off her feet. Her ballerina slippers dangle from her toes. She loses them as she kicks. Her nails draw blood on my arm, but I feel nothing.

"Who did it?" I grit out.

"Lennert," she says on a gurgle.

The guy who dropped off the photo. I make a mental note to kill him.

"Who told you?"

She doesn't answer.

233

I shake her. Her lips are turning a shade of purple. Her eyes are bulging.

"Who the fuck told you?"

"C–Clive."

The smell of piss fills the air. A trickle runs down her leg.

There's another gurgling sound. My phone rings, breaking my trance. I'm not sure I want to let her go. I want to kill her badly, but the ring is persistent, and it's the ringtone I only use for Cowan. The fucker must be psychic.

I drop her with a snarl. She falls to her knees, clutching her throat. Silencing the call, I go down on my knees to put us at eyelevel.

"You don't tell a soul about this," I say menacingly, poking the blue marks I'd left on her scrawny neck, "or I'll make you suffer in ways you didn't know existed."

She lifts her gaze to me, but instead of fear, I'm met with triumph.

"You touch her again," she croaks, "and she's not only ugly, but dead."

I straighten, reeling away from the evil promise in her words. The girl kneeling in front of me is not the blabbering, blushing innocent who yacked my ear off about her roommate and nail varnish color. She's a Monkey in the making, a true heiress to his throne. I don't think Monkey realizes what a good candidate she is. With someone like Lindy, he doesn't need me to take over the reins.

I back away from her in disgust. "You know I'm going to kill Lennert and Clive, right?" Let their deaths be on her conscience.

She regards me calmly. "Yes."

I can't look at her for another second. "Clean yourself up."

My lip curling with loathing, I walk from her room with one purpose in mind–get to Jane. In the hallway, my phone rings again. Cowan.

"What?" I bark into the phone.

"Jane's in hospital."

"I know." I'm about to snap in a dangerous way. "I'm on my way."

"Stop."

The single command does exactly that. It stops me in my tracks. "What did you say to me?" I'll kill anyone standing between me and getting to that hospital.

"I said stop and listen."

My pulse starts racing. The horror of the image plays over in my mind. I only saw her face. What if other parts of her body are mutilated? "How is she?"

"Brian–"

"How the fuck is she?" I yell.

"If you calm down, I can tell you."

My chest heaves. I drag in as many breaths as it takes to lower my voice. "Tell me."

"She's stable. Got her face stitched up and she's being treated for shock."

"That's it?" Every nerve in my body shakes, waiting on the verdict. "No other injuries?"

"Nothing else."

"I know who did it."

"Yes. That's why I'm calling. Have you killed anyone?"

"Not yet," I grit out.

"Are you somewhere private?"

I glance behind me. The door to Lindy's bedroom is still open. The vacuum is still sounding from downstairs. Cowan warned me about bugs, which is why he gave me a secure phone and why I never talk in the house.

"Hold on," I say through clenched teeth. I go outside into the vast garden until I'm outside a transmittable radius. "You can talk."

"I took Jane's statement. The man who attacked her was masked. He wore gloves. My men are combing her place with a fine toothcomb as we speak. So far, there's no evidence."

"I know who did it!"

"I can't make an arrest without evidence. All he said was that it was a message from Lindy."

"Lindy already admitted it."

"We're going to get them, Brian. I promise you the guy who did this will pay, but if you screw it up now in a blind rage, your cover is blown. Our mission will be fucked. We'll be back to square one with nothing to go on, and Monkey and his cronies will still be free."

I'm fuming, burning with a need to avenge what they did to Jane. "I can't let it go."

"We won't, but you have to be patient. If you fuck this up, the deal's off, and you're on your own."

If I fuck this up, Monkey will kill me before Cowan can slap cuffs on me and drag me to prison. I'm no good to Jane dead. Everything inside me rebels at the knowledge, but Cowan is right. The only way forward is to put Monkey away and pull down his business. I'll bide my time. It doesn't mean I'll let this go unpunished.

"Fine." The word is almost inaudible.

"I can't hear you, Michaels."

"I said fucking fine!"

"That's better. Do I have a rat, or don't I?"

"Yes," I hiss.

"Good. Go have a drink and calm down."

The line goes dead.

I want nothing more than to go to Jane, but I can't see her, now less than ever. As long as these fuckers follow orders from Lindy and Monkey, I can't go near her. I don't doubt for one second Lindy will follow through with her threat. It was there in her eyes as she serenely sacrificed two men's lives.

I kick a stone, sending it flying. I feel like ripping out every rose bush in the pristine flowerbed until my hands are bleeding from the thorns, but I only shove my phone back in my pocket and let another layer of steel slip around my heart. When I'm done with the Williams', they'll be sorry they were born.

---

*Jane*

MY SUTURES COME out one week later. My face is awful to look at, but I suppose that was the point. A scar in the shape of a V runs across my cheek. It's an angry red and swollen. The doctor says it'll fade some with time. He offered me the number of a plastic surgeon, but I don't see the point. For who am I going to make myself presentable? I don't mind looking at my disfigured face. It'll be a reminder of what I almost sacrificed in the name of love, should I ever have an inclination to be so foolish again. I'm done with love. I gave everything I had to Brian, and that's where it'll stay. I can never love like that again. I don't want to love like that again. I'll cherish the memory like a treasure, buried in a deep, inaccessible part of my soul. The rest of me will move on.

Detective Cowan said they didn't find anything in my house that can aid in identifying my attacker. No DNA. Not even a hair. Despite the fact that Dorothy had my place cleaned, I can't go back there. I stay in a guest bedroom at Dorothy's house. Abby offers to come live with me again, but I'm not going to use guilt or pity to sway her decision.

Life goes on. I receive a handsome payout from Toby, about two years' worth of salary. I give notice to the rental agent and sell everything to a pawn shop except for my clothes. Finally, I'm left with nothing but personal belongings. No house, no furniture, no job. No husband. No child to take care of. No baggage. Just the clean slate of my future stretching in front of me.

Throwing my two suitcases in the trunk, I hug Dorothy goodbye and drive to the old house, Debbie and Francois' house, and now Abby's. I've told Abby about my plans–or rather my lack of plans–over the phone, but saying goodbye is much harder in person.

Abby wraps her arms around me. Francois is standing to the side, giving us space.

"You're sure you're going to be okay, Mom?"

"Of course."

"Send me a postcard."

"I will."

"I love you."

"Love you too, honey."

"I'm not going to make a scene. I'm just going to go inside before I cry." She blows me an air kiss, a tear already slipping from the corner of her eye.

I smile at her, drinking in her profile until she disappears into the house.

Francois walks up to the car. "Any idea where you're going?"

I shrug. "Where the road takes me."

"You're sure about this?"

"I need to get away for a while."

"I understand." He hesitates. "This wasn't my intention."

"It was Abby's choice. She wants to be here when her brother is born. When she's ready, she can come live with me again."

He brushes his fingers through his hair before shoving his hand in his pocket. His voice is strained. "Debs is a good woman. If it seemed she wanted to alienate you and Abby, it's only because of her insecurity. It's not easy on her being the second wife. She was trying hard for Abby to like her. Too hard, maybe."

"I'm not blaming Debbie. This is where Abby's school and friends are. Right now, this is what's best for her."

"I appreciate that you're letting her. I thought after the paternity test..." He shakes his head, as if wanting to rid it from an unpleasant thought.

"You're a good father. You and Debbie will be great parents."

"When I said it wasn't my intention, I didn't mean just Abby. I meant everything that's happened–your job, your friends, your home, losing Brian..." He swallows. "Your face."

The silence stretches, because I can't talk about Brian. No one understands, except the ones who share our secret. I can't let Francois in on the secret of shameful photos and the many reasons why a man would stalk a woman or why a jealous fiancée would send a butcher to make a point, but I sense he has more to say, so I wait. It's never been easy for Francois to talk.

"You know why I left you, right?"

His hesitation stretches all the way back to the day in Kream when I asked him for a reason and he denied me. Not that it matters, any longer, but I let him get it off his chest.

"Debbie loves me in a way you never could. She looks at me like you used to look at Evan."

"I'm sorry I couldn't be what you needed."

"It's not your fault. I knew what I was doing the night I sneaked into your room. I knew exactly what I was doing when I slept with you without using a condom. It was a gamble. I hoped you'd fall pregnant. I hoped you'd grow to love me as much as you loved him. I'm just sorry you paid the price for the risk *I* took."

"It's in the past. We've moved on."

He nods with a sad smile. "Yes, we've moved on."

"Take care of Abby. Dorothy will visit her often."

"You don't need to worry."

"I don't. Call me if there's anything."

"Take care on the road, Jane. Oh, and I owe you an apology for Brian. I'm sorry for thinking the worst of him when Abby lied. I'm sorry if things between you didn't work out because of that. You deserve to be happy."

Not wanting to drag the moment out longer, I get into my car. Francois lifts his hand in a farewell as I pull away from the curb.

It's strange how my old life seems so long ago. Back then, I had this beautiful house, a family, friends, and a good job, but it was make-belief. I may not have much now, but at least it's real.

Cutting across the quiet neighborhood, I head toward the highway. It's not until I hit the four-way split that I make a decision.

I'm going north. I'm leaving the love I've found in this city behind. There was a time I believed it was a love beautiful and pure, but now I know it's a love tainted with obsession and tarnished with lies. But sometimes an impure love is the greatest thing we'll ever accomplish. It's not perfection that matters, but how deep our feelings go. It's existing at the center of someone's world, even if just for a few fleeting minutes against the rough bark of a tree.

I drive for four hours before I hit the small mining town of Pilgrim's Rest that dates from the gold rush era. It's a place where I used to come on holiday as a child. Being from Cape Town, my parents didn't seek out the beaches in summer. When the tourists flocked to Cape Town in their hordes, we escaped inland. My dad liked playing golf and fishing for trout. My mom spent her days hunting for treasures in antique shops while I basked in the sun with my books. There's a string of touristy restaurants and pancake houses lined up in the main street, but it's the run-down bar at the end that catches my fancy.

Seeing that the whole town is a national monument, the buildings date from a time when every man had a dream and gold nugget in his pocket. Wooden walls are topped with steep, corrugated iron roofs. The bar is no different, except that it's more rustic. The walls are made out of rough logs and the floors are unsanded. The name is painted in pink letters over the roof. Panties. When I push the swing-doors back, I understand why. Hundreds of panties are pinned to the ceiling. It's a rainbow of colors in all sizes and shapes, from lacy thongs to flesh-colored granny panties. I'm grinning up at the display as a female voice says, "You have to take yours off and pin it there if you'd like to enter. Tradition."

A smile tugs at my lips for the first time in two weeks. "That's a strange entry fee."

The scar pulls, reminding me it's still fresh and unsightly, but the lady behind the bar doesn't seem to mind.

"Daisy." She holds out a hand.

Accepting the handshake, I take her in. She has coal-black hair and arms the size of a wrestler's.

"I'm Jane."

"What brings you to town?"

"What doesn't?"

"Mm-mm. If you don't want to take your pants off here, you can shimmy out of your panties in the bathroom."

"Are you serious?"

"Mm-mm."

Shaking my head, I go to the ladies' to return commando, my thong swinging from my finger. "Now what?"

"Now you pin it where you like, sweetheart. Here." She hands me a pin. "You can use a barstool to reach."

I take a place of honor between a hot pink French bikini and a crotchless number.

"Burger?" Daisy asks. "It comes with a free beer."

"Sure."

I take a place by the bar. It's then that I see the for sale sign. My mother used to say if you follow the signs, you'll never lose your way.

"How much?" I ask.

"Fifty rand."

"No, I mean this." I point at the sign.

"The owner wants a couple of million. The down-payment is half a mill."

I've got one point two million in my account, thanks to my retrenchment. If that's not a sign, I don't know what it. Besides, I've always preferred the countryside to the city. It's thrillingly freeing to make an impulsive decision, to throw all caution to the wind and live flat-out in the moment like there's no tomorrow.

It's exhilarating to simply say, "Yes."

Daisy puts a beer in front of me. "Sorry, sweetheart, what was that?"

"Yes. I'll take it."

# 12

*One year later*
*Jane*

There's a slump between the afternoon diners and the evening customers who come in for a party. I let Daisy finish up the cleaning and take a well-earned break on the swing-bench on the porch. The sunset is orange brushstrokes over a purple sky. At night, the stars are so bright the Milky Way looks like a thick blanket of diamonds draped over the sky. It's quiet here. Except for the crickets and the occasional frog, there are no sounds of cars racing down the highway or police sirens in the distance. Crossing my ankles on the rail, I stretch and drag in the clean air. It smells of pine and cedar. I can never get enough of filling my lungs. I don't take a single breath for granted.

My soul is content. My heart is at peace. I stopped looking when I drove away from Pretoria a year ago. I stopped swimming upstream so hard and allowed the current to gently drift me along. This is where I washed up. Pilgrim's Rest. Ironically, I'm like one of those pilgrims who found their resting place. Finally, I can tick a couple of those boxes on my to-do-before-I-die list. I've retired to the countryside. The bar isn't a Michelin restaurant, but I like the home cooking. It's honest. No frills. What you see is what you get. I get to do what I love most–cooking–while finishing a correspondence degree in Food Science. Oh, and I'm taking Italian classes. Well, sort of. My kitchen help, a native girl from Naples, is teaching me to cuss up a storm. I even like the rowdy clientele and late-night singing. I made new friends, including Daisy, who is my bartender / bouncer. Not even the big folks mess with Daisy. She's got a black belt in karate, and she can throw knives like she throws darts. I'm not living in a city of boutiques, architects, and posh private schools, any longer. I'm just the owner of a run-down bar in a bohemian town where no one gives a rat's ass about my age or scars. It's not that the people here aren't curious about my past. It's that they stopped asking questions I don't answer.

Abby comes to visit every second weekend and holiday. She loves it here, but not enough to settle indefinitely. She enjoys the big city vibe too much. Hank, her brother, is the cutest thing since squirrels. I've babysat him on a few occasions when Debbie and Francois needed a weekend break. It's good to see Abby happy. She dotes on her brother, and now that he's started walking, he follows his big sister and Dusty everywhere.

Dorothy comes out here once a quarter to fish trout, her latest hobby. During those holidays, she stays in the guest bedroom upstairs, adjoining mine. My quarters are humble, but cozy. I still think of Brian, but it's not a blooming ache that opens up and bleeds every time I poke my fingers into the memory. It's a bitter-sweet reminder of life's yins and yangs, of the darkness that stretches beyond the light, and the light that can't exist without darkness.

My mind drifts to him, as it often does, in these silent moments between the rush of living and the quiet of longing. Evan was my first love, but Brian was my soulmate. The yin to my yang. It's not until the figure hiking up the road is only a block away that I notice him, so lost am I in my thoughts.

He's got a familiar gait. The way his boots pound the tar is both lithe and powerful. It evokes contrasting sensations of happiness and loss. I can't quite put my finger on it, but then it dawns on me like a feather drifting gently down to the ground. It comes to me slow and sweet as understanding blossoms in my chest and heats my belly. His unusual length and the color of his hair remind me of the very object of my thoughts. His body is more muscular, and the highlights in his hair lighter, giving the blond a sandy hue, but the way he moves as he shifts a duffle bag on his shoulder is achingly familiar. I tense and relax at the same time. My body is confused, not knowing how to react to the jarring signals my brain is sending, but my mind is clear. My mind knows who is coming up the road, walking toward me with a lazy stroll even as every muscle in that manly body is drawn tight. His lips are curved in a smile, exposing one dimple, but his fingers clench around the strap of the bag. He's a contradiction of cues, a whole lot of yins and yangs twisted together.

He stops in front of the porch and drops the bag to the ground. A small puff of dust rises up in the air. Resting his hands on his hips, he regards me from guarded eyes.

"Hello, princess."

---

### Brian

I'VE BEEN LIVING for this moment for one, long year. If I'd been living it my whole life, I'd still not be prepared. I stare at the woman I've lost on every physical and emotional level. It's like a dream, yet, nothing has felt more real. The sheen of perspiration on her skin is real. The smell of her grapefruit perfume is real. So is the way her chest gently rises as she inhales. Most of all, so is that scar she earned because of me.

The woman who died twice. I carry the medical report in my pocket like a shrine to remind me of miracles and that nothing is impossible. Something as rare as what we had is worth fighting for. She's worth fighting for. To hell with the how and why. To hell with the age between us.

For a long moment, we look at each other. Jane is even more crazily beautiful than I recall. The imperfection of the scar draws an eye to her beauty, highlighting her stunning features. She looks younger. Country living suits her. There's a strawberry blush to her cheeks and a bronze hue to her skin. Her hair has grown to just past her shoulders. She's wearing denim cut-offs and kick-ass cowboy boots with a matching hat. Her tank top is too tight for my liking. I can already imagine the other men's eyes on her. She's got her legs crossed and propped up on the rail, her stance not tensing one ounce at my unannounced presence. Any other woman who shares our kind of history would've chased me off her property, but not Jane. She's too considerate, fair, and empathetic. More than that, she's confident. She's over me. She doesn't need to chase the hurt away. My confidence takes a knock, but I'm here to do what I have to do, and I'm not leaving until it's done.

I look around the building. It's rustic. The log walls and unsanded floorboards aren't what I imagined. I still associate Jane with expensive architecture and refined cuisine, although she doesn't need the brands to make her the lady I remember. Even in shorts and boots she exudes an air of soft sophistication with that undercurrent of dark desires only a man like me who shares her tastes can sense. My gaze runs over the name of the bar painted in pink letters over the corrugated iron roof.

"Panties?" I'm amused and more surprised. What kind of a name is that?

A slight smile tugs at her full lips. "Go grab a beer inside. Tell Daisy it's on the house."

I narrow my eyes a fraction, loving her guts. She's not only enjoying bossing me around, but also making a point of showing me I'm on her turf.

Picking up my bag and dumping it on the porch, I make my own statement. I'm here to stay. She barely gives the gesture any notice, nothing more than a cursory glance from the corner of her eyes. It's as hot as a furnace in these parts, and I can do with a beer after hiking the last few kilometers from where my lift has dropped me. Pushing my palms on the doors, I swing them open. They make a squeaking noise. I make a mental note to oil the hinges. The interior is dark and cool, a welcome refuge. The tables and benches reflect the exterior in their homely design. Checkered tablecloths cover the tables, and potted cactuses are the center decoration. There's a karaoke system and a jukebox in one corner. Nice. Snug, but it's the hundreds of panties on the ceiling that catches my attention. Ha. Hence the name.

A woman with coal-black hair looks up from the bar. Her eyes light up with interest as they roam over me. "Howdy, stranger. What can I get you?"

"You must be Daisy."

She leans an elbow on the counter. Her arms are almost as big as mine. Tattoos cover the skin from her wrist to her shoulder, which is visible under a strappy top. "Do we know each other? Because I'm sure I would've remembered."

"I'm a friend of Jane, and I'll have two beers, please."

"Ah." She straightens. "You're taken. Lucky bitch."

I won't bet my money on the *taken* part, but I'm going to put everything I've got behind getting there.

She hands me two cold lagers. "Jane's favorite. Unless you want something different?"

"This will do fine. Thanks."

She salutes me with two fingers as I make my way back outside. Leaning on the rail, I twist off the caps and hand Jane one.

She tilts back her head and takes a big swallow. The way her throat moves forces my dick to attention. I can't help it. She's always had this effect on me. Even before I met her in person. I'm just glad my tools are still functioning, because I haven't had a spontaneous hard-on since *that* day. I still can't bring myself to say it. The day she walked away from my engagement party. The last day I saw her. She's a miracle. Still a princess. And I want her. Irrevocably and immediately. My body starts pulsing until every nerve ending has taken notice. I haven't touched another woman since Jane. The only way I settled my urges was with hand jobs, and now that she's in front of me in flesh and blood, I both want to not lay a dirty finger on her and tear her apart with my cock. Her pussy, only inches away from me, reminds me how unfulfilling those hand jobs were. My desire for her hasn't waned one bit. It grew worse. In an effort to cool down, I down half of the beer. She's on a quarter of hers before she speaks.

"How did you find me?"

"Dorothy. Although, I always kept tabs."

She nods in a way that doesn't tell me if she approves or disapproves.

"Where's your truck?"

"Sold it. I hitchhiked here. Walked part of the way."

Her eyebrows rise. "Thinking of hanging around, then?"

I give the bar another glance. "I could do with a job."

"What happened to Orion?"

"I resigned."

"Your mom? Sam?" Her gaze slips to my bare ring finger. "Lindy?"

This needs some explanation. I sit down next to her. She doesn't make space for me, but she doesn't chase me away, either. Our hips are touching. Her skin burns me through the layers of our clothes.

"Jane…"

At the soft utterance of her name, she turns her head an inch toward me.

I wipe a sweaty palm on my thigh, clutching the beer bottle like a buoy. *"That* day..."

*Say it, damn you. Get it the hell over with. Take your guilt and fucking own it.*

I take a deep breath. "The day I almost..." I check myself. No use beating around the bush. "The day I *killed* you, I called my mom and told her to close the hatch."

Jane's fingers twitch on her bottle. I need to touch her. I need to soothe her, make up for too many things that don't have words, but I have to take it slow. Resting my arm on the backrest of the bench, I let my fingertips casually, accidentally, graze her shoulder. She tenses. Regretfully, I ease up, moving my hand away just far enough so I'd still touch her if she shrugged or lifted her shoulder.

"She couldn't do it. She couldn't cross the lawn and close the hatch to prevent you from drowning," I say softly. "That's the day I realized it couldn't carry on like that. I realized you were right. I had to do something to help her."

Her voice is quiet but attentive. "Did you?"

"I booked her into an institution that deals with cases like hers. She didn't like it, but she understands now."

"Is she better?"

"She lives in her own flat in Hatfield with Sam. She has a steady job and friends. She's been sober for a year."

"That's good." She sounds sad in a nostalgic kind of way, as if she doesn't like where her memories are taking her. "I'm happy for her."

"She has a great therapist. He reckons they can stop their sessions this autumn."

"It must've cost a fortune."

"Toby paid well."

She chuckles. "He did." Slowly, she turns her head toward me. "Why did you resign?"

Her eyes say I had a great thing going. True, but nothing

compares to her. Nothing is worth anything if I can't share it with her.

"I gave up my studies."

She discards her bottle on the floor, jumps to her feet, and walks to the rail. Leaning on it with her elbows, she stares at the darkening mountaintops in the distance. "You shouldn't have done that."

I leave my beer next to hers and follow her to the rail, molding my body around the air between us. The only point of contact I allow myself is to brush her hair over her shoulder, but I retract my hand when her body freezes up.

I push forward, laying my life at her feet. "It took me a year to get my life in order, a year to sort out my mother and Sam and the thing with Lindy so I could get back to you."

She flings around, her earlier serene expression sparkling with anger. "You shouldn't have done it, Brian. I've gotten over you."

It hurts like a lance rubbed with poison through the heart, but I gladly take the pain. I'll take anything to have this moment, to get another chance.

"I'm over you," she says again.

I wince. "I know."

"Then why did you come here? If it's for absolution, you needn't have bothered. I don't blame you for what happened. I don't blame you, because I've moved on. You should've, too."

"I came here because I'm not over you."

Her eyes cloud over. The lovely blue turns into a stormy gray. "No."

She tries to move around me, but I plant my palms on the rail on either side of her body, caging her in.

"There are things you need to hear."

She turns her head away. "No."

"Don't be afraid of the truth. The truth is all we've got. I'm going to give you what I couldn't the day Sam's phone call and the storm interrupted us, what I couldn't give you the night Clive walked in on us at the country club. I'm going to give you what you deserve."

"Brian..."

I grip her chin and turn her face back to me. This way, she can't hide *her* truth and the way it brims in her eyes. She can't hide her pain and love from me. I know her too well, this woman who invaded my heart and life. My everything. My obsession then, my obsession now. I itch to kiss that scar, to show her that I love every old and new part of her, but what needs to be said can't wait.

"I met Benjamin in Oscars."

"I know. He told me everything."

"Let me finish. He showed me a photo of you and asked me to help him avenge his dead friend who you'd allegedly cheated on. I only found out later he's Evan's brother when I saw his poster on a lamppost. He offered me a lot of money to sleep with you."

She flinches and tries to pull away, but I hold on.

"He offered me fifty grand to sleep with you and give him photos as the proof. I said no. The truth is, from the minute I saw that photo of you my curiosity was piqued. My gut stirred. I was already obsessed without even having seen you in person. I had to meet you. I had to see if the reaction that photo had on me would be the same in reality. I can't explain it. I can't justify it. I just knew I'd regret not looking you up for the rest of my life. I stalked your house. It looked deserted. The lights were dark, and the garden was overgrown. I thought maybe you'd moved. Maybe it wasn't the right address. Diving into your pool was an irrational decision I made on the spur of the moment after one beer too many in a bar. I wanted to be in your space, to feel what it felt like around the things that were *you*. I never expected you to be there that night, but I'm glad you were. I'm glad you came outside in your tight T-shirt and pants. I'm glad you cooked me breakfast. Every moment I spent in your company, every minute I was around you was premeditated, but not for fifty grand. The grand prize was *you*. It was making you mine."

"Brian, stop."

From the furrow between her eyes and the quivering of her lips, I know this is hard for her to hear, but I've got to lay this out between us. She has a right to know.

"I fell for you before I met you, when I met you, and every day after. I couldn't tell you about Benjamin. I knew you'd bail, and I couldn't lose you. Yes, I watched you on the security feed. Yes, I jacked off to the images of you, but I never showed another soul. When you brought me those photos, I was boiling with rage. I knew Benjamin had hired someone else for the job. I promised I'd cut off his fingers if he harmed you, and I don't break my promises."

Her eyes widen in alarm. "Please tell me you didn't amputate Benjamin's fingers."

"I almost did. I found the scumbag before he skipped the country, but he told me you'd made peace. He told me about the camera he'd hidden in the house, and how Dorothy had made him destroy the photos and films."

She lets out a breath.

"There's more. I'm not a good man. I killed two people."

"Your mother's assailants," she whispers. "I put two and two together."

"Cowan found the gun that would've incriminated me in the cellar after what happened to you, so I cut a deal. In exchange for walking free, I delivered Monkey Williams, Lindy's father, who ran a crime syndicate in the north and west. I wore a wire and got Cowan the evidence he needed to shut the whole mafia operation down for good. Monkey had me in a corner. He made me witness a murder and blackmailed me to marry Lindy. This was the only way I saw out. It took us a year to get enough evidence to wipe out the syndicate."

I wish she'd say something, but she's only looking at me, deadly quiet.

"Monkey's in for life. Lennert, the guy who cut you up, got

killed in a shootout with the cops. Clive pulled a gun. Got shot in the heart. He was the one who told on us. Eugene and Albert left the gang before things got heated. Lindy was charged with the murder of three men she'd commissioned. She won't be seeing anything but brick walls and orange jumpsuits for the rest of her life. Staying away from you for a year damn well nearly killed me, but I had to do it to keep you safe. Lindy threatened your life. I owed Cowan to finish the job and honor our deal."

"What about your engagement?" she asks softly, a lingering pain simmering in her eyes.

I'm going to take that pain away. That's the sole objective of the rest of my existence.

"I swear I never touched Lindy. I didn't lay a finger on her except for the day I was forced to put a ring on her finger and the day I almost strangled her when I found out what she'd ordered Lennert to do to you. I'm sorry. More than I can ever express. The whole engagement thing was a farce, and I made sure everyone knew it the day Lindy went to prison.

"I needed to tell you this so you know I'm coming to you clean. No more secrets. I know I fucked up, and I'm going to work harder for you than ever. I betrayed your trust, but I'll win it back, if it's the last thing I do, because there's one thing you can't argue. We belong together. You may be over me, but if we both try, you can fall for me again. We can start over." I glance back at the bar. "Here. Anywhere you like."

She shakes her head, already retreating mentally from me. "You forgot an important factor. No matter what we lived through and survived, the difference between us is still twenty-three years."

I wipe the hair from her forehead, framing her face between my hands. She's straining against me, trying to pull away when I bring my lips closer to the white lines that mar her cheek.

"Please, don't," she whispers.

"I own this scar." I press my lips to it. "I own it because I'm the cause of it." I look into her eyes so she can see the truth in mine. "You've never been more beautiful."

"Brian."

"You have to hear this. Before the accident, I would've used everything in my power to keep you, even blackmailing you with those damned photos myself."

Her eyes flare, but I continue mercilessly.

"I didn't only lose you. I had to let you go. I set you free so that I could claim you back the way it's supposed to be."

I'm clinging to the fact that she's not pushing me away. I'm clinging to the way her chest rises and falls faster, to how her nipples grow hard under her top. Looking down, I'm met by her delectable cleavage and the white lace of her bra peeping out from under the strappy T-shirt. My already hard dick strains in my jeans. Leaning closer, I let her feel the effect she has on me. Damn, it feels good where the little hard pebbles push against my chest. I want to dip my fingers between her legs to test her, but I have to slam on some brakes.

With a whole lot of difficulty and some more, I pull away.

Her eyes are hazy, like when she's battling with lust, but they're also uncertain. "What do you want me to say, Brian?"

"Say yes. Say you'll give me another day. Another week. I'll take anything. Whatever you're willing to give."

Her gaze flitters to the bar. "It's hard work. Long hours and little pay."

Hope blooms in my chest. "I'll take it."

She bites her lip. "It'll have to be a sleep-in position. It's a small town. There aren't any other flats for rent."

"Is that where you sleep, up there?"

She nods.

"Then I'm in."

"Without checking it out first?"

"I don't need to check it out. I'll be in your bed, and I know exactly what'll be there."

A glint of humor creeps into her eyes, a little bit of light that expels the shadows. "You're pretty sure of yourself, aren't you?"

I'm going to work on that, until there are no more shadows in those midnight blue eyes. "I'm sure of my feelings where you're concerned."

She looks down at her toes, seeming to weigh my answer. Letting her out of the cage of my arms, I drop them by my sides. I'm done playing and manipulating. I'm done forcing. This has to come from her.

The wait is excruciating. She can send me packing all over again, or she can let me in and give me another chance. The wheels must be turning in her head. She studies my face as she chews her bottom lip. Ever so slowly, she raises the tips of her fingers and runs them over my knuckles. I hold my breath. It's a fragile caress, and my whole future balances on which way that small gesture of affection is going to tip. Our gazes remain locked as our fingers intertwine. I'm not sure who took whose hand first. It just kind of happened, this small gesture that holds all the meaning in the world.

"On one condition," she says, already tightening her hand around mine.

"Anything." Whatever it takes.

"It's all or nothing."

My heart stutters with a leap of joy. A year's agony peels away as I press my lips to hers, tasting her bottom lip with a soft nip.

"I'll take all," I say, letting the dam burst inside of me and crushing our mouths together.

There's surrender in the kiss, but also domination. We're both surrender. We're both domination. We're two of a kind wound together by fate.

Our love is stronger than age and secrets.

Our love was meant to be.

# EPILOGUE

*Jane*

"**D**ammit."

I'm leaning over the dressing table in our bedroom, trying to fit the butterfly part to the earring, but I'm shaking slightly. It's the rush and emotions.

"It's not considerate to look more beautiful than the bride," a deep voice says from the door.

I catch Brian's profile in the mirror. He's leaning in the frame, looking ravishing in beige slacks and an open-collar linen shirt. I take a moment to appreciate him. He's more muscular than when he was younger, thanks to the DIY he does in Panties and the house he's practically building with his own hands on our new property, a quaint stretch of land next to the river. He still has the advertising exec in him, enough so his company is thriving. Clients fly from Windhoek and Cape Town for a chunk of his genius. It wasn't always easy. In the beginning, he travelled a lot. Since he employed a manager at his franchise company in Johannesburg, we get to see each other every day. We go to bed together and wake up together, and still it never seems enough. I can never get my fill.

He pushes away from the frame and closes the distance. "Let me."

Taking the obstinate earring from my hand, he fits it effortlessly. His hands slip down my sides over the apricot-colored silk of my dress to find purchase on my hips.

There's admiration in his voice as he tilts our foreheads together. "God, you're beautiful. This dress…" His gaze moves over me. "I'm not sure I can let you out wearing this. I can see your nipples."

I lean against him, ridiculously happy. "Where's your sense of voyeurism now?"

"Do you have a jacket?"

It's scorching hot outside. Is he joking? No, there's no mocking light in his eyes.

"The dress was Abby's choice. Come on, we're going to be late." I bend down to fit my shoes, but he holds me back.

"You know I love you, Jane Logan, don't you?"

I melt as I always do for him. "I know."

"Tell me."

"I love you, too."

"That's better."

He kisses me and goes down on one knee, fitting first one and then the other shoe. His palm lingers on my calf under the long skirt of the dress. The way he stares up at me tells me everything I need to know. We've had our share of darkness, Brian and I, but it only brought out our light. He straightens slowly, dragging his hand up to the underside of my knee, the back of my thigh, and finally my buttocks. His gaze never leaves mine as he straightens the skirt and pulls the thin strap of the top back onto my shoulder.

Hand in hand, we make our way downstairs. The tables are set up on the lawn of Panties, overlooking the river. I want to have a last look to make sure everything is perfect. Jasmine and Sam are putting the finishing touches to the flowers. They did a great job with bouquets of wild flowers. Their dresses match mine in color. Only the styles are different.

"This looks beautiful," I say. "Thank you, Jasmine."

"It was mostly Sam."

Sam punches Brian on the arm. "Where's your tie?"

He grunts. "Abby said casual."

My God, I still can't believe it. My baby girl is getting married. "I'm going to check on the food."

Brian grabs my wrist. "It'll be fine."

"I just—"

"Everything will be delicious. Checking on the caviar mousse one more time isn't going to make it set faster."

I let out a shaky breath. He's right. Anyway, the guests are arriving. Daisy is already showing them to the chairs arranged in front of the garden gazebo where the exchange of the vows will take place. Francois and Debbie arrive with their three kids in tow. She's seven months pregnant with their fourth. We make our way over the lawn to greet them.

"How are you holding up with the heat?" I ask Debbie.

"Oh, God." She rolls her eyes. "You don't want to know."

"Is the guesthouse comfortable enough?"

"It's great," Francois says.

"Maybe you should draw the line at four," Jasmine teases.

"She looks so damn pretty when she's expecting," Francois says, "I can't help wanting to keep her in a permanent state of pregnancy."

Debbie swats his arm. "I swear to God, this is the last baby you put in me."

"Famous last words," Sam says on a chuckle.

I look at Francois. "Ready? She's waiting for you inside."

We all glance to where the groom is standing near the gazebo.

"Poor Henry." Sam snickers. "He's as nervous as I've ever seen him."

Dorothy comes rushing up, her heels sinking into the lawn. She holds a stylish Queen Elizabeth hat on her head with one hand. "Oh, my gosh. Am I late?"

"Just in time." Brian offers Dorothy and me his arms. "Shall we take our seats?"

We install ourselves while Francois goes inside to wait with his daughter before walking her down the aisle.

Brian puts a hand on my knee, his fingers toying with the silk. "I have a surprise for you," he whispers in my ear.

I glance at him. "For me? Why? What's the occasion?"

"Your birthday."

My birthday isn't until another two months. My fingers involuntarily move to the scar on my cheek. I proposed to have plastic surgery to make the ugly mark less unsightly, more as a gift to Brian than to myself.

Brian catches my fingers. "Don't." He kisses my fingertips and then the scar. "I own this. You said you didn't mind it. Does it bother you?"

"No. I was thinking more of you."

"I love every part of you. You don't need plastic surgery to make you more beautiful to me. What I love the most, plastic surgery can't alter."

What have I done to deserve this beautiful man? "If it's not that then what's your surprise?"

He smiles down at me. "I'm taking you to Rome."

My breath catches. "You are?"

"Just you and me. In June, when it's summer in Italy. One whole month."

"Brian…" I swallow away a sudden bout of emotion. "A month! I don't know what to say."

"Say you'll come with me."

"What about Panties and your job?"

"That's why I have a manager. Daisy runs this place just as well as you do, and Sam already agreed to help out during her varsity holiday."

My soul expands at his consideration. "You thought of everything, haven't you?"

"Is that a yes? Will you come with me?"

"Of course, I will."

"Good. That means I don't have to put my kidnapping back-up plan into action."

My body takes notice. "Hold on. You were going to kidnap me to Rome?"

"Blindfolded, bound, and naked," he says on a dark whisper, "in a chartered plane. I was going to have my way with you many times over. It's a long flight."

My abdomen clenches, and my love spills over. "In that case, I'll have to decline."

His lips curve into the most wicked of smiles, exposing his sexy-as-sin dimple. "I was hoping you'd say that."

The notes of the wedding song fill the air. Abby steps from the veranda door, arm in arm with Francois. She's the radiant bride I wished upon her. She's everything I ever wanted for her–happy and in love. As the music rises like a cloud to the sky and tears of joy build in my eyes, Brian takes my hand in his. Our fingers interlock. I can argue that he's too young or I'm too old, but love knows no boundaries or age. I prefer to say he's as old as he should be, and I'm enough.

~ THE END ~

# ALSO BY CHARMAINE PAULS

**DIAMOND MAGNATE NOVELS**
*(Dark Romance)*

**Standalone Novel**
*(Dark Forced Marriage Romance)*
Beauty in the Broken

**Diamonds are Forever Trilogy**
*(Dark Mafia Romance)*
Diamonds in the Dust
Diamonds in the Rough
Diamonds are Forever
Box Set

**Beauty in the Stolen Trilogy**
*(Dark Romance)*
Stolen Lust
Stolen Life
Stolen Love
Box Set

---

**The White Nights Duet**
*(Contemporary Romance)*
White Nights

Midnight Days

---

**The Loan Shark Duet**

*(Dark Mafia Romance)*

Dubious

Consent

Box Set

---

**The Age Between Us Duet**

*(Older Woman Younger Man Romance)*

Old Enough

Young Enough

Box Set

---

**Standalone Novels**

*(Enemies-to-Lovers Dark Romance)*

Darker Than Love

*(Second Chance Romance)*

Catch Me Twice

---

**Krinar World Novels**

*(Futuristic Romance)*

The Krinar Experiment

The Krinar's Informant

---

**7 Forbidden Arts Series**

*(Fated Mates Paranormal Romance)*

Pyromancist (Fire)

Aeromancist, The Beginning (Prequel)

Aeromancist (Air)

Hydromancist (Water)

Geomancist (Earth)

Necromancist (Spirit)

---

# ABOUT THE AUTHOR

Charmaine Pauls was born in Bloemfontein, South Africa. She obtained a degree in Communication at the University of Potchefstroom and followed a diverse career path in journalism, public relations, advertising, communication, and brand marketing. Her writing has always been an integral part of her professions.

When she moved to Chile with her French husband, she started writing full-time. She has been publishing novels and short stories since 2011. Charmaine currently lives in Montpellier, France with her family. Their household is a lively mix of Afrikaans, English, French, and Spanish.

**Join Charmaine's mailing list**
https://charmainepauls.com/subscribe/

**Join Charmaine's readers' group on Facebook**
http://bit.ly/CPaulsFBGroup

**Read more about Charmaine's novels and short stories on**
https://charmainepauls.com

**Connect with Charmaine**

**Facebook**

http://bit.ly/Charmaine-Pauls-Facebook

**Amazon**
http://bit.ly/Charmaine-Pauls-Amazon

**Goodreads**
http://bit.ly/Charmaine-Pauls-Goodreads

**Twitter**
https://twitter.com/CharmainePauls

**Instagram**
https://instagram.com/charmainepaulsbooks

**BookBub**
http://bit.ly/CPaulsBB

**TikTok**
https://www.tiktok.com/@charmainepauls